SHE SAW
THE KISS COMING

As Paul pulled her closer, every part of her sang a welcome. It had been so long. The thought skittered through her mind while other sensations took precedence. His mouth, full and demanding . . . his taste, his body, heady and exciting. She clung to him, wanting to know again the passion that only he had been able to arouse in her.

Paul had kissed her almost on a dare, a challenge he couldn't refuse. But in moments, that had all been forgotten. The contrasts of Christine had always fascinated him. His body pulsed in total recall of those moments. She was everything he'd ever wanted and he'd done without for so long. Could he ever get enough of this woman? What man could discipline himself not to touch fire of this magnitude? He had once, and should never have touched her again.

Paul drew back. "It's time I took you home," he said quietly.

No, Chris thought, moving slowly toward the doors. It was past time.

ABOUT THE AUTHOR

According to Patricia Cox, humor was definitely a prerequisite when she had to cope with four children under the age of ten and write a humorous column for the *Detroit News*. Her literary career began, though, at the age of sixteen when she wrote a teenage gossip column in the *Akron Beacon Journal*. Patricia makes her home in Arizona with her husband.

Books by Patricia Cox
HARLEQUIN AMERICAN ROMANCE
217–FOREVER FRIENDS

THE FOREVER CHOICE

PATRICIA COX

Harlequin Books

TORONTO • NEW YORK • LONDON
AMSTERDAM • PARIS • SYDNEY • HAMBURG
STOCKHOLM • ATHENS • TOKYO • MILAN

To Susan Warren,
who taught us all
a great deal about compassion,
with love from Mom.

Special thanks to Captain Frank E. Schaffer,
retired of the Phoenix Police Department.
For all his wonderful insight.

Published July 1989

First printing May 1989

ISBN 0-373-16303-7

Prologue

Rain, so unusual for late May in Arizona, splashed heavily against the window as Paul Cameron lay in his second-floor hospital room staring out at the date palms swaying in the wet wind. The bullet that had entered his rib cage had exited cleanly out the back without hitting a vital organ. Again, he'd been lucky. Chris hadn't thought so.

Christine Donovan. Paul shifted slightly, remembering her pale, frightened face as she'd stood looking down at him just a short time ago. Her deep blue eyes had been ready to overflow, and her hand had trembled as she'd touched him.

"The doctor said you're going to be as good as new in no time," she'd told him, sounding unconvinced. He'd tried to talk, but the aftermath of surgery had him too drugged to answer, so he'd just nodded. She'd gripped his fingers, then bent her head. He'd felt her tears falling on his hand and knew she'd been reliving another such bedside vigil. Only her policeman father hadn't survived.

Paul blinked as a flash of lightning lit up the midnight sky. He'd been attracted to Christine from the first moment he'd laid eyes on her. And had been warned by her brother and his best friend, Mike Donovan, to bide his time with Chris. He'd known that her father's death had greatly affected her, known she was hesitant about getting involved with a self-assured, somewhat arrogant man who was on his way up in the police department. But Paul had fallen hard for her and had gone after her the same way he'd pursued whatever else in life he wanted—with a single-minded persistence.

He'd seen a certain wariness in her eyes yet he'd known from their first evening together that Chris wanted him, too. Six months ago they'd become lovers, and Paul had never been happier. He was a rising star on the Phoenix police force, doing work that challenged him. And he'd earned his promotions despite the fact that his father was a U.S. senator with a lot of political clout. And he had Chris.

For the first time in his life, Paul was seriously considering marriage. Then, a couple of weeks ago, something had changed. Chris had become cool and distant, yet refused to discuss why. Tonight, he'd planned a nice, quiet dinner at their favorite restaurant, where he'd hoped to draw her out. Only on the way there, his police radio had warned of a robbery in progress nearby, and instinctively, Paul had hurried to the scene.

It had been raining steadily when they'd arrived, minutes before the first blues, and he'd cornered one young punk by the front door. But Paul hadn't seen the second man leap out of the evening shadows in time to avoid the bullet that had ripped into his side. As the squad cars pulled up, he'd sunk to the wet cement, fighting the blackness. The last thing he remembered was Chris holding him, her eyes huge and horrified.

A clap of thunder brought Paul back to the sterile room and the too-sweet smell of anesthetic. Chris had stayed with him until the doctor had insisted she go home to rest and come back in the morning. But her last words worried him.

"Take care, my love," she'd whispered. "Please take care of yourself." And she'd walked out the door.

That had the eerie foreshadowing sound of a goodbye scene, Paul thought hazily as his mind began to cloud again. He'd have to talk with her tomorrow, find out what she'd meant. His heavy eyes closed at last. Yes, tomorrow.

CHRISTINE DONOVAN STOOD in the sheltered courtyard of her aunt's home halfway up Camelback Mountain and stared at the winding roadway where, minutes ago, a taxi had brought her home from the hospital. She leaned against the trellised bougainvillea, scarcely noticing the rain that dripped from the heavy plantings. Her hand twisted a lock of her shoulder-length black hair as her mind reached a final decision.

It was time to leave. The insurance company she worked for had offered her a transfer to its San Diego office, and she'd rolled the idea around in her mind for several weeks now, ever since her little chat with Senator John Cameron, Paul's father. She'd been shocked and disturbed by his request, had in fact wanted to slap his smug, self-confident face. She'd had no intention of giving in to the senator. But tonight, she knew she had to take the transfer. She looked down at Paul's blood that had stained her pink suit as she'd held him while they'd waited for the ambulance. She was in love with him, but she knew she couldn't go through another scene like the one tonight.

Chris turned troubled eyes to the cloudy night sky, which was as murky as her thoughts. Her aunt would be upset by her departure and her brother would be confused and quietly critical. It couldn't be helped. Neither really understood.

Tonight she'd painstakingly relived the evening she and her mother had rushed to another hospital then stood in another antiseptic corridor for hours while another man had struggled to live. Sergeant Patrick Donovan had died in surgery, and the light had gone out of her mother's eyes.

For years, Mary Donovan had lived with fear, and then she had to live with loss. That wasn't the life Chris envisioned for herself. It would seem Paul's father would win, after all.

Raindrops splashed relentlessly on the red-tiled courtyard, and Chris inhaled deeply. She hated to leave the home she'd grown so fond of. Her mother had died a year after her father, and her aunt, Maggie Muldoon, had made Chris feel like the daughter she'd never had. But she'd adjust to life in another town. Life, after all, was filled with necessary adjustments, and Chris, for the most part, had handled her share.

There was only one adjustment she couldn't make, and the only way to handle that was to remove herself from the problem. Loving Paul Cameron would cost her more than she was willing to pay.

With a last glance at the distant lights of the valley shimmering through the damp mist, Chris slowly made her way to the door. Yes, it was time to move on.

IN ANOTHER PART OF THE CITY, rain beat against the fourth-floor windows of a beige stucco office complex. The lone figure in the building bent over the books spread out on the desk, barely noticing the storm outside. The small lamp threw just enough light onto the accounting pages as the changes were made, slowly and with much care. Altering records wasn't easy. It took skill and know-how so suspicions wouldn't be aroused.

A great deal was at stake. Even one small mistake would be costly. This sort of thing involved detailed planning, patience and time. But that had been clear from the beginning. Yet it would be worth it. The trick was not to rush, to get greedy or careless. Slow and steady, and a desperate dream would come true.

There was a slight sound outside the closed door, and the figure froze, eyes raising. No one else should be here at this time of night, in this part of the office complex. One night watchman lazily roamed the production area, but months of careful checking had ascertained that he never wandered to the accounting section. No, no one was there. It was just nerves or the storm. The eyes returned to the page.

Next to the open ledger, smoke curled from the ashtray—sweet, acrid, almost cloying in the small room. Several butts already lay inside the clay container that was carefully emptied each night. This cigarette, too, would soon become ash and join the pile, forgotten by the smoker whose concentration was absolute.

The details had been worked out months ago and now it was time to put the plan into action. No one would get in the way now.

A crack of thunder reverberated through the empty building. The figure hunched over the desk ignored it, set aside the ledger and opened the next one.

Chapter One

Deafening. The sound in the large, windowless room was deafening. Paul Cameron heard none of it as he narrowed his eyes and concentrated on the target fifty yards ahead of him. Slowly, he squeezed the trigger, and the next bullet ripped from his snub-nosed .38 to hit the bullseye, emptying the final chamber.

A yank on the pulley brought the dangling paper target over to the enclosure where he stood. He noted with grim satisfaction that all six shots were close to dead center. Not bad for a cop who, in eight years on the force, had actually had to fire his weapon only twice at anything other than paper targets.

Stepping back, he began to reload, then changed his mind. Enough for today. Sometimes when he was keyed up, he could work off his frustrations and shut off his thoughts by losing himself in the intense concentration of target practice. Today, after twenty minutes, he knew it wasn't working.

Paul thrust his gun into his shoulder holster and removed his protective earmuffs. Despite the air-conditioning, his face was damp. He wiped it dry with his handkerchief. Shooting was not really something he enjoyed, but he knew every cop had to be prepared.

Shrugging into his jacket, Paul turned to see the desk officer approaching him.

"The captain wants to see you in his office, Sergeant," the officer said.

"Thanks, Charley." Paul clapped the older man on the shoulder and walked toward the exit. With a nod, he handed his targets to the range master in the booth and strolled through the connecting corridor to the main building of downtown police headquarters.

Paul made his way to the second floor offices, stopping to greet an occasional friendly face. He knew he was known around the precinct as a cop's cop, a relentless investigator, someone who always got his man. Few of them knew the man behind the badge, and Paul liked it that way. As he walked, his mind was on his work, which dominated his thoughts as it did his life.

He approached the girl seated outside the captain's office. He flashed a grin of appreciation at the curvaceous blonde's obvious attributes. Good old Mike always managed to find secretaries who were efficient, as well as easy on the eyes. "You're looking terrific today, Millie. The captain in?"

She gave him an answering smile. "Not yet, Sergeant. But he said you could wait inside."

Nodding his thanks, Paul entered the familiar office, strolled over to the double windows overlooking the downtown street three stories below and saw they were still tangled with morning traffic.

Ironic, he thought as he stared out at the unseasonably damp May morning. It had rained on that last day he'd seen Chris Donovan two years ago, and it was raining today when he'd likely see her again, if precinct scuttlebutt was right. And it was seldom wrong. Sometimes before the assignment report was in the hands of the officer, word mysteriously got out about the case and who'd probably be assigned. The speculation often annoyed Paul, yet he had to admit it was usually on the money. He turned from the window and eased his long frame into the chair facing Mike's desk.

Captain Mike Donovan, the brass nameplate read. He still keeps a cluttered desk, Paul noted, despite the fact that he was head of the Phoenix Detective Bureau for six months now. An old friend, a good friend and now his commanding officer. Paul didn't begrudge Mike's rapid climb up the ladder, acknowledging that he was no slouch himself. His recent promotion to detective sergeant made him, at thirty-two, the youngest man on the force to reach that position in the shortest period of time. And he hadn't come from a long line of cops the way Mike had.

Mike was a politician's policeman. A born diplomat. Paul was a street cop; he got the job done.

The door opened, and his friend walked in, his broad Irish face moving into a warm smile. Paul stood to shake hands with him.

"Sorry to keep you waiting, Paul." Mike sat down in his deep leather chair. "I seem to be running a little late this morning."

"No problem." Paul slouched back into the chair, his eyes on Mike. A full four inches taller than his own six feet, the captain was a big man, very solid with coal-black hair, a thick mustache and kind gray eyes. A man who invited trust and confidence, the type who lulled people into dropping their guard easily with his deceptively low-key ways and almost lazy interest. Which was their mistake, Paul thought, for Mike was one of the shrewdest cops he'd ever known.

The captain took his time, shook a cigarette from a crumpled pack, put his lighter to it and blew smoke toward the ceiling. It was a tactic he used, whether to put the person at ease or make them nervous as hell, Paul wasn't sure.

"I take it you've read the report I left in your box."

"Yes, I have." The investigating officer who'd initially answered the call had turned in a clear, concise report to the Detective Bureau for follow-up. Paul had read it all with a sinking feeling and a sense of certainty. "Sorry to hear there's a problem at your aunt's company. I thought she'd have smooth sailing now that Jeremiah Green was back in her life. They're getting married soon, aren't they?"

Mike nodded. "Right. The wedding's what uncovered the embezzlement, actually. Maggie wanted to turn some stock over to the bridegroom and ordered an independent audit. The auditors discovered the theft, which evidently has been going on for some time."

"She's been in business now what, ten or fifteen years?" Paul asked, making mental notes. He thought he'd better remember what the report said, even though Mike had probably assumed Paul wouldn't want to be put on this case. The captain was well known for not allowing personal feelings to interfere in police decisions.

"Closer to twenty," Mike went on, leaning back. "Interesting story. I don't think I've ever told you. Maggie had tried all sorts of businesses but nothing had clicked for her. Then one day she met this guy—probably at a bar—and he turned out to be a chemist. She'd saved her money so she backed him and opened this small cosmetics company."

"And she'd had no previous background in it?"

"None. Anyhow, this chemist came up with a new perfume, and she hired a publicist to spread the word. They named the company Lady Charm, and the damn thing took off. The rest, as they say, is history. The first chemist died, and she's had several since, each inventing something that makes her piles of money."

"She's something, all right."

"Yeah, Maggie's always been ahead of her time. Not just starting a brand-new business on a shoestring but adopting a baby as a single parent thirty years ago. Of course, her attorney arranged it privately, but it still took some doing."

"Sounds like her bridegroom's stepping into a gold mine. What's old Jeremiah do?"

"He's retired, but I don't think he ever made much money. He was a professor, I think. When he popped back into Maggie's life, I warned her to go slowly, and she did for a while, then she suddenly announced she was marrying him. I guess she got tired of waiting after being in love with Jeremiah for forty years."

Paul let out a low whistle. He'd met the flamboyant Maggie Muldoon several times through his friendship with Mike, but he hadn't known much about her past. "Forty years. What broke them up, do you know?"

Mike shrugged as he knocked an ash from his cigarette. "Family interference. The Greens are from Boston, tracing ancestry back to the *Mayflower* and all that. No money, but they considered themselves bluebloods. Probably still do. Maggie was beautiful but poor and Irish to boot."

Paul smiled. "From what little I've seen of her, I'd guess that Maggie's always been something of a maverick. And the Greens wanted someone tamer for Jeremiah?"

Mike nodded. "Right. His family had picked out a girl with the right background, and they ordered Jeremiah back. He listened, married her and lived to regret it, or so he's told Maggie. He claims he never forgot his first love, and when his wife died last year, he came back to her. Pretty amazing, eh?"

"To carry a torch for four decades? Yeah, amazing."

Mike studied Paul through a haze of smoke. "So what do you make of the report, of the embezzlement at Lady Charm?"

"That's a lot of money not to be noticed sooner in the regular audits. Got to be an inside job, probably close to the top. Someone patient and methodical who's planned it long and carefully and undoubtedly has a lot at stake."

"I think you're right." Dropping his gaze, Mike snubbed out his cigarette. "I'd like you on this case."

Paul shifted slightly, searching for the right words. "I'm real close on the Lowell case. Al and I've been on it for three months. I hate to let that go right now."

"Al can handle the Lowell stakeout. I can assign him a junior grade and you can check with him periodically. I want you to give priority to Lady Charm."

Well aware he was losing ground rapidly, Paul decided to give it another shot. More than an assignment was involved. His peace of mind was in jeopardy. "Margaret Danforth has really come a long way as an investigative detective. Wouldn't you think she'd do better handling something like this, a women's cosmetics firm?"

Crossing his arms, Mike leaned forward on his elbows. "Lady Charm is a business, one that a private audit has revealed as having four hundred thousand dollars missing from company funds. Embezzlement has no gender. This is my family involved here. I want the best cop. And you're that person."

Damn but the man made refusal next to impossible. And he knew it. Time to strip it down. Leaning back, Paul steepled his fingers and looked at Mike. "Badges aside for a minute?" he asked.

Mike nodded, his eyes on his friend.

"I'm sure you went over the report as thoroughly as I and that the name jumped out at you, too. Or maybe you knew about it from Maggie. Chris is the insurance investigator on this?"

Again, Mike nodded.

"Why?" Paul asked. "Why is she coming all the way from San Diego to investigate an embezzlement in Phoenix when Southwest Insurance Company has an office right here in town? I can't believe that all their local investigators are on other assignments."

Mike shrugged. "Maybe she's also the best there is. Is working with Chris going to present a problem for you?"

He'd never lied to Mike and didn't see any point in starting now. "Hell, yes, it's going to present a problem for me." Paul rose and walked over to stand at the window.

The rain was letting up but it was still a gloomy day, perfectly reflecting his dark thoughts. He didn't need this right now. Or ever. He had his life in order, comfortable with his job and dating Susan Blake, someone uncomplicated and undemanding. Why did this have to happen now?

Paul fingered his mustache, remembering how, like his father, Chris hated it. Had that been why he'd grown it after she'd left, as some silly act of rebellion? he wondered. Perhaps he'd wanted to show both of them that he was his own man, making his own decisions. He heard Mike clear his throat, dragging him back to their conversation.

"You know I wouldn't ask you to do something I wouldn't ask of myself," Mike reminded him unnecessarily.

Yeah, he did know that. Taking a deep, bracing breath, Paul turned. Their work wasn't easy, on either side of the desk. If an officer was a professional, he didn't let emotion get in the way of assignments. He'd work with Chris and set aside his personal feelings. Mike was only doing his job, and he'd do his. With effort, he put on a small smile. "When do you want me to start?"

Mike's face didn't register surprise, Paul noted. His friend knew him well.

"I told Maggie you'd be over this morning, after the briefing."

Paul struggled to keep his face expressionless. He wanted him to go over there now, when there was not even time to prepare himself. Maybe that was best. Nodding curtly, he moved to the door.

"Report only to me on this one," Mike called after him.

"Right." Paul left, closing the door behind him.

As he walked toward the stairs, in his mind's eye Paul saw a woman with jet-black hair, pale skin and deep blue eyes. A black Irish beauty, his father had said of Chris the first time he'd met her. Paul felt a spurt of fresh anger. Christine Donovan had hurt him like no other woman had. He'd do well to keep that in mind over the next few weeks of the investigation. He wasn't anxious to see her again, but Mike had left him no other choice. He would make sure she didn't know how he felt about their reunion.

Two years, he thought as he pushed through the door to the parking lot. A long time. He couldn't help wondering if those two years had changed her, as they'd changed him.

FULL CIRCLE. SHE'D COME full circle, Chris thought waking up in her mother's old bed. She'd been born in it twenty-eight years ago, had spent countless nights in it since her mother's death and this morning had awakened in it again, the big four-poster dominating her old room in Aunt Maggie's house. When she'd moved away, she hadn't planned to be back in it so soon. Or perhaps ever. Certainly she hadn't thought she'd return in an official capacity, as well as on a much-delayed personal visit. An oddly disturbing visit. Yes, full circle.

Scooting out from beneath the light sheet, Chris stood and stretched, going up on her toes, arms high in the air, feeling her pale blue nightshirt rising to skim along the backs of her legs. She yawned expansively and realized she never slept quite so well as when she was home in this bed. Home. A Freudian slip or a subconscious choice? she wondered. Her home was in San Diego now, yet a part of her still considered Maggie's house home.

Chris hadn't called Maggie "aunt" since her midteens, seeing her more as a dear friend than a relative. Maggie was very special, the woman who'd been like a mother to her even before her own had died. It had been Maggie who'd told her about "that time of month," as she'd called it. Chris smiled, remembering her later explaining with a straight face about boys and French kissing and sex, then asking with a raised brow if she had any questions. Maggie with her compassion, her warmth and her innate charm. And her bright red hair, her snapping blue eyes and her whiskey voice. To this day, she represented home.

Chris walked to the terrace doors and, opening them, strolled outside under the overhang. The rain was stopping but moisture still dripped from the leaves of the royal palm trees that bordered her second-story balcony. She inhaled deeply, filling herself with the familiar desert scents—warm clay tiles, fragrant honeysuckle and sweet oleander. The late May heat would soon suck up all remnants of rain, and the persistent sun would break through the thinning clouds. In an hour, it would look as if it hadn't rained in months, which it probably hadn't before yesterday. So different from her coastal apartment outside San Diego. It was good to be back.

A quick knock at her bedroom door had Chris turning. The door opened, and a short, heavy-set woman with a thick, dark braid down her back, wearing a broad smile entered quickly and placed a black lacquered tray onto the small table by the chaise lounge.

"Mendosa!" Chris cried out as she walked toward the woman with outstretched arms. "It's so good to see you."

"*Nenita*, it is wonderful having you back with us." Mendosa hugged Chris to her ample body. "Too long you have stayed away, Christina." Pulling back she said, "Why?"

"Many reasons." Chris blinked back a rush of emotion hearing Mendosa's pet name for her, meaning "dearest child." She'd been only fifteen when she'd moved in with her aunt. Mendosa had been with Maggie many years before that. She was housekeeper, companion and friend, and Chris had sorely missed her tender, loving care.

Mendosa was too kind to press for details. "You arrived very late last night, yes?"

Nodding, Chris stepped back. "Nearly midnight. My flight from San Diego was delayed. I talked with Maggie for a short time, then fell into bed." She smiled wanly. "You're looking good, not a day older."

"And you, *nenita*, are even more beautiful." Mendosa indicated the tray she'd brought. "Come, have some coffee."

"Thank you." Chris sat on the edge of the chaise and let the bustling little woman pour the coffee, knowing how pleased she was to fuss over her.

Mendosa perched on the end of the unmade bed, her dark eyes dancing. "So you've not met the bridegroom yet?"

Chris swallowed a sip of coffee and shook her head. "No. Tell me about Jeremiah."

"Oh, he is tall, very handsome. There is much love in him for Maggie, I think."

"Good. If anyone deserves to be happy, it's Maggie."

The woman nodded in agreement. "She is so happy. He brings her gifts almost every day—jewelry, flowers and this magnificent alabaster egg."

Chris raised her brows in surprise. "A Faberge egg?"

"Yes, yes, that is what Maggie called it. Simply beautiful."

Mike had told her on the phone that Jeremiah was far from wealthy. How very odd that he could afford such gifts. Chris sipped her coffee, thinking she was anxious to meet Maggie's long-lost love. She'd been exhausted last night and glad to postpone seeing everyone until today. Now, she was eager to get updated.

"And how's Teddy?" Chris asked. Maggie's adopted son was only two years older than Chris, yet they'd never been particularly close. Teddy hadn't been good friends with Mike, either, seemingly preferring his own company. His indulgent mother had had him educated in Europe, which perhaps had made him a bit of a loner. Chris wondered if he still was.

"He don't come around much. He's too busy with his new wife. That man crazy about that woman, for sure."

Chris had been as surprised as anyone when Maggie had phoned about a year ago to inform her that Teddy had eloped. His wife's name was Diane, and she also worked at Lady Charm, having been lured away from a large firm on the West Coast, where she'd been a marketing expert. Maggie had given a small reception following their wedding, but Chris hadn't flown in for it. She hadn't felt ready to face everyone at the time. But she was curious to meet Diane Muldoon. She leaned toward Mendosa. "You don't care for her?"

"She's okay. A cool one, that lady. You never know what she's thinking." There was a faint trace of disapproval in her voice.

Chris smiled. "Not like me, right? You always seemed to know what I was thinking."

Mendosa shook her head a little sadly. "Not always. I didn't know you would leave and not come back for two long years."

With a sigh, Chris swung her gaze through the open balcony doors. The clouds were disappearing, and the sun was already breaking through. It would be a nice day after all. She turned to look back at the dear lady who'd helped her through so many crises in her earlier years.

"I had to go, Mendosa, and I wouldn't have come back now if Maggie didn't need me. I hated to leave so abruptly but . . . it's a long story."

Mendosa leaned to pat her hand. "I know. The policeman, right?"

Yes, Paul Cameron. Paul with his flyaway hair, his dark eyes that seemed to see straight into her and those hard, strong hands. Chris cleared her throat, stood and put on the best smile she could muster. "I got over Paul a long while ago. The move to San Diego was the right decision for me. We were wrong for each other." She reached into the dresser drawer for underwear. "I suppose I should take a quick shower. Is Maggie downstairs already?"

Mendosa stood and picked up the tray. "Oh, yes, for hours now. She is still an early riser. She ask me to tell you she's waiting to have breakfast with you on the terrace."

"Please tell her I'll be right down."

"I will. I'm glad you're here. Maggie has been very upset. This problem with the company—it's terrible." She shook her dark head.

"Yes, I know. Hopefully, with Mike's help, we'll be able to get to the bottom of things quickly." She started for the bath.

"Christina," Mendosa called from the doorway, "I think you should know. It's not Mike who will be working on the embezzlement case with you, so Maggie told me only this morning."

Chris stopped, then slowly turned back. "Paul?" She saw Mendosa nod and felt her shoulders sag. She should have guessed. She'd heard of his recent promotion. Mike would want the best for Maggie, and Paul had always been outstanding. She took a fortifying breath. "I'm sure we'll have no trouble working together. We're both profession-als.''

Mendosa's shrewd, dark eyes studied her a long mo-ment before she nodded and quietly opened the door. "I will tell Maggie to expect you shortly."

Chris leaned against the doorjamb and sighed. Perhaps she shouldn't have persuaded Mark Emery, her manager at Southwest Insurance, to assign her the investigation. He'd certainly been reluctant, and it hadn't been because she was a member of the family involved. She'd known for some time now that his feelings for her were stronger than hers for him.

Mark, with his sense of humor and gentle eyes, was ex-actly the kind of man she should fall in love with but somehow couldn't. She hadn't encouraged him, but none-theless he'd persisted. Reluctantly he'd let her take this case, and here she was. And where did she go from here?

Of course, representing her company or not, she'd had to come. Maggie was in trouble and needed her, for moral support if nothing else. Still she couldn't help wishing her aunt lived in a city far from Phoenix, far from Paul Cam-eron.

She'd been as honest as she knew how to be when she'd told Mendosa that she was over him. She'd adjusted well in the two years she'd been gone and had made a good life for herself in San Diego. She dated occasionally, had several good friends and loved her job. She admired, respected and even liked Paul, but that was all there was between them now. He, on the other hand, might still be upset at the way she'd left so abruptly. But he would undoubtedly hide his feelings well, being the professional he was. Paul would only be a problem during her stay in Phoenix if she let him become one, and she was determined not to do that.

They would work together in a calm, adult way. Wonderful theory, Chris thought as she went into the bathroom. Now if only she could hold up her end of things.

Chapter Two

Maggie Muldoon was seated at her glass-topped breakfast table contemplating her dish of prunes when Chris came out onto the terrace. Shielding her bright blue eyes, Maggie rose and stretched on tiptoe, trying to adjust the umbrella so she'd be more shaded.

"I'll get that for you," Chris said as her long-legged stride carried her quickly across the flagstone patio.

"Thank you, Christine," Maggie said as she resumed her seat. "The sun's barely out, and I have to hide from it. I'd kill for skin like yours."

Angling the umbrella and locking it in place, Chris smiled to acknowledge the compliment and took the chair opposite her aunt. She'd always loved the terrace where she and Maggie had shared many a breakfast. Several tiny desert wrens hopped along the balcony ledge, cocking their heads in anticipation of a morning treat while their friends chirped in nearby trees. "What a lovely morning."

"Yes, isn't it? Would you like some coffee, dear? Oh, no, it's coffee ice cream you prefer, isn't it?" A low laugh rumbled from Maggie's throat. "I'd nearly forgotten."

Chris laughed with her. "I used to prefer ice cream for breakfast. Mendosa brought me a cup of coffee already, but I'll have another, thank you."

With a flick of her carefully manicured hand, Maggie signaled and within minutes a silver coffee server was fetched by a smiling, dark-eyed woman who quickly withdrew.

"She's new, isn't she?" Chris asked as she filled her cup. "But not too much else is different around here." Somehow, that thought reassured her.

"Her name's Carmella, and she speaks about six words of English, but she's a hard worker and a darling girl." The Irish brogue Maggie had picked up years before at her mother's side was still somewhat in evidence. "And she's the only new one since you left. How did you find Mendosa to be? She's been nervous as a cat since I told her you were coming."

"The same as always. I've missed her."

Maggie pushed aside the uneaten dish of prunes with a look of distaste. "Mendosa never changes, thank God. I find the older I get the less easily I adjust to change. What about you, Christine?"

"I'd say you're telling me tall tales, Maggie me girl," Chris said, deliberately mimicking her aunt's accent. "It's a lot of changes you'll be seeing once Mr. Jeremiah Green moves in his duds in a few weeks."

Maggie laughed out loud. "Oh, but it's good to have you back."

Chris smiled as she picked up the delicate, hand-painted glass near her aunt's plate and turned it over. "A signed Lalique. This is lovely."

"A gift from Jeremiah. I take my Metamucil in it." Maggie frowned. "The things you have to do as you get older to keep your body happy are endless."

"Fifty-nine isn't old. Besides, aren't you about to become a bride?"

Faint color moved into Maggie's face. "Isn't that astounding, at my age? I wonder what that dear man sees in me now. I was beautiful once, but..."

Reaching over, Chris squeezed her aunt's hand. "You're even *more* lovely now." She'd missed this, sitting on the sunny patio, easy affection, lazy conversation. Maggie had visited her twice in San Diego, but it hadn't been the same as being with her here.

"I'm glad you're back," the older woman said softly.

"So am I," Chris answered, seeing her aunt's eyes fill as she blinked her thick, false eyelashes. "I'd have come back for your wedding, you know. You didn't have to stage an embezzlement to get me to return." They'd purposely avoided business talk last evening, but they couldn't side-step it much longer.

Taking a sip of coffee, Maggie's face became serious. "Ah, yes, the embezzlement. You've read the reports, I imagine."

Chris nodded. "Do you have any ideas?"

"None whatsoever, I'm afraid, and they say it's been going on for well over a year, right under my nose." She shook her head, her red hair stacked high on her head moving lightly in a soft breeze. "I can't believe it yet. I'm not a careless businesswoman, and we've been showing a steady profit. How could I *not* have missed four hundred thousand dollars? Incredible!"

"Don't blame yourself. Our office has investigated several embezzlements, and some very shrewd people, like you, have been taken in by smart thieves. But we caught them in the end, so how clever were they?"

"Not clever enough, I'd say," said a voice from the archway.

Chris caught the scent of expensive cigar coming closer as she turned her head in the direction of the man walking toward them, smiling at Maggie. Since hearing of Jeremiah Green's existence and the story of their rekindled love, Chris had tried to imagine a man her aunt would wait for for forty years. Nothing could have prepared her for the real thing.

In his early sixties, Jeremiah was quite tall and built solid with the smallest hint of a paunch. "Nattily clad" was the only expression that came to mind to describe his attire. He wore a white silk shirt, brown linen slacks and hand-tooled leather boots. At his throat was a muted paisley scarf tied in ascot fashion. His thinning, silver-blond hair was combed just so, and his ruddy cheeks spoke of his love for the sun. His eyes were an innocent blue and clenched between his full lips was a long, thick cigar. Removing it, he ran a hand along Maggie's shoulders and leaned down to give her a big, noisy kiss. Chris felt a little as if she should applaud his entrance.

Jeremiah swung his attention to her. "And this must be the lovely Christine." Before she could speak, he leaned forward, picked up her hand and gently kissed it.

Chris struggled to contain a bubble of laughter. How utterly old world and romantic. "It's good to meet you, Jeremiah."

"Isn't he charming?" Maggie asked, giving him a radiant smile as he seated himself next to her.

"Yes, charming." Chris watched, mesmerized, as the two of them intertwined hands on the tabletop and gazed into each other's eyes. Love of this magnitude, at any age, was something to behold. Had she been this . . . this giddy? she wondered. No, she decided, and she was much too private for such a display.

She'd known Maggie Muldoon all her life, knew her to be a tough businesswoman, a loving mother, a warm and giving person, always there when someone needed her. But she'd never seen her blush and stammer and turn teenager in front of her very eyes. Quite a transformation. Chris sipped her coffee.

Maggie poured a fresh cup for Jeremiah. "Would you like some breakfast, dear? Something tasty, not these dreadful prunes I should be eating. How about you, Christine?"

"Not for me, thank you," she answered.

"I believe I will," Jeremiah said, hopping up. "I'll just dash to the kitchen and tell Carmella myself." And off he went.

"Isn't he absolutely priceless?" Maggie asked in her husky voice as she watched him leave the patio.

Priceless? It wasn't the word she'd have used, Chris thought. But she was hard put to come up with a better one, at least one she could say out loud. "He's quite a gentleman," she finally said, hoping she didn't sound too inadequate.

Maggie didn't even notice. "He likes to drink Pink Squirrels, to swim in the nude and to go bird-watching. Can you imagine me doing any of those things?"

Chris tried to choke back her reaction to a couple of colorful mind pictures. "Actually, no, I can't."

Maggie sighed. "I shouldn't doubt he'll get me to try all three. Amazing man."

Chris had noticed a slight accent and wondered if it were real or affected. "Was Jeremiah born in the East or was that a trace of Britain I heard in his speech?"

"Born in New England, but, yes, he does sound British, doesn't he?" Maggie raised sparkling eyes to her niece. "Do you know how glorious I feel since he's come back to me? Every day's a treasure, every one."

If only it would last for her, Chris thought with a small tug of irrational fear. Did this overwhelming feeling ever last, for anyone? "I'm so very glad for you."

Inside, she heard the echoes of the doorbell and the shuffling of feet as someone moved to answer it. Probably Mike, Chris decided.

She loved her brother dearly but knew that a rush of disturbing memories would walk in with him. They often talked on the phone, but carefully steered clear of controversial subjects, such as her sudden departure from Phoenix and Paul Cameron. At least *she* did, and she ignored Mike's veiled references. When he had made captain, she'd been elated, pleased he was mostly desk-bound now and out of danger. But she still fervently wished he were in another line of work and was unable to hide that from him.

"You look a little tired," Maggie went on. "Did you sleep well?"

Chris smiled indulgently. It had been some time since anyone had fussed over her. "I always sleep well under your roof," she said softly, then saw her aunt look toward the arched entrance behind her.

"They said I'd find you both out here," a deep voice said.

Not Mike's, Chris thought with a start. But a familiar one, even after all this time. So he'd come right away. She'd thought to postpone this meeting until she and Maggie had gone over things in the office. But it seemed that was not to be. Turning, she swung about, her gaze colliding with eyes dark brown and guarded. Then they warmed as he shifted to smile at Maggie.

"Paul Cameron." Maggie rose and extended her hand. "How good of you to come right over."

"You're looking lovely, Maggie." Paul walked to the table and took her hand. "Congratulations on your impending wedding." Though he hadn't seen much of her, he sincerely liked Mike's feisty aunt.

"Thank you. It's been too long since we've seen you. About a year, right."

"More than that, I think."

She'd forgotten how rock solid he was up close, Chris thought, studying him. The breadth of his shoulders under the light tan sportcoat seemed wider than she'd been remembering, his hips slimmer in well-fitting black slacks. His blond hair worn regulation short was still wind-tossed, his face a bit narrow and angular, his generous mouth saving it from looking hard. His lips were full, hinting of passion, and she knew how grandly he could deliver on that promise. And there was a new addition, a mustache, giving his face a kind of rakish air. She'd never much cared for mustaches, thinking they usually were worn to make a statement. Certainly Paul didn't need to make one. She wondered why he'd decided on growing it.

"You remember Christine." Maggie looked a little nervous at reintroducing two people who'd once meant a great deal to each other.

Paul adjusted his smile. "Of course. How have you been, Chris?" He took in the morning-fresh look of her in white slacks and yellow blouse, her skin free of makeup, and he tried not to recall other more private mornings that they had shared. She obviously hadn't been expecting him so soon. There was a wariness in her eyes, those huge blue eyes that dominated her small face, eyes that could make a man forget his name.

Chris found her voice. "I'm fine, thank you. And you?"

Waving Paul to a chair, Maggie answered for him. "Paul's doing wonderfully well. Did you know he made detective sergeant recently?" Glancing up, she raised auburn brows. "Coffee, Paul?"

Chris tried to look pleased. "I believe Mike mentioned your promotion. Congratulations."

Paul accepted the coffee and took a sip, feeling a little pleased with himself. He couldn't tell what she'd been expecting but he'd give her charming if it killed him. She wasn't quite sure how to respond to him on this new professional level. Good. He'd wanted to put her a little off balance. It was about damn time the ball was in his court.

Hesitantly Chris glanced through the archway. "Isn't Mike with you?"

"No, dear," Maggie said, answering for him again. "Paul's the investigating officer on my case." Her eyes seemed to implore Chris to understand that she had nothing to do with Mike's decision.

"Yes, I know," Chris said with just a touch of annoyance. "I just thought Mike would—"

"I'm sure he'll be calling you later," Paul said.

Maggie scooted back to her chair. "Excuse me a moment while I see what's keeping Jeremiah."

Not only was he here too soon, but she was left alone with him. Chris squared her shoulders as she sipped her coffee and studied him from under her lowered lashes. Paul had always been a sharp dresser. He hated ties, preferring casual clothes, but he wore them with style. She remembered once accusing him of being a Fred Astaire fan, often wearing colored socks to match his shirts, much as the dancer had. Today, his shirt was a bright yellow and, as he crossed his legs, she smiled at his yellow socks. "You're looking good, Paul. Success seems to agree with you."

He acknowledged the compliment with a small smile as he leaned forward, elbows on the table, and rested his chin on his clasped hands. "Where's that California tan I expected to see?"

Chris shrugged. "I don't seem to have much time for the sun. And I suppose you're too busy rounding up all the bad guys in black hats to spend much time outdoors." Beneath his cool exterior, there seemed a barely camouflaged tenseness, a slight weariness in the way he held himself, which was new and seemed out of character.

"Yes, though I still get out to ride my horse occasionally. We never did ride together, did we?"

"No, we never did." It was starting, reminders of the past. Chris swallowed more coffee.

Paul congratulated himself. This wasn't so difficult, making small talk while the many angry questions he wanted to hurl at her churned inside him. But he wasn't going to ask those questions, he'd promised himself. Because he really didn't give a damn about her answers. He'd almost wandered afield just now, asking about riding. He would stick to the business at hand. "So, what do you make of the embezzlement?"

Chris shook her head slowly, relieved to be on safer ground. "Four hundred thousand dollars is a lot of money. I've read the insurance claim, but there's not much information there."

Paul sat back, placing his left ankle on his right knee. "No, there isn't."

She raised her head questioningly. "Someone fairly high up in the executive ranks, would you imagine?"

He nodded. "That would be my guess at this stage. They've used several outside CPAs and auditing firms, but I think we can rule them out. The company books never leave the premises, so it would have to be someone who had easy access, someone who would come and go at all hours without arousing suspicion. Probably someone Maggie trusts implicitly."

"I have a feeling that's a long list to check out. Maggie's always prided herself on hiring people she could trust. Only one got by her, it would seem. How do you want to go about the investigation?"

A voice from the doorway interrupted Paul's answer.

"Buttermilk, darling," Jeremiah insisted, walking toward the table. "The difference is buttermilk." He carried a large plate laden with food while Maggie followed, hanging on his every word. "Biscuits *must* be made with buttermilk to be light and fluffy."

Jeremiah took his chair and Maggie sat down, her gaze never leaving him. Love lit up her face, peeling off the years. As Chris and Paul watched, Jeremiah tore off a buttery section of biscuit and lovingly fed it to her.

"Now, you see, that's scrumptious." Leaning toward her, he kissed her smiling lips. "And that's scrumptious, too."

"Too much cholesterol, dear," Maggie informed him, the pleasure in her voice taking the sting from her mild scolding. "You know it's bad for you."

Jeremiah beamed at her and blushed. "I love it when you worry about me."

The man actually blushed, Chris realized. When had she last seen a male color? Back in high school. Maybe "priceless" *was* the word for Jeremiah, at least in her aunt's view.

Maggie looked around the table as if suddenly realizing there were others present. "Forgive my manners, please. Jeremiah, this is Detective Sergeant Paul Cameron, the officer who's going to be investigating our case. Paul, I'd like you to meet my fiancé, Jeremiah Green."

"Nice to meet you." Paul rose and shook hands.

"My pleasure, young man," Jeremiah answered, offering a firm grip.

So this was the bridegroom, Paul thought. His practiced eye took in Jeremiah's expensive clothes, a row of imported cigars in his shirt pocket, boots that would easily cost an average man a week's pay. Jeremiah's smile didn't seem to reach his cool blue eyes. And he had soft, manicured hands. However he'd gotten his costly clothes, it hadn't been through manual labor. Mike had told him that Jeremiah's family had a name but little money. In forty years, he could have made a bundle through wise investments or come into some cash by inheritance. Or was

Maggie keeping him in grand style? It would bear looking into. As far as Paul was concerned, no one at this point was above suspicion.

Jeremiah swallowed a healthy mouthful of food and made an appreciative sound. "Aren't you having some breakfast, Sergeant?"

"Coffee's fine, thanks."

Shoveling in another goodly portion, Jeremiah shook his head. "You young people have terrible eating habits. Don't you agree, my dear?"

As Maggie nodded, Chris realized that she'd most likely agree to whatever Jeremiah thought these days. Hard to believe her sensible, hard-sell aunt had become so smitten.

"You're looking a little thinner, Christine," Maggie observed, pouring more coffee all around.

"I'll have to disagree with that," Paul interjected, his dark eyes on Chris. "I wouldn't change a thing." He took a deep breath, wondering what had made him state the obvious when he hadn't intended to say a word.

Compliments. He'd always been generous with them, Chris remembered. Yet the look on his face hinted that he'd spoken before careful thought and now regretted it. She'd let him off the hook and return to business. "Did you bring the police report with you?"

She was probably unaware that her hand was busily twisting a long strand of her hair, Paul thought as he recognized the familiar habit. He remembered she'd done that only when she'd been a little nervous. The thought made him smile as he reached inside his jacket, withdrew the folded report and handed it to her.

Chris leaned back, concentrating on reading.

"I've had the office next to mine at Lady Charm cleared out and made ready for the two of you," Maggie told Paul. "There are two desks, comfortable chairs, phones, a filing cabinet. Whatever else you may need, my secretary, Ginny, has been instructed to get for you.''

"That sounds perfect," Paul said.

Chris looked up, sensing an underlying anxiety in her aunt's words. After all, an embezzlement was not an everyday occurrence. "That's sweet of you, Maggie, and I'm sure I'll be spending time there," she said. "But I imagine Paul will be working out of his office at police headquarters. This can't be his only case." Having a police officer on the premises would only make Maggie more nervous. And having *this* particular one constantly around wouldn't do much for Chris's nerves, either.

So she didn't want him near her, Paul thought. Too bad, because he intended to be. Let her be uncomfortable for a change. Besides Mike had made it clear that he had little choice in the matter. "The captain feels strongly that this case should take priority over my others for the time being," Paul said in his most reasonable tone. "I'll be reporting in frequently, of course, but I'll be available to share the office with you, Chris."

The captain. She'd forgotten her brother, the good captain. Inadvertently, and with the best of intentions on Maggie's behalf, Mike had made sure she and Paul would be together continually. She hadn't counted on that.

Smile in place, Chris stood. She would show Paul just how adaptable she was. "Fine. I'll get changed, grab my papers and drive in with Maggie so we can set things up."

Maggie frowned. "Oh, dear. I won't be going in till late afternoon today, if at all. Jeremiah and I have some wedding things to attend to. Unless, of course, you absolutely need me." Her voice held a note of apology. "Paul, would you mind driving Chris in? Dear, would that be all right?"

Chris ground her teeth and hoped no one noticed. More time spent together. She could, she supposed, rent a car, but that would be pressing a point. She plastered on another weak smile.

Seeing her discomfort restored some of Paul's good humor. She wasn't any happier about their arrangement than he was. He was determined to be pleasant no matter the price. "No problem. I'm still driving my old Mustang, and I promise not to put the red light up on top or turn on my siren."

Big of him. Chris could see no way to bow out gracefully. Her only outward reaction as she turned to leave was a slight narrowing of the eyes, which she was certain Paul didn't miss. "I'll be ready in ten minutes."

Upstairs, she again questioned her wisdom in insisting on this assignment. She remembered Paul's old '69 Mustang, the one he'd lovingly restored. She'd be riding in it again, steeped in memories, knee-deep in nostalgia. With determination, Chris yanked open the closet door. She couldn't run away this time. She'd handle it, that's all.

"WE'LL NEED PROFILES on all employees from Personnel," Paul said as Maggie's secretary took notes. "For those who had access to accounting records in even the smallest way, we'll need their entire file. The first shortage appeared—" he glanced down at his report, then back up "—nearly two years ago. We should have all accounting records from that time to the present, including ledgers, year-end reports, financial statements, income tax returns, fiscal projections. I want to see the independent audit, previous audits, sales reports and cost sheets."

"Very good. Anything else?" Ginny asked.

He smiled, hoping to soften the tall order. "It's a lot of work, I know, but once we have all that, hopefully we won't have to impose too often on your time."

A short, middle-aged woman with a cap of prematurely gray curls, Ginny returned his smile. "It's no problem. I'll have some of it by this afternoon, the rest within a couple days.''

"Great. Chris, can you think of anything else?"

Glancing up from the papers she was reading, she gave Ginny a smile. "No, I think that's it for now."

With a nod to both of them, Ginny left the room.

"As soon as I get the complete employee list from Personnel," Paul said as he turned in his swivel chair to look at Chris, "I'll run a check on everyone, just as a precaution, to see if anyone has a police record."

"Good idea. Let me finish reading this police report, and then we can set up a schedule for the interviews."

Shifting his gaze around the large, comfortable office Maggie had had prepared for them, Paul decided it was a big improvement over his own cubicle at police headquarters. Thick, pale gray carpeting, a couch in muted stripes, touches of salmon and creamy beige, two thriving green plants and a huge window that provided an inspiring view of jagged mountains and blue sky. Four-stories high, the stucco building that housed Lady Charm, its plant and offices and vast parking lot, spread over five acres. Not bad, Maggie Muldoon, he thought, mentally tipping his hat to the woman who'd worked long and hard for it all. She deserved some happy time, some carefree years. Finding the embezzler would take those faint strain lines from her face, the nervous quiver from her voice, he was certain.

Paul's interest returned to Chris seated at the other desk. Her long, black hair was pinned up off her neck, giving her a businesslike, remote look. Her tailored white linen suit worn with a blue silk blouse projected the same no-nonsense image. Only her scent—something dark, heady and expensive—hinted of the real woman beneath.

His mind took him back to the day he'd first inhaled that fragrance, the day he'd first kissed her. They'd met at a party Mike had given in his new apartment one rainy night.

Chris had had car trouble so he'd offered to drive her home. They'd stopped for coffee and had been shocked to find they'd spent two hours exchanging life stories. At her door, he hadn't been able to resist kissing her. She'd pulled back from him with a look of surprised pleasure, then had leaned in for another taste. That had been the beginning and...

Paul threw down his pen. He hadn't allowed himself to remember pleasant beginnings in a long while. It was healthier for him to remember sour endings so he wouldn't have to face another. A smart man didn't let himself get burned twice by the same match. If only he wasn't cursed with a damnably keen memory, especially now that the subject of his musings was only ten feet away.

The opening of the door interrupted Paul's thoughts, causing him to look up. A tall man wearing brown slacks, his shirtsleeves rolled up, his pale blue eyes skittish, stepped in. His narrow face broke into a shy smile as he spotted Chris.

"Teddy!" Chris rose to hug her cousin, stepped back to look at him. "It's good to see you."

"You, too, Christine," Teddy said in a soft voice. "You've stayed away too long."

"Perhaps." He was the same as she remembered, only a bit paler. She noticed new strain lines around his eyes and a nervous twitch at the corner of his mouth. A faint odor of strong tobacco clung to his somewhat rumpled clothes, and there was a thin sheen of perspiration on his broad forehead. The embezzlement was taking its toll, Chris decided. Even as a young man, he'd never handled stress well. Turning, she included Paul. "I'd like you to meet Detective Sergeant Paul Cameron. Paul, this is my cousin, Teddy Muldoon."

"Nice to meet you." A firmer grip than he'd have imagined, Paul thought, shaking hands with the heir apparent.

Or was he, now that Jeremiah was on the scene? Odd that he'd never met Teddy before now, though he'd known both Mike and Chris for several years. A man with a low profile.

"Same here." Teddy gave him a guarded smile before turning back to Chris. "Have you talked with Mike yet?"

Chris leaned against her desk, crossing her ankles. "No, but I hope to see him soon. Maybe we can all get together at Maggie's. I'm anxious to meet your wife."

A frown appeared on Teddy's face, and he smoothed his thinning red hair back nervously. "I don't know. Diane might have other plans."

Other plans? She hadn't even mentioned a particular date, Chris realized. Either Diane wasn't terribly social or Teddy was being overly cautious.

Thrusting his hands into his pockets, Teddy looked from one to the other. "You're both working on the case?"

"Yes." Paul rose and went to stand next to Chris. "I hope we can count on your help."

"Oh, sure. Maggie already asked me to be available. What do you need?"

You could tell a lot about the relationship between two people by what they call each other, Paul thought. Teddy called his mother by her first name. Not Mom or Mother, but Maggie. He wasn't sure yet what that indicated but perhaps he'd be able to find out in time. "Nothing right now, thanks. But after we get the personnel files, maybe you can give us a rundown on some of the questionables. You've been with Lady Charm a long time, so you probably know everyone who works here."

"I started here full-time after I came home from college. I guess you could say I know everyone."

"That'll be a big help," Chris added, wishing he didn't look so uneasy. She couldn't remember when she'd last seen her cousin relaxed.

"Perhaps I can be of assistance also."

Three pairs of eyes swung in the direction of the voice coming from the open doorway. Chris watched a slim blonde, beautifully dressed in a rose-colored silk chemise, stroll in. She was small with lovely features and green eyes that assessed thoroughly. In one hand she held a cigarette in a long, gold holder, and before anyone spoke, she reached out her other hand toward Chris.

"You must be Christine Donovan. I'm Diane Muldoon."

Chris hoped her surprise didn't show as she shook hands. In her wildest dreams, she'd never have imagined this cool, sophisticated woman as Teddy's wife. "I'm happy to meet you."

Diane's eyes turned a shade frosty. "It's too bad you couldn't have made it in for our reception. It was quite a party." She inhaled deeply and studied Chris through the smoke.

"Christine's job keeps her very busy," Teddy said, defending his cousin.

"I'm sure it does," Diane murmured, not even glancing at her husband. Her green gaze moved to Paul. "Nice to have you with us, Sergeant Cameron. If there's anything I can do to expedite your investigation, you'll find me across the hall."

Diane had finally managed to find a smile, Chris noted, and she gave it to Paul. But then, she looked like a woman who easily dismissed other women yet had a keen eye for most men.

Paul found her hand cool and dry. "Thank you. I'll keep that in mind." So she already knew who he was. A woman who prided herself on doing her homework, he thought. No warmth in her eyes, no softness in the stiff way she held her body. It would be wise not to underestimate Diane Muldoon.

As if she'd just noticed him standing awkwardly nearby, Diane looked up at her husband. "Are you taking me to lunch, darling?" she asked.

It was the voice, Paul realized. Matter-of-fact, as if she'd asked him to pass the salt. No inflection, no suggestion of humor, no enthusiasm. A very controlled lady.

Shuffling his feet, Teddy nodded, looking boyishly pleased. "Sure, I'll take you to lunch."

"See you two later." Diane turned and walked out. With a self-conscious wave, Teddy followed her, closing the door.

"Interesting couple," Paul commented as he returned to his desk. "Why didn't you come back for their wedding reception, just about a year ago, wasn't it?"

Hard to take the detective out of the man, Chris thought. Ever ready with more questions. She sat down and rubbed a spot just above her left eye. Already the beginning of a headache, and it was only late morning of the first day. "Like Teddy said, my job keeps me quite busy."

Too simplistic an explanation, Paul thought, but he decided not to press. He needed Chris's cooperation throughout this investigation, and zeroing in on her motives, past and present, was not the way to get it. The sooner this case was solved, the better off they'd both be. He decided to switch the focus to Maggie's son. "Considering his position in the company, I'm surprised to find Teddy so . . . so nonassertive."

Chris nodded in agreement. "Even less assertive than he used to be. He's always had a problem with self-image, despite being showered with Maggie's love. Perhaps it stems from growing up without a father."

"You lost your father at an early age, and you're pretty assertive. I grew up without a mother and . . ."

"But you have a very assertive father." Chris frowned, thinking of John Cameron, the senior senator from Arizona. Assertive wasn't the only word she'd use to describe his father, and none of them were kind. She brushed away the thought and returned to the subject of her cousin. "I'd hoped that marriage would improve Teddy's sense of his own worth. But Diane . . ."

"Isn't quite the kind of woman you expected Teddy to marry?"

"No, not at all. Don't you see them as an unlikely couple?"

"Yes, but it's hard to say what attracts one person to another."

Chris slid her gaze to Paul, but he was staring out the window thoughtfully. Why was she suddenly looking for double meanings in his words? "Are you planning to interview Teddy and Diane, too?"

Paul swung around and pulled out a yellow pad. "Everyone. It's too early to rule out anyone. Isn't that how you usually work, a process of elimination?"

"Yes."

"Are you going to have a problem questioning these people, some who are relatives, others who are friends?" If she was hesitant, he needed to know.

Would she be able to ask tough, direct, perhaps disturbing questions of Teddy and Diane and the others? Chris asked herself. Everyone, Paul said. Yes, that's how it had to be done. She'd just have to set aside her feelings. She was good at that, wasn't she? "I don't anticipate problems. Even though I lived with Maggie, I hardly know most of the people here at the office."

"If you do—" The ringing phone interrupted Paul. He picked it up. "Cameron."

"Paul, this is Maggie. Did you find everything you need?"

He caught the hesitancy in her voice and tried to sound reassuring. "Yes, everything's fine."

"Oh, good. I'm feeling a bit guilty not being there on your first day. But we've so many arrangements to make, and there's something Jeremiah wants me to see way across town. If you need me, though, I can—"

"We're managing very well. Ginny's been great. You just enjoy your day." He heard Maggie sigh her relief.

"Thank you. And, Paul, please take Chris to lunch. I worry about her. She looks thin and more tired than I'd expected. I wanted her here with me, yet I hated dragging her back, if you know what I mean."

He knew, all right. "I'll do that, Maggie."

"And perhaps tomorrow, if you both have the time, I can take you on a tour of the plant. Would you care to see how we make our cosmetics?"

Paul could think of nothing he'd care for less. "That sounds good. I'll mention it to Chris."

"Fine. And the lunch is on me. Take her somewhere special, will you?"

"Don't worry, I will. Talk with you later." He hung up, scarcely realizing he was frowning. He wished Maggie would stay busy with her wedding arrangements and quit interfering. She wasn't making this easier on either of them.

"Is anything the matter?" Chris asked, noticing his annoyed expression.

"Not really. Your aunt's feeling a little guilty not being with us."

Chris smiled. "Yes, she would."

Paul stood. "She's worried about you and wants me to take you to lunch."

Chris sat back and shook her head. "She needn't pass her mother-hen ways on to you. Besides, I usually skip lunch."

"I know. And you skipped breakfast. Ginny won't have the first set of files here for another hour at least. Come on, I'll buy you an enchilada. I know this great place not far from here." Probably not as grand a place as Maggie would have chosen, but he had no intention of accepting her offer of payment anyhow.

Well, why not? Chris thought. They were just two business associates sharing a lunch. Still...

Paul's gaze skimmed her from head to toe, his expression assessing as he saw the hesitancy in her eyes. "Maggie's right. You're too thin. Downright skinny, I'd say."

She rose to his bait and reached for her handbag, letting her expression tell him she knew exactly what he'd done. "All right, let's go."

"Good. I'd hate to disobey a direct order from Maggie."

"I'll just bet you're a stickler for direct orders."

"Matter of fact, I am, for those brave enough to give them to me."

She reached for the doorknob. "That lets me out. I'm not very brave."

"I wouldn't say that," Paul said, his eyes on hers. "You're here, aren't you?"

She had no answer to that, Chris decided as she walked out the door.

THE RESTAURANT WAS SMALL, noisy and fragrant with mysterious kitchen smells. Muted Mexican music thrummed in the background. Recognizing Paul, a tall, bearded waiter with a big, toothy grin hustled them to a corner table miraculously vacant in the noontime frenzy. He seated them with a flourish, then left to fetch a pitcher of water.

"You must come here often," Chris observed, dipping a crisp corn chip into a bowl of thick, red salsa before bringing it to her mouth. "Mmm, delicious."

"I bring all my skinny insurance investigators here. Irving here fattens them up."

"Irving?"

"Irving Gonzales, at your service, ma'am," the tall waiter said as he returned to pour ice water for them. "What'll it be, Sarge, the usual?"

Paul glanced at Chris. "You willing to risk it?"

"Sure, let's go for it."

Paul nodded to Irving, who scooted off to the back. "Your experimental nature pleased him. His mother's the cook."

Chris took a long drink of water to quench the fire she'd swallowed, then gave Paul a suspicious look. "Irving's mother is the cook? Where's his father, doing dishes?"

Paul swallowed a crunchy chip before answering. "No, he's doing time in prison."

"And you put him there?"

"Sure did. Ever since, Mrs. Gonzales has fed me free of charge, as long as my system can handle her chili peppers."

"Why, Sergeant, payola?" She shook her head, smiling. This was comfortable, almost like the old days. She'd always enjoyed Paul's company. "I don't know whether to believe you or not. You always did tell whoppers."

The tables were small, their chairs close together, their arms almost touching. All around, the voices of diners ebbed and flowed, leaving them in a cozy cocoon of privacy. Leaning forward, the smile left Paul's face. "This is no whopper. I didn't want to be put on this case, and I don't think you were too pleased to return either, were you?"

Perhaps it was best to get a few things said, discussed and set aside so they could get on with the job at hand. "I was a little concerned, wondering if we could work together." She raised his eyes to his. "Weren't you?"

"At first. Then I thought it over and realized we're nothing to each other anymore. Just a man and a woman, a detective and an insurance investigator, working on a case. Nothing more, nothing less.''

She caught the bitterness in his tone. She'd known she'd hurt him. She'd not known how deeply. But he was right. They were two professionals who had a job to do. "Exactly. Polite strangers who'd known each other once, but no more.''

Paul tried to keep the resentment from his voice. "Why did you leave so suddenly, without a word?''

She should have known he wouldn't just let it go. He wanted his pound of flesh. "I wrote you, I tried to explain.'' His silence told her that that feeble explanation wasn't enough. Perhaps she did owe him more. "I couldn't handle the pressure, Paul. I saw no solution except removing myself from the problem.''

"And *I* was the problem?''

She watched her hands fold and unfold her napkin. "Yes.''

"Self-imposed pressure then.''

"Isn't that the worst kind? After that night, when I saw you shot, when I held you in my arms, I knew I wasn't cut out for that kind of life. No matter how much I cared...''

"And so you ran away.''

She raised her eyes at last, wondering if he'd ever see how much that decision had cost her. "I never meant to hurt you.'' Briefly, she saw the banked fury in his eyes and knew he'd resurrected his rage to cover up the pain.

"I think it was a little easier for you. You were the one who left, not the one left behind. You didn't have to get over the anger and the hurt.''

"No,'' she said softly. "All I had to get over was you.''

Irving chose that moment to set before each of them a steaming plate of Paul's usual—chilis *relleno*, cheese enchilada, refried beans and rice. "Something to drink, folks?'' he asked as he looked from one silent face to the other.

Chris recovered first. "Iced tea, please," she said, wondering if she'd be able to swallow anything since her appetite had suddenly vanished.

"Make that two." Paul picked up his fork and jabbed at his food. He shouldn't have brought it up, he thought, taking in a very hot mouthful. Why had he let her know how hard it had been for him, how hard it still was seeing her again? He was a man forcefully in control of his life, of every facet of it. Except this one slender, slip of a woman. But he would master his feelings for her, too. He would *not* let her get to him again.

With some effort, he made his voice calm and level. "Is today the first time you've met Jeremiah?"

She swallowed carefully and latched onto the neutral topic. "Yes," Chris answered. "He's a bit overwhelming, isn't he?"

"That he is. He and Maggie are so different, yet they seem compatible. And she's waited forty years for him. Amazing." Paul looked up and smiled his thanks as Irving placed iced tea in front of them. He squeezed fresh lemon into his. "Did Maggie talk about him a lot when you lived with her?"

Chris took a sip of tea and shook her head. "Hardly ever. Oh, I knew there'd been someone she'd cared for as a teenager from stories my mother had told me. And I thought it was so romantic, star-crossed lovers and all that. But, of course, I was too young to realize how much pain she'd been through. We were close, but Maggie seldom spoke of Jeremiah to anyone. Occasionally I'd find her staring off into the mountains, looking sad and a little wistful. Yet when I'd go to her, she'd brighten immediately, looking grateful that I'd interrupted her lonely thoughts. Maggie's a remarkable woman."

"She may have met her match in Jeremiah. He's one of a kind."

Thinking of Maggie's comments about Jeremiah's penchant for nude swimming, Chris hid a smile. "I think he's made her come out of her shell a bit. She had a colorful youth, but she'd settled down in recent years. He's revived all that spirit she'd probably forgotten."

"I wouldn't have picked Maggie and Jeremiah as soul mates, but then it's impossible to tell what attracts one person to another, don't you agree?"

Twice now, he'd mentioned that. Lifting her eyes, she noticed again the slight cleft in his chin, noticed and remembered the way her lips had so often been drawn to the small indentation. She set down her fork and decided to give him an honest answer. "No, I don't agree. Not in every case."

Paul raised questioning brows as he scooped a mound of rice into his mouth. "How so?"

This sort of innuendo fencing was what often happened in the months they'd dated, Chris recalled. They'd always been on the opposite sides of controversial issues, but both had enjoyed the debates. Paul's keen mind had been one of the things that had drawn her to him. There was always a danger to this type of conversation, but there was also an excitement in sharing innermost thoughts. She hadn't done that with anyone since she'd left Phoenix.

"I know exactly what attracts me to someone," she said. "Don't you?"

"Why don't you tell me?"

Despite his earlier attempts at catching her off guard, he was as wary as she. That thought gave her courage. She hated walking on egg shells, especially for the several weeks this investigation would probably take. Best to get it all out. "I don't think I need to stroke your ego, Paul. You certainly must know I was very attracted to you. That was never the problem."

Was attracted, she'd said. He watched her play with a loose curl of hair and wondered why neither of them could leave it alone. They were like children scratching at a bothersome scab that wouldn't heal. "Then what was the problem?"

"As I said earlier, I became very uncomfortable with your career choice after what I'd been through with my father, and you seemed to thrive on it. I was getting too serious about you, thinking forever and happily-ever-after thoughts. I don't want to love a cop. It's as simple as that." She wasn't going to mention her chat with John Cameron. Paul obviously knew nothing of it and there seemed no point at this late date. Besides, his father wasn't the real reason she'd left.

She'd found the secret to turning love on and off. How simple, how wonderful for her, Paul thought. He drained his tea and signaled for another before he turned narrowed eyes on her. "Danger's a relative thing. A CPA with a safe desk job can step off a curb and get run over by a bus. You're afraid to let yourself care, afraid you'll be hurt, afraid to live. Fine. I hope you find some nice, quiet, safe man to marry, and I hope you both live to be ninety. Somebody like good old Mark Emery. I'll bet he has dental checkups twice a year, jogs daily and has a low cholesterol count."

She wasn't going to allow him to get her angry. "How do you know Mark?"

"I met him a couple of times before he moved to San Diego."

He had no business asking about her personal life—not any longer. Chris put on a confident smile. "Matter of fact, Mark *is* still in my life. He's a terrific guy. We run together, not jog. There's a difference."

"Peachy." Paul accepted his fresh glass of tea and gulped half before setting it down. This was exactly what he'd promised himself he *wouldn't* do. Why had Maggie suggested this lunch, and why had he been dumb enough to go along with it? He cleared his throat, gathering his thoughts, absolutely determined to show Chris that he didn't give a damn about her personal life.

"I have a serious question to ask you," he said, watching the suspicion leap into her eyes.

"What's that?"

"Are you going to finish that enchillada? It's a shame to see it go to waste."

Feeling enormously relieved at the change in subjects, Chris exchanged his plate with hers. "Here, growing boy. You're going to need your strength this afternoon." If he could switch from serious to silly so easily, she'd show him she could, too. "Who do we interview first, and how do you want to go about it?"

Paul took a bite before answering. "The way I've set it up, we go with either the chief bookkeeper, Nancy Evans, or the chemist, Steve Thorn, this afternoon. We can probably fit both in, provided they're available." Finishing, Paul sat back and wiped his mouth.

"I think Maggie's asked everyone to be available."

"I'd like you to take the first person and seat him or her alongside your desk and ask the questions, which we'll go over together beforehand. Meanwhile, I'll be at the other desk, messing around with some papers, but actually listening to the conversation. Taking notes while people talk makes them nervous and causes them to clam up. If we both listen, one might catch something the other missed. Then, for the next interview, we'll reverse the roles. What do you think?"

"Sounds good, boss."

"I'm not your boss, Chris. We're partners." He offered his hand. "Can you handle that?"

It was the best they could manage at this point. She gave his hand a quick shake. "Sure, although I wouldn't be surprised if you leave me totally in charge this afternoon."

Paul rose and guided her to the front door. "Why's that?"

"With all that hot food you consumed, you may be out of commission in another hour."

With a smile and wave at Irving, he opened the door for Chris. "Not old iron gut," he told her.

Chapter Three

"I hope I'm not late," Nancy Evans said, wearing a worried frown as she came in precisely at two o'clock.

Chris rose to greet her. "Right on time. I'm Chris Donovan, and that's Detective Sergeant Paul Cameron. We're pleased you could spare us the time."

Nodding shyly toward Paul, Nancy seated herself in the chair Chris had set alongside her desk.

"I have a few general questions," Chris said, sitting down and opening the folder that had been sent by Personnel. "And a few specifics on the ledgers that I hope you can answer for us." Right out of Central Casting, Chris thought, smiling reassuringly at the small woman with the thick glasses and wispy brown hair.

"If I can."

It took Chris less than an hour of conversation to determine that Nancy was an expert in her field and knew her books inside and out, that she was nearly thirty-five and that she was painfully shy and nervous by nature. Chris deliberately hadn't read Nancy's personnel file beforehand, preferring to form her own impressions.

Throughout the questioning Paul hadn't said a word, his head bent to a pad he was writing on. Yet Chris had caught him studying Nancy surreptitiously with occasional glances. He'd even made a phone call, speaking in low tones, but had otherwise remained in the background. It pleased Chris that he'd not interrupted. Partners. A new thought.

"You're really on top of these books, Nancy," Chris told the woman as she closed the final ledger. "Who do you think is behind this embezzlement?"

Nancy sat back, her eyes on her hands held tightly in her lap. "I don't know."

"But you must have some ideas. Who had access? Who could have altered these books without anyone noticing for months?"

"Lots of people have access. I just don't know." Nancy stood and glanced around the room. "Do you mind if I have some water? Arizona's so dry, I drink quarts of water every day."

"So do I. Help yourself." Chris was thoughtful as she watched Nancy eye Paul timidly, then skirt his desk and quickly fill a paper cup from the water cooler. Drinking deeply, she crumpled the cup and returned to her chair. Was this quiet, self-effacing woman capable of grand theft? On the surface, it wouldn't appear so. But experience had taught Chris that criminals came in all sorts of wrappings.

"Do you think it's possible that someone came in, let's say at night, and altered your books in such a way that you wouldn't know it for some time?"

"No." Nancy shifted in her seat, clearly uncomfortable with that thought.

Chris arched a brow. "No? Not possible?"

"Not probable. There's security who patrol at night. How would this person get past them?" Nancy shook her head. "No."

"Let's suppose it was someone known to the guards, someone who works here, whose presence at unexpected hours wouldn't be questioned?"

Nancy appeared to think that over before swinging her myopic gaze to Chris. "Sometimes the men on duty have a dog with them."

"Dogs can get used to a person's scent." Watching closely, Chris saw Nancy dismiss that thought also as she toyed with the paper cup. She wasn't going to get anywhere pressing this woman. She did want to pursue something else that had her curious. It was really none of her business, but... "I'm surprised you haven't gotten your CPA certification, Nancy. Are you planning to?"

The bookkeeper made a self-conscious swipe at an errant lock of hair as she shook her head. "I'd planned to, once. But I had to go to work, and we just didn't have the money for more schooling. Then my mother died, and there was my younger brother to take care of. Now, it seems a little late."

"I remember Maggie telling me about a program here at Lady Charm, something about continuing education toward a degree or further professional development while you work."

Nodding, Nancy tossed her crumpled paper cup into Chris's basket. "Yes, I almost signed up for it but... well, I might be getting married soon." The blush crept up her neck, the added color making her small face almost pretty.

"How nice," Chris said as she stood. "But you can do both. You certainly have a thorough knowledge and a quick mind." As far as her work went, but she seemed deliberately vague or naively evasive on other questions.

Nancy stood and gave Chris a small smile. "Thanks, but I'm not sure Steve will want me to continue working after... after we're married. Do you need me for anything else?"

"That's about it for now. We'll sift through all this and if we have any further questions, we'll call you. Thanks again."

"Sure, anytime." With a quick nod toward Paul, she scooted out the door and closed it quietly behind her.

Letting out a deep breath, Chris sat down and turned to Paul. "Well, what do you think?"

He was thinking that Chris handled herself very professionally. She'd asked the questions they'd gone over plus several new ones, yet had known when to back off. She had a natural instinct for compassion that appealed to his sense of fair play. But then he'd expected her to be good at her job.

"Odd little mouse of a woman," he said, rising and stretching, then walking over to her desk. "You probably deal with bookkeepers more than I. How'd she impress you?"

Chris played with her pen as she spoke. "On a first impression, she's typical. Male or female, most of the bookkeepers I've met seem very much at home with numbers, ledgers, and yet are oddly insecure with people and personal relationships. Maybe it's because numbers never lie, two and two are always four. They deal in a world of absolutes. Figures can be relied upon and people can't."

"Interesting observation," Paul mused as he perched on the edge of her desk. "She seemed uneasy, almost jumpy. Did you catch that?"

"Yes, but that could be because you're an officer of the law and I'm an insurance investigator reviewing her books. That's enough to make anyone jumpy and nervous."

"I suppose. We'll have to check out those night guards. Why do they have dogs with them only some of the time?"

Chris massaged the back of her neck absently. "I'll ask Teddy. He can probably help us there."

"You have a headache?"

She frowned. "Probably just tension. I left in a hurry, and the last couple of days have been hectic."

Tension. He could relate to that. He'd been more tense today than on some dangerous stakeouts he'd been on. "Need some aspirin?"

"I think I'll wait and see if it gets worse." Chris continued rubbing, remembering another time and another place when she'd complained of a headache and Paul had taken the pins from her hair and massaged her head with his long, sensitive fingers. In short order, he'd chased away the pain, and she'd turned in his arms, reaching for his kiss and—

"Steve Thorn is due any minute," Paul said as he checked his watch and adjusted the chair alongside his desk where the chemist would sit.

With genuine effort, Chris brought herself back to the matter at hand. "I'll be able to see Steve clearly from there and— Steve! Say, didn't Nancy say she was getting married soon, to a man named Steve? Do you suppose Steve Thorn could be that man?"

Paul sat down and reached for the Thorn file. "We'll soon find out."

"You're not going to ask him such a personal question, are you?"

"Not directly. We'll see how it works out. You're a more gentle interrogator than I am."

Chris added a couple of random thoughts to Nancy's file while she waited. It was ten minutes after the hour when Lady Charm's chief chemist gave a quick knock on the door and briskly strolled in. Perhaps he'd gotten involved in a project he couldn't easily leave, she thought, or he was someone who was perennially late. Maybe he just liked to keep people waiting. He made no apologies, just shook hands with both of them as they introduced themselves and sat down where Paul indicated.

He was a slight man, Paul noted, bordering on thin, with neatly combed brown hair and a sallow complexion. He wore a striped shirt, designer jeans and a leather belt with a large, silver buckle. A package of cheroots was wedged into his shirt pocket. He looked arrogant, self-assured and obviously annoyed.

"How long have you been with Lady Charm?" Paul began.

"That information's in my file," Steve answered, nodding toward the folder on the desk.

"I haven't had a chance to read your file. I'd like you to tell me."

Steve sighed, an exasperated sound. "Five long years."

Paul caught the emphasis on "long." An unhappy employee? "All of those as chief chemist?"

With a look of impatience, Steve raised his pale blue eyes to Paul's face. "If you'd care to check my credentials—when you have the time—you'll find that they're impeccable, my background unblemished. *Of course*, I hired in as chief chemist."

The sarcasm wasn't lost on Paul, but he kept his features bland. He'd dealt with resentful subjects before. Was Steve just a pompous ass with an elevated sense of his own importance, or did he have legitimate reasons for sounding bitter?

"And before coming here, where did you work?"

Steve seemed to reach for a tiny shred of remaining patience. "Sergeant, I don't have time for all this. Why must I sit here and repeat information that's already in my file?"

Folding his hands on the desk, Paul slowly leaned forward. Even to the keenest observer, Chris thought as she watched him carefully, only his eyes had changed from moments before. They'd gone steely cold.

"Mr. Thorn, we are dealing here with an embezzlement of some magnitude. Someone has deliberately and methodically altered the books of this company over a period of some months and siphoned off over four hundred thousand dollars that didn't belong to him. Or her. My job,

along with Miss Donovan, is to find that someone. No one
at this firm—I repeat, *no one*—is too busy, too important
or above suspicion at this point. We can do this with your
cooperation or without. We can do it here or downtown at
police headquarters. Your choice. But we will do it, Mr.
Thorn. Do I make myself clear?''

Steve shifted slightly on the chair, but he wasn't about to
give in easily. ''Wouldn't it make sense, in the interest of
time, to read the personnel files on everyone *before* you
question them?''

Paul allowed himself the smallest of smiles, though it
didn't reach his eyes. ''I won't tell you how to make your
perfumes if you don't tell me how to run my investigation.'' He took a calming breath because inside he was
seething. ''Now then, before coming here, where did you
work?''

Chris found two aspirins in her purse and got up for a
drink of water. She saw Steve's angry eyes watch her as he
all but spat out his answers to Paul. She returned to her
desk and sat doodling on her pad as Paul dragged Steve's
reluctant memory back through his education, his job history, the cities he'd lived in and enough background to fill
two files. Though Paul's methods weren't hers, she had to
admit that within half an hour, the cockiness Steve had
strolled in with had diminished considerably.

''Do you ever have occasion to go into the accounting
department?''

''Rarely.''

''But you have been there?''

''Inasmuch as I've probably been in every nook and
cranny in the entire complex over five years, yes, I've been
in accounting.''

''Who do you think did the embezzling?''

''I haven't a clue.''

''Do you know Nancy Evans?''

Steve shifted his gaze out the window, appearing bored. "Of course."

"Who in this company do you feel is capable of embezzling?"

For the first time, Steve allowed himself a tiny smile. "Many."

"For what reason?"

His eyes were wearily disdainful. "The obvious reason. Money. Most everyone's underpaid."

"Are you saying that nearly everyone at Lady Charm is underpaid?"

"Yes. Except for a . . . a privileged few."

"How would you know, Mr. Thorn, as a chemist and not working in payroll, what anyone is paid and whether they consider that pay satisfactory or not?"

"People talk."

"Directly to you?"

"Check with the employees if you don't believe me."

"Are you ever social with other people who work here?"

"No, never. Except when Maggie has everyone over to her place, and that's not often."

"Are you planning on being married soon?"

That stopped him. His eyes narrowed, and his mouth all but dropped open. "Who told you that?"

"Are you?"

"No, not that it's any of your business." His thin fingers drummed on the desktop. "Look, am I being accused of something here?"

Paul's voice was maddeningly calm in the face of Steve's anxiety. "I told you. Everyone is under suspicion until they're cleared. Who is your immediate superior?"

"I report to no one. I work with Maggie."

The man's ego was staggering. Paul tried not to grit his teeth. "Do you ever compile reports on new products, experiments, things like that?"

"Yes."

"Who do you hand them to, Maggie?"

"No. Teddy Muldoon. How many more questions?"

Paul leaned back. "That'll be all—for today."

Stiffly Steve Thorn stood. He couldn't resist a parting shot. "Are you going to warn me not to leave town?"

"Why, Mr. Thorn," Paul said with a smile, "you've been watching *L.A. Law* too long."

His eyes flinty, Steve walked past Chris without a word and left the room, closing the door hard behind him.

"Whew!" She let out a deep breath. "That was some interview."

Paul shook his head. "That guy's got a real chip on his shoulder, to say nothing of an ego the size of the Grand Canyon."

"He's a real piece of work, all right. I don't think he's the Steve Nancy spoke of. He's not her type."

Frowning, Paul turned to gaze out the window. "I'm not sure. Steve's shrewd. He deliberately misled us with some of his answers."

"Is that why you jumped around questioning him, trying to catch him off guard?"

"Yes. I'm not sure it worked. He's really cautious."

"Maybe Maggie could give us some insight into him. She's the one who hired him. I wonder if she'll make it in today."

"Ginny heard from her and told me that Maggie and Jeremiah decided to have a long, late lunch but she'll be in tomorrow."

"Good for them."

"Yeah," Paul agreed under his breath, wishing he and Chris had taken a leisurely lunch, wishing ... He shook his head as if to dislodge thoughts along those lines. It was self-defeating to try to recapture the past. He opened the file.

"I've got to write my notes on Steve before I forget my impressions."

Chris began clearing away her papers. "If you don't need me anymore, I think I'll call a cab and go back to Maggie's, maybe take a swim."

Paul began writing, but he wasn't concentrating. He was remembering a day long ago when he and Chris had taken inner tubes and gone tubing on the Salt River east of town. A lazy, fun-filled day when they'd waded in the chilly water and cooked hot dogs, then sat on a blanket counting the stars at nightfall. He clenched his teeth. He should instead be remembering the empty days and nights after she'd walked away from him, remembering the anger, so he wouldn't soften and let her get to him again.

He heard her click shut her briefcase. It was good she was leaving. He'd work better without her distracting presence. He began scribbling his notes.

At the door Chris turned to look back at Paul. He was already absorbed in completing his report. Work always came first with him. It had before, and it probably always would. She felt sorry for a woman who might try to compete with his commitment to his career. He was a man married to his job, and a dangerous one at that. The most a woman could hope for with Paul would be second place, not an enviable position. She'd definitely made the right decision in separating herself from him.

Still, irrationally, she wished they could talk as old friends would. She'd buried the past and, if only Paul would, they could work companionably together, instead of with this underlying tension she knew they both felt. Somewhere she'd read that two people who'd once been lovers could never be friends, yet she wasn't sure she believed that. She sighed, deciding that seeing him only for the investigation would probably be best.

Chris opened the door. "See you tomorrow."

"Right. I'll set up the next interviews."

"Fine."

Quiet. It was suddenly so very silent in the small, stuffy room. Paul wrote rapidly, thinking he'd finish up and get out of here. He'd stop in at the station, see if Mike wanted an update and check on his other cases. Maybe afterward he'd call Susan, pick her up for a bite to eat. Susan was a buyer for a busy department store, yet she was not at all intense and could always make him laugh.

There was a knot of tension at the back of his neck, but he chose to ignore it. Work would make it disappear faster than any pill. At the precinct, there'd be action, noise, lively confusion. Here, it was too damn quiet.

CHRIS STOOD ON THE DIVING board of Maggie's pool and tested its resilience, bouncing lightly. Satisfied, she raised her arms, stepped into position, took a high jump and dived neatly into the shimmering water.

Refreshing coolness eased over her entire heated body, a bit of a shock to the system, but a pleasant one. Only half an hour in the noonday summer sun and her skin was hot, damp and itching for a plunge. She let the momentum carry her to the far side of the pool. It was Saturday, her first day off since arriving a week ago, and she was glad for the chance to relax.

After six laps, she emerged at the shallow end and let the water drip from her, smoothing back her long hair with one hand as she climbed the steps out onto the Kooldeck. She picked up her towel, lay back down on the lounge chair and turned her face to the sun as she closed her eyes.

Maggie and Jeremiah were off somewhere, Mike had phoned saying he'd stop over later, the household staff was busy, and Chris was glad to be alone. It had been a grueling week, and she was in need of some quiet time. Leaning toward the small table, she poured herself a glass of ice water from the insulated pitcher and took a long drink. Arizona took the moisture out of a person like a sponge. She'd forgotten that. Paul had begun to kid her about the amount of liquid she drank, steadily depleting the bottled water in their office.

Paul. His day off, too, and he was working at the precinct. Catching up on his other cases. Chris wondered if all those hours were really necessary, wondered if he ever stopped to smell the roses.

They'd made progress in their workload this past week, interviewing an endless stream of people. They'd conferred with Teddy, Diane and Maggie, gathered reams of reports and still hadn't found a solid lead. Someone very clever had stolen that money, Chris thought as she reached for her sunglasses, but somewhere a small mistake had been made. She was certain she and Paul would find it.

At the sound of the patio door sliding open, she looked over her shoulder and saw her aunt coming out. Despite sharing the same house, they'd seen very little of each other, except for the afternoon Maggie had spent showing Paul and her around the plant.

Chris was not surprised that Maggie was so knowledgeable about how the cosmetics, the perfume and even the newer products were made, even though she'd gradually turned over much of the operation to Teddy and Diane. And nearly everyone knew her by her first name, greeting her warmly as they'd strolled through the labs and down the production aisles.

She'd enjoyed seeing that facet of the business, but Paul had looked somewhat bored, though he'd tried not to show it. Chris smiled now as Maggie, who thought herself too short, came toward her balancing on impossibly high heels. Glass in hand, she sat down in the chair opposite her.

"Don't get too much sun, dear," she warned.

Chris rubbed her pink nose. "Mmm, I'd almost forgotten that the sun in the desert is so much stronger than in California."

"It's very becoming, your rosy cheeks."

She watched Maggie take a tiny taste of the Irish whiskey and wondered how such a small woman could drink such strong liquor. As far back as she could remember, Maggie had steadily sipped her favorite drink yet had never shown the effects, with the possible exception of a somewhat husky voice. "And where were you all morning?" she asked.

Maggie placed her glass on the table and settled herself in the shade of the umbrella. "Jeremiah and I had brunch at this wonderful little outdoor spot. After that, we went shopping. He's the only man I've ever known who loves shopping almost as much as a woman." Maggie fingered the necklace she wore and leaned toward Chris to show her. "Look what he bought for me."

Chris examined the filigreed gold chain with half dozen rubies delicately interwoven. "It's beautiful," she said. And obviously very expensive. Again, she wondered where Jeremiah got his money. She'd talked with him casually several times over the past week and had found him to be intelligent, witty and charming. But he didn't seem to exhibit much business acumen. Chris wished she didn't have this nagging feeling that something wasn't quite right about him. Sometimes his eyes looked deliberately evasive. "What does Jeremiah do at Lady Charm?"

"Oh, this and that. Mostly helps me. He's a love, but a businessman he's not."

At least they were in agreement on that. "What did he do before coming here?"

Tucking in a strand of hair that had escaped her topknot, Maggie smiled. "He taught archaeology at one of those Ivy League schools back East. The stereotypical absentminded professor, I might add. He can remember the names of hundreds of rocks but can't remember where he left his glasses. He loves to talk for hours about fossils and ancient artifacts."

A dignified profession that his family probably approved of heartily. "You mean like Harvard or Yale? I understand professors make quite a bit at Ivy League schools." That would explain his ability to lavish Maggie with gifts.

Maggie chuckled as she reached for her drink. "My, no. It was a small, private finishing school. His retirement income wouldn't keep Jeremiah in cigars." She sipped her whiskey.

Certainly not in imported cigars, Chris thought. Did that mean Maggie was giving him money? Surely his pride wouldn't permit that. Then where did his money come from? Maybe it would bear looking into, without her aunt's knowledge, of course.

"Do you know where we're planning to go next year?" Maggie asked, her blue eyes dancing.

"No, where?"

"To Egypt, on a dig. Won't that be fantastic? We'd go there on our honeymoon, but I don't want to be away that long right now with all this mess at the company."

An Egyptian dig. She was like a child at Christmas. Jeremiah was a lucky man. Chris hoped he was everything Maggie thought him to be. Caring for someone that deeply could make you vulnerable. Drawing up her legs, she hugged her knees and stared into the depths of the pool, suddenly somber. So damn vulnerable. "How did you manage all those years without Jeremiah, loving him like you do? How did you ever let him go in the first place?"

Maggie's smile was wistful. "The person who's left behind has no choice but to accept the situation and make the best of it. The person doing the leaving has all the choices."

Hadn't Paul said something similar earlier in the week? "I don't agree. You had choices, too. You could have learned to care for someone else, forgotten Jeremiah."

Maggie shook her head. "If only it were that simple. Do you remember how strongly your mother loved your father? It was the same with me. You can't make yourself stop loving someone and decide to care for another. It just doesn't work for some people. You can bury your feelings, go on with your life, but they'll surface again. Though Jeremiah left me alone for four decades, I couldn't forget him." She leaned forward and touched her niece's arm. "I suspect you're a great deal like both your mother and I."

Chris's sigh was ragged. "No, I haven't your strength or Mom's patience. I can't see myself waiting forty years for a man, and I'd never sit patiently each night, wondering if I'd ever see my husband again."

"Not every police officer gets killed in the line of duty like your father did, Christine. Surely you're smart enough to see that."

"Even if they don't, it's the waiting, the worrying, daily. That's no way to live."

"Is spending your life alone any way to live for a beautiful, caring woman who has much to offer some good man?"

"It's not such a bad life, Maggie. Besides, I'm not sure the kind of man I want exists."

"Perhaps you should learn to take a few risks, dear. Loving is always a gamble. You can't order a man tailor-made, the way you would a new outfit."

Chris smiled. Is that what she'd sounded like? "Now you're laughing at me."

Impulsively Maggie stood and enveloped Chris in a hug. "Of course not. I'd never laugh at you."

"Can I get in on that?" a low, rumbling laugh asked from behind them.

Maggie straightened and smiled. "Michael! It's about time you showed your face."

Michael Donovan gave his aunt a hug that nearly lifted her feet from the pavement. "Now, Maggie, if I came around too often, you'd get tired of me." He turned to Chris, who was smiling as she rose. "Well, little sister, living in California certainly agrees with you. You look terrific."

Moving into his arms for a long moment, Chris let herself absorb the warmth of Mike's embrace. He was so big, so solid that just being near him reassured her always. "You never change," she said as she leaned back to look at him. "A constant in a shifting world. It's good to see you."

"You, too," Mike said as he eased into a wrought-iron chair. "As I mentioned on the phone, I'm sorry I couldn't make it earlier. It's been a busy week at the station."

Chris dismissed his apology with a wave of her hand. "Not to worry. I've been pretty busy, myself."

"Those long hours aren't good for you, Michael," Maggie fussed. "All work and no play are going to make you a dull boy. Would you like a cold drink?"

"No, thanks, Maggie," he answered, smiling at her lovingly nagging ways. He looked Chris over. "So, how's it feel to be back home again?"

Shrugging into her white coverup and adjusting it over her black swimsuit, Chris hid a smile. Mike had never accepted her move from Phoenix as permanent. "It feels fine. And are you turning into a dull boy or are you squeezing in a little fun?"

"Now and again. Man cannot live on a steady diet of murder and mayhem without an occasional diversion."

"Am I going to get to meet one of your diversions while I'm here?"

He shrugged noncommittally. "Maybe. What about you? How's your love life?"

"Michael, really!" Maggie said. "That's a bit personal, wouldn't you say?"

Laughing, Chris shook her head. "It's all right. He's been asking me that question since I was sixteen. One of these days, I'm going to shock him and start talking."

"I'm all ears," Mike said, grinning.

"Oh, you two." Maggie drained her glass and stood. "I've got to freshen up. Jeremiah and I are invited to a pool party this afternoon. Will you be all right for dinner alone tonight, Christine?"

"I'll manage just fine. You have a good time."

"All right. I'll see you later, dear." She patted Mike's head. "I'll have a dinner party soon and we'll get more chance to visit."

"Great. Enjoy yourself."

Chris watched her aunt hurry inside and smiled. "I hope she keeps her clothes on at this pool party."

"What?"

"She told me that Jeremiah loves nude swimming."

"No!" Mike laughed out loud as Chris nodded through her chuckles. "I can't believe it, either. It seems old Jeremiah's loosened Maggie up a bit."

"Kind of sounds like that." Stretching out his long legs, Mike eyed his sister. "And how's the investigation going?"

Chris rubbed suntan lotion on her legs. "I'm sure Paul's filled you in."

"I want to hear your version."

Chris gave him a mock scowl. "You don't trust your own man? Shame on you, Captain. My version doesn't differ, I'm sure. It's been mostly preliminary interviews and fact gathering so far. Except for a few vague impressions, we know precious little more than we did when we began last Monday."

"Something will start to click soon, some fact will fall into place, another won't add up and you'll zero in. You know how these things go—you creep along, then suddenly, all hell breaks loose.''

Chris patted lotion on her face. "I know. But I'd really appreciate a break soon. For Maggie's sake.''

His gray eyes studied her, quietly probing. "Is that the only reason?''

Chris shot him a quick look. "Of course. What other reason would I have?''

Mike's expression was unreadable. "Paul sings your praises. Tells me you really know your job.''

"He's just being polite.''

"Paul isn't one to give compliments out of politeness.''

She needed to change the subject. "Maggie looks good, doesn't she?''

Mike waited a heartbeat before answering. "She's handling all this a lot better than I'd have predicted.''

Chris smiled. "She's in love. That's foremost on her mind. She wants this solved and over, but she trusts us to do our jobs. Meanwhile, Jeremiah's around to make her forget.''

"What do you think of Diane?''

She wrinkled her brow as she thought that over. "Well, she's not terribly friendly. And Teddy follows after her like a puppy.''

"He's no puppy. He recently bought a sailboat, keeps it docked in San Diego and takes off alone whenever the mood strikes him. I understand she stays home alone.''

Alone. Chris didn't think Diane looked like the type to stay home by herself, but she didn't want to worry Mike by voicing her impression. "San Diego? He goes there and he's never called me?''

"I guess he hasn't.''

"I wonder why—''

"Christina, telephone," Mendosa called from the doorway.

"Thanks. Excuse me a minute, Mike." She walked through the French doors into the hushed coolness of the family room and picked up the phone. "Hello?"

"I'm glad I caught you," Paul said. "I need your help."

Not on her first day off, Chris moaned to herself. "How's that?"

"One of Nancy Evans's bookkeepers quit very suddenly, I discovered late yesterday afternoon. She's moved to Sedona, and it's kind of hush-hush. I talked with Nancy, and she seemed a little upset but didn't say anything helpful. I think we should drive up there—it's only two hours—and talk with the lady."

Chris glanced at the clock on the wall, frowning. "Are you sure this trip is necessary?"

"We won't know that until we talk with Dora Phillips."

His voice was businesslike and detached. Two hours to Sedona and then back. Something told her this wasn't wise. Something else told her she couldn't refuse without admitting she didn't want to be alone with him. Getting over Paul was one thing. Being cloistered with him for hours was another.

"All right. What time do you want to leave?"

"Can you be ready in an hour?"

His abrupt tone indicated he looked on this as nothing more than a business trip. "Yes, an hour."

"Good. I'll pick you up."

Chris hung up the phone and went out to Mike, still wearing a thoughtful frown.

"Anything important?" he asked as she sat down on the edge of the lounge chair.

"It seems Paul's learned that one of the bookkeepers quit suddenly and moved to Sedona. He's picking me up shortly, and we're driving up to interview her." She took a quick sip of water before turning bemused eyes to her brother. "Why does Paul feel compelled to put in eighteen-hour days plus weekends, do you suppose?"

"Do you know his father, the senator?"

Oh, yes. She knew John Cameron, all right. "I met him once. He didn't like me, and the feeling was mutual."

"Oh, John's not so bad. He lost his wife to cancer, and his younger son seems a bit shiftless. So he pushes a little hard on Paul."

"I don't see why Paul lets his father run his life."

Mike frowned. "I don't think he does. John didn't want Paul to go into police work. He wanted him in law. So Paul works doubly hard trying to show his father that he made the right choice. Being a senator isn't enough for John. He's got his eye on an even higher office, I think. If not for himself, then perhaps for Paul. What's wrong with that?"

"I still think the man's a barracuda."

"Maybe." Mike's shrewd eyes narrowed. "Why do you care?"

Chris reached for her towel. "I don't." She adjusted her sunglasses, needing the protection. "Why did you put Paul on this case with me?"

"Because he's the best man I've got and always brings them in." He gave her a look as if to soften his words. "You walked away from Paul once, Chris, but inside, you're still battling him. He's still there, isn't he?"

"My brother, the psychoanalyst." Chris averted her gaze as she stood. "Sorry to cut our visit short, but I have to shower and change."

"No problem," Mike said as he walked in with her. "I'll drop in again in a day or so. Let me know if you learn anything new."

She headed for the stairs. "I will. Take care."

"Chris?"

She turned. "Yes?"

"Keep your guard up." Mike let himself out the front door.

Slowly Chris climbed the steps. Now what did he mean by that? she wondered.

DORA PHILLIPS HAD THE KIND of face that invited confidences and trust—open and friendly. Her brown, curly hair had a touch of gray, and her brown eyes had a trace of humor. She looked over Paul's I.D. and invited them into her small stucco house on the southern edge of Sedona.

"Please excuse the mess," she said as she ushered Chris and Paul past boxes and cartons still unpacked. "Would you like something cold to drink?"

They opted for iced tea, and when they were all settled around the wooden kitchen table, Dora leaned forward, her candid eyes on Paul's face. "I'm not sure why you came all this way to talk with me. Is anything the matter with the way I finished up at Lady Charm?"

"No," Paul answered, "but I'm sure you're aware that we're investigating an embezzlement and that the accounting books were involved. We didn't get a chance to interview you before you left, so we do have a few questions."

Dora crossed one sturdy leg over her other and nodded. "Fire away. I have nothing to hide."

Chris asked a couple of general, inconsequential questions about her bookkeeping position, which Dora answered with ease. Then, she decided to get to it. "We're curious why you left so suddenly. Was there some problem?"

Dora took a deep breath, as if she really didn't want to explain but had little choice. "Henry, my husband, loves the cooler weather here in Sedona. We bought this place years ago, but we were only able to come up on weekends because we both worked in Phoenix. Henry got fed up and made a sudden job change to a Sedona company and called a moving van. I had no choice but to go along with him."

Chris frowned. "Something must have happened at Lady Charm. You didn't even turn in the usual two weeks' notice. You jeopardized your reputation, your future recommendations by walking out like that."

Dora nodded, looking a little chagrined. "I know and I hated to leave Accounting shorthanded. But I couldn't handle a two-hour commute in each direction. Nancy wasn't happy with my decision, but she said she'd give me a good recommendation if I needed one. I'm looking for a job up here now."

"What do you think of Nancy Evans?" Paul asked, hoping to open her up.

"I'll say this much, Nancy really knows her stuff. I've worked in a lot of places, and she's one hell of an accountant."

"Would you have any reason to believe she might somehow be involved in the embezzlement?"

"Nancy? Never. She's too honest. She's awful flaky about her personal life, but not her job."

Chris sat up a little straighter. "How do you mean, 'flaky'?"

Dora toyed with her iced-tea glass. "Well, I hate to tell tales here but, for a woman in her mid-thirties, Nancy talks about her love life like a teenager. Maybe she never had a boyfriend when she was younger." Dora shook her head. "She drove me crazy with her never-ending chatter."

Chris tried to hide her surprise. "What kind of things did she tell you?"

Dora sighed. "More than I wanted to hear, I can tell you. She's wild about some guy. She talked about him all day at work, then she'd call me at home evenings, sometimes weekends. Henry got awfully tired of it. So did I."

"Do you know who he is?"

"No, she never did say."

"Someone in the company?"

"I don't know, but I doubt it."

"Did you ever notice a man come into the accounting department and be overly friendly with Nancy?"

"No, I've never seen her be anything but shy and uncomfortable when a guy came in. Yet when she talked about this one man, you'd think she was describing a movie star."

Chris couldn't reconcile what she was hearing with her impression of Nancy Evans. "But was she telling you fact or fantasy?"

"At first, I thought she was making the whole thing up. But then she started talking about a wedding and bringing in bridal books. I think she's got someone, all right." She looked up at Paul as if suddenly a thought had occurred to her. "Do you suspect Nancy or perhaps this man of the embezzlement?"

"We don't suspect any one person at this time, Dora," Paul assured her. "We're trying to eliminate people. The logical place to begin is Accounting."

"Of course. I'm sorry I can't be of more help, but I really don't know anything else."

Paul stood, and Chris followed suit. Dora led the way to the front door. "If you think of anything," Paul said, "here's my card and a number where you can leave a message. Please don't hesitate to call me."

"All right."

"Thanks for your time," Chris said with a smile. She walked to the car as Paul said his goodbyes. When he got in beside her, she glanced at his profile. "It seems our little Nancy's full of contrasts."

"I'll say. Why would she confide details of her love life to Dora Phillips and never mention the man's name, yet tell you his name was Steve the first time you met her?"

"I can't figure that one, unless it was a slip of the tongue."

"Or unless Dora knows the man in question and Nancy was afraid she'd say something to him." Paul started the car. "It's hard for me to picture timid little Nancy Evans involved in a tempestuous love affair."

"Haven't you heard that still water runs deep?"

His dark eyes bore into hers. "Yes, I believe someone once proved that to me."

She remembered, too. Paul had been her first lover, and her last, though he probably would never believe that. She'd been shy and a little afraid, and he'd been so gentle, so loving. He'd unleashed a sleeping passion in her that had thrilled them both. But that had been then, and this was now. Chris looked away.

Paul backed out of Dora's driveway. "Do you mind if we make a quick stop? I board my horse not far from here. I'd like to see how he's doing."

"No, I wouldn't mind at all," Chris answered, glad to postpone the long ride.

"It's still plenty light out. Sam has lots of horses on his ranch. We have time for a ride, if you like."

To climb onto a horse and go like the wind, to forget everything else. She very much wanted to do that. "I'd like that."

Chapter Four

The horse's name was Wildfire, and he'd earned it honestly. A huge stallion, he stood pawing the ground restlessly while Chris stroked his thick, chestnut mane. "He's beautiful," she whispered, not wanting to startle the animal with a loud voice.

She'd been riding since she was ten, and though she'd never taken a lesson, she could hold her own on most any mount. Growing up in horse country, where some of the finest Arabians and quarter horses in the world were bred, she'd taken full advantage of the availability. Set free on horseback, Chris felt at home, in control, alive. "You're truly magnificent," she told Wildfire.

"You sure you can handle him, little lady?" Sam Bosley asked with a questioning glance toward Paul. "He can be a handful."

A retired Phoenix police officer, Sam now raised and boarded quality horses on his spread just outside Sedona. He welcomed Paul and several others from his old precinct, offering the use of his ranch and his horses, even loaning them riding clothes when necessary. Paul knew Sam was a cautious worrywart.

"She can handle him," Paul assured his friend. He knew from Mike what a skilled rider Chris was, and he knew Wildfire, having acquired him a year ago. He gathered the reins of the fidgeting black stallion he would ride, one of Sam's own stock. "I'll take full responsibility."

Still skeptical, Sam scratched his balding head and handed Chris the reins. "Take care, miss."

She gave him a dazzling smile. "Thanks. I will."

"Ready to roll?" Paul asked.

She raised a booted foot into the stirrup and swung easily atop Wildfire. Patting his thick hide, she leaned down to whisper soft words into his twitching ears. Straightening, she smiled at Paul. "Ready."

He'd known she would prefer mounting herself though both men had been available to give her a hand. He climbed up and maneuvered his horse through the fence gate as Chris nudged Wildfire to follow.

The terrain stretched out in front of them, rough with patches of crab grass, low-growing tumbleweed and huge saguaro cacti dotting the landscape for miles. In the distance the breathtaking red rock formations loomed and captured the afternoon sun shining from a perfectly cloudless sky. Chris swallowed a lump in her throat at a quick surge of happiness, the likes of which she hadn't felt in far too long.

"You lead and I'll follow," Paul told her. Expert rider though he knew her to be, he wanted to be able to keep an eye on her.

Chris didn't need further prompting. Over the hard-packed red clay they moved at an easy canter, horse and rider as one. Then she let Wildfire have his head. The scrubby trees rushed past in a blur as the heated wind caressed her face and sent her hair flying about her head. She forgot the scorching sun and the borrowed clothes already sticking to her, forgot the embezzlement, her job and her life back in San Diego. She even forgot Paul and the disturbing memories that surrounded him. Instead she concentrated on the pleasure of being open and free and a little bit reckless.

A short distance behind her, Paul's eyes rarely left Chris's small frame atop the huge animal. He watched her hair dance and twirl, making her look wild and untamed. And maybe she was, on the flip side of the coin. Her conservative, professional side was in charge most of the time. But set her astride a powerful horse and her gypsy nature evidently came to the fore. She leaned into the stallion as she laughed into the wind. Riding, it seemed, aroused in her a passion that she showed to very few.

It was a full half hour before Chris slowed, bringing Wildfire finally to a halt. Paul dismounted and helped her down. They walked the horses slowly toward a stream, letting them cool off. Finding the water very shallow, Chris shook her head.

"Slim pickings, fella," she told the snuffling horse, who nonetheless dipped his head and lapped up some liquid.

Paul tied both horses' reins loosely to a barren tree trunk and, with a heavy sigh, flung himself down on a nearby patch of sparse grass. "Lady, you sure know how to wear out a man."

"You ain't seen nothin' yet. We still have to ride back." She smiled at his groan. "Out of shape, and you an officer of the law?"

"I don't pull much mounty duty these days."

Chris lay down beside him, rolling onto her stomach and picking up a blade of grass to chew. She wondered how often he took an afternoon and just frittered it away doing something nonproductive like enjoying himself. Not often, she'd wager. "But you do pull a lot of duty, though I suspect you're at fault on that score. Why do you work so hard, Paul?"

He raised his arm to shield his eyes from the sun. "We up-and-coming types have to keep at it so some young whippersnapper doesn't unseat us."

She ignored his attempt at levity. "Do you really enjoy your work that much?"

"Most of the time."

"That sounds as though some aspects don't please you."

Paul fixed his gaze on a distant tree, bleaching in the sun. Sure, some aspects didn't please him. The paperwork could be staggering, but he knew that's not what Chris meant. He didn't mind the grueling detail work, the stakeouts in one-hundred-plus temperatures or even the risks involved. He'd known all that when he'd become a cop. What bothered him were the vagaries, the almost capricious injustices he'd witnessed at times in the courts. That and the politics involved in getting ahead. He wondered how much of that he should tell her.

"All jobs have some negatives. I'm not crazy about the politics of police work. Mike handles that far better than I."

"At least moving up in the ranks got him off the streets."

He turned to her with a look of amusement. "I'm not exactly walking a beat either, Chris."

She sighed as she threw away the weed. "Maybe not, but you still get involved in dangerous assignments. This case is probably the mildest one you've worked on in months. As I recall, you always were drawn to risky situations."

They'd been over this ground before, Paul thought, and each knew where the other stood. Why was she bringing it up again? "I take the assignments as they come along."

Did he? Or was he trying to make a name for himself, as Mike had hinted? She sought his eyes, wondering if she should explore the subject, then decided not to. "How's Pete doing?"

At the mention of his brother, Paul shrugged. "Hopefully he's got his act together. He seems to have outgrown his vagabond tendencies. He's just finished law school and plans to take the bar exam next week."

"I suppose your father will want him to go to Washington."

"He did once. I'm not so sure now."

"Following in a father's footsteps isn't the answer for everyone."

"I must remember to have you explain that to Dad sometime."

No, not her. She'd tried to explain something to John Cameron once. And had failed miserably. "Isn't he encouraging Pete?"

Paul let out a long breath. "He's convinced Pete will fail again, either the exam itself or later in actual practice."

Chris couldn't prevent the groan. "I'm sorry, but that's terrible. How can Pete succeed if his own father sees him as a failure?"

Paul sat up. "You have to understand. Pete's disappointed Dad over and over."

But you haven't, have you? The dutiful son who always excelled. "At least, he has you."

He stared into her eyes a long moment. She hardly knew his father, yet whenever she spoke of him, her voice changed, became cooler. He'd have to discover why. But not today. "That's enough serious talk." Paul rose to his feet. "Let's head back, take a quick shower and get something to eat. I'll buy you the best Western dinner in town. Provided you don't injure my pride and beat me back to the ranch."

"All right, I'll let you win. But only by a nose."

He offered his hand and pulled her up. Only she lost her footing on the uneven ground and had to grab him to keep from falling. Suddenly, she was hard up against his chest, so close he could feel the beat of her heart.

Chris became very still; even her breathing stopped as her body went rigid. *Please let go of me,* her eyes implored him, but she couldn't make herself say the words.

He wanted her, she could tell. And that knowledge started a burning excitement in her. She should steer clear of this—but did she have the strength?

Paul's hands on her back were damp and not as steady as he'd have wished. He swallowed hard. "Be honest with me, Chris. Do you feel anything?"

No, she wasn't going to let herself get trapped. She couldn't push away from him without hurting his feelings. She could simply refuse to play the game. "Yes," she said, trying for an innocent tone. "Hunger. I'm really hungry. Where is this restaurant?"

Slowly Paul let her go, half pleased she'd defused the situation, half angry with her. "Not far." He helped her mount.

"Good. Let's go." And she nudged Wildfire into motion.

COWPOKE ANNIE'S WAS ALMOST a landmark, a rustic eatery family owned and run, popular with townfolk and tourists alike. A checkered cloth lay on the corner table they were given, and a thick white candle flickered in a glass holder, lending a soft glow.

"I remember coming here with Mike and my parents years ago, when we were both teenagers. It's hardly changed."

"That's what I like about it," Paul said as the waiter handed them oversize menus. After ordering a very good wine and a tremendous amount of food, he turned his attention back to the woman across from him.

Sitting in his office this morning, Paul had convinced himself he needed her along to question Dora Phillips, needed her special perspective. Sitting across from her now, watching the candlelight turn her skin golden, he knew he'd lied to himself. He'd simply *wanted* her along. Even as he acknowledged the fact, he wasn't certain he could stop his own destructive behavior.

"Tell me about your life in San Diego," he prompted.

"There isn't much to tell," Chris said as the waiter brought the chilled wine and poured each of them a glass.

"Tell me anyhow," Paul insisted as he took a sip, enjoying the cool tartness which flowed down his throat.

"I live in a third-floor apartment, not too far from a park and close enough to town that I can walk to work."

"But you don't," he guessed, knowing how she hated to do exercise in the morning.

"No, I don't. But occasionally, when I have some paperwork to catch up on, I bicycle over on a Saturday."

Again, the flip side of the coin. "And does that shock Mark Emery, having his best agent arrive in blue jeans on her bike?"

Chris took a long sip of her wine, absorbing the taste. She set down the glass and turned her gaze on Paul. "Do you know Mark that well?"

He knew that Chris had started working part-time for Southwest Insurance while still attending college and that Mark had just been made manager of the Phoenix office. Single, attractive and, rumor had it, very hung up on Chris, Mark had transferred to San Diego only six months before the night Paul had been shot and Chris had decided to move. Had he persuaded her to follow him? Paul wasn't sure.

"I spoke with Mark yesterday on the phone about the case. He seems to miss you."

She'd talked with Mark yesterday, also. He hadn't mentioned speaking with Paul. Chris spread her napkin on her lap. "He said that?"

"No. I read between the lines and picked up on it."

She reached for her wineglass, held it between both hands, her eyes meeting his over the rim. "You're picking up on something that isn't there." It wasn't exactly the truth, but she wanted to lead him away from this. The man was too intuitive. The detective in him, she supposed. She didn't much care for him dipping into her personal life.

"Do you still enjoy investigative work?"

"Yes."

"Is there an attraction for Mark? Do you go out with him?"

"I have dated him on occasion," Chris said, answering the second question and ignoring the first.

"Do you like the weather in San Diego better than here?"

"Sometimes." Suddenly, she laughed out loud, releasing the tension that had been mounting. He was so transparent. "Now I know how poor Steve Thorn felt. Diversionary tactics and all. Why do I get the feeling I'm under the lamp in the interrogation room?"

Paul's smile was lopsided, hinting at self-derision, a quality she hadn't associated with him before. He tipped his glass to her.

"Touché."

Chris smiled in acknowledgement. "Why don't you just come out and ask me what you want to know and stop this artful fencing?"

He put down his glass and raised his eyes to hers. "Is there anyone in your life right now, a man you're interested in?"

So that was it. Already he'd shown her glimpses of a buried anger and a dormant desire that didn't please him.

But why would he care if she had someone else? "No. Is that all, Sergeant?"

"Yes, for now." Careless. Paul cursed himself for having revealed more than he'd intended again.

"But that doesn't mean—"

"Ah, dinner's here," Paul said, smiling at the waiter who'd arrived with their food, silently applauding the man's timing. "I'm starved, and I know you are, too."

The sly fox, Chris thought, watching the waiter put heaping plates in front of them. Mike had been right. Paul was undoubtedly the best in his field, getting information out of people that they hadn't meant to share, even the ones who were on to him.

The dinner was delicious, and they finished the entire bottle of wine. Paul suggested a walk along the main street of the town till his head cleared. The sun had left the sky and taken the heat of the day with it. Strolling comfortably side by side, they stopped in art galleries, browsed in specialty shops and wound up in a quaint little store that sold genuine Indian jewelry and artifacts. While Chris studied a collection of hand-painted bowls and vases, Paul made a hasty purchase and pocketed it until they were back in his Mustang, ready to start home.

"I have something for you," he said, turning toward her. They were parked on a quiet side street not far from the dim glow of an old-fashioned street lamp. Reaching into his shirt pocket, he handed her the small box.

"But when...the Indian store! Paul." He'd always been generous. She'd almost forgotten that. She saw a softness in his eyes, as unexpected as the cooling night breeze that drifted in through the open car windows.

"Open it."

A delicate silver necklace, interspersed with small chunks of the rich turquoise that was so prevalent to the area. Chris held it up to the streetlight and smiled. "It's lovely. Thank you."

"Just between us partners," he said as he took the necklace from her. "Turn around."

Chris lifted her long hair and held it high as he fastened the gift around her neck. She turned back toward him and looked down. It hung low, nearly to the opening of her blouse. She looked up, and his eyes told her he liked what he saw. Then he raised his gaze to hers, and she saw more.

He hadn't set out to buy her anything, to shift their relationship to that more personal level. Yet when he'd spotted the necklace, he'd wanted to see it next to her skin. Paul didn't regret the purchase for it suited her. He wondered if he'd regret the gesture.

Pleasantly relaxed, Chris leaned back. When he moved closer and slid one arm along the back of the seat, she didn't stop him. His eyes held hers captive as he raised a hand and ran the backs of his fingers down her cheek and along her jaw.

"You have beautiful skin, did I ever mention that? The Irish usually freckle."

"I freckle sometimes."

"I hadn't noticed." Her fragrance teased his senses. This was inviting trouble, Paul knew, yet he seemed unable to resist. He moved his hand along her throat, tracing the necklace as it fell almost to the swell of her breasts. He felt her breathing deepen. *All I had to get over was you,* she'd said. But was she really over him?

Vaguely remembered sensations flooded Chris, and a once-familiar weakness stole over her. Catching her breath, she stopped the progress of his hand with her own, moving it away from her skin. "Paul, this isn't wise. We're working partners only, remember? We want different things from life. Touching is going to cloud our thinking."

"Sometimes," he said as his other hand tightened on her shoulder, "you have to pass through some clouds to reach the clarity of the open sky."

"No," Chris said, more firmly this time.

He sighed somewhat wearily. It was there again, the distance she was determined to put between them. He should have been pleased and instead found himself growing angry. "Are you going to run again, Chris? That's your answer when you experience feelings you think you can't handle, isn't it?" He let her go, moving back to his side of the car. "Just like your mother, always hiding, afraid to face things head-on."

Chris saw red. "You leave my mother out of this. With a father such as yours, you have no business talking about anyone." She turned from him, seething.

Frowning, Paul put a hand on her chin and forced her to face him. "What do you mean by that?"

She shook free of him. "Never mind. Take me home."

"Not until you explain."

Chris groped for the door handle. "Fine. I'll take a cab."

"No." He settled himself behind the wheel. "That won't be necessary." He started the engine with a less than steady hand. Damn! A good detective knows when to back off, that he has to stay dispassionate, uninvolved. A smart man should, also. He shifted the car into gear and drove toward the highway.

Leaning back against the headrest, Chris shut her eyes. A close call. She'd convinced herself all week that she was over Paul Cameron. Sure she was. Until he touched her. She'd wanted him to stop, yet had wanted him to continue. And then she'd opened a large can of worms. What on earth was the matter with her?

Paul drove with one hand casually draped over the steering wheel, certain Chris couldn't see that his other hand was tightly clenched into a fist. "We'll drop this discussion for tonight because we're both tired. But we *will* discuss it again.''

Chris didn't answer, just sat still as she struggled with her ambivalent feelings while Paul maneuvered the car toward Phoenix. She was sure he wouldn't forget. It promised to be a long, hot summer.

CHRIS HAD NEVER BEEN FOND of Monday mornings. It was the one day of the week where she had to *make* herself get going. Because she knew her weakness, she set out even earlier than usual. She'd borrowed Maggie's Mercedes and driven to Lady Charm's offices, hoping to beat Paul in and look over the appointments he'd set up for the day.

She swung into Maggie's parking space and climbed out. Already, the heat that would build steadily throughout the day was noticeable as she made her way to her office. Paul's car was nowhere in sight, and she was relieved.

The ride home from Sedona had been silent and strained. Chris had feigned sleep to avoid conversation, but she knew she hadn't fooled Paul. He'd walked her to her door like the gentleman he was, but his eyes had been dark and distant, and he hadn't made a move to touch her. As lovers, they'd been wonderfully matched. As partners on this case, they worked well together. But friendship between the two of them, it seemed, could only last a couple of hours before memories of their past would intrude or emotional eruptions occur. Chris moved gratefully into the air-conditioned building, wishing things were different between Paul and her, yet she felt fairly certain they never would improve.

She'd been in her office a good ten minutes before she noticed it. Relishing the quiet time, she'd taken some things from her briefcase and gathered a couple of files that Ginny had left for her and sat back, prepared to read, when something made her glance at the typewriter on the stand next to her desk. A single white sheet of paper was partially rolled into the machine. There was one line of typing on the page, all in capitals. With a pounding heart, Chris read the message: GO HOME OR YOU'LL BE SORRY.

For a moment she considered the possibility of a prankster, then discarded that notion. If not, then it had to be a warning. The embezzler? Who else would want her to go home? Was the message intended for her or for Paul? Probably both. Chris drew in a deep, shaky breath as the office door opened.

She looked up as Paul walked in, his face bland. The thought occurred to her fleetingly that he, too, was sorry about their flare-up last Saturday. Then she saw his features change as he noticed her expression.

"What's the matter?" Paul asked. She was pale beneath her light tan, and there was a shocked look about her eyes.

Chris clasped her hands tightly in her lap. "Someone left us a message in the typewriter over the weekend."

He moved quickly beside her and leaned over to read the single line on the page. A threat, brief and to the point. Damn! He touched her shoulder. "Are you all right?" He saw her nod. "Looks like we've hit a nerve with someone."

"Someone quite bold it would seem. Who else would take a chance at being seen entering or leaving our office?"

Paul frowned in concentration. "The office doors around here are rarely locked. People come and go all day, delivering papers, picking up documents and mail. Obviously it's someone familiar who can walk into the building without suspicions being aroused. Which verifies our theory that it's an inside job."

"But you mentioned leaving here around six Friday, and I arrived a little after eight this morning. So evidently it's someone who comes in on weekends or works late evenings."

"Maybe. It only takes a minute to type one line." He leaned closer to examine the page. "Did you touch the paper?"

"No."

"Fingerprints are really difficult to pick up off bond paper, but I think I'll send it to our police lab to double check. Have we got a manila envelope somewhere?" He waited till Chris took one from a drawer and handed it to him. Touching only a tiny corner of the page, he removed the sheet and inserted the paper in the envelope. "I think I'll have the typewriter dusted for prints, too, though I imagine our thief was careful enough to use gloves."

"I don't think it was typed on this machine," Chris said. "I used it last week, and the *Y* is chipped just a shade. It wasn't in the note."

"Very observant," Paul commented. "I'll order a sample testing of all the typewriters at Lady Charm."

"He could have typed it on a machine at home and brought it here."

"That's possible, but we have to eliminate the obvious first. And *he* could also be a *she*." He noticed her color was better now. "Are you sure you're okay?"

Chris nodded. "Yes. I've just never been threatened quite so bluntly before."

Paul sat on the edge of her desk. She was handling her fright, but her eyes still looked concerned. The threat was probably intended more for him than her, but he could understand her fear. "Haven't you ever investigated a case where you've run across someone who saw you as the person who might expose them?"

Chris sat back, forcing herself to relax. Perhaps she had overreacted to the note. "I suppose so. The closest I ever came was last summer when I was investigating a claim on a very expensive yacht that had mysteriously caught fire only weeks after we'd written a very large policy on it. The owner had a somewhat unique method of diverting my attention from ferreting out all the facts."

"And what was that?"

She laughed, remembering the case. "He kept asking me out to dinner, sending me flowers, even an expensive case of wine."

"Bribery yet. Did you go out with him?"

"No. I even sent back the wine."

"Was he responsible for the fire?"

"He sure was. He was also responsible for my discovering his involvement. He loved to brag about himself, and during one of his many phone calls, he told me he'd once owned a large sailboat and had kept it moored on the French Riviera. I got to thinking about that and checked with our sources overseas. Sure enough, that boat had gone up in flames two years before."

"Quite an insurance racket." He glanced at the envelope containing the typewritten note. "Our embezzler's not that subtle. It's been my experience that white collar criminals such as embezzlers are seldom really dangerous." Some of them, of course, were but Paul felt she needed some reassurance right now.

"I'll try to take comfort in that fact." She glanced at her watch. "I saw on the appointment sheet that you've scheduled us to interview Angela Knight at lunch today. Have you met her?"

"Briefly on Friday."

"Is she as beautiful as she looks in the ads?"

Paul ambled over to his desk. Angela Knight was Lady Charm's model, most recently seen purring over a bottle of their most publicized scent, Forbidden. Beautiful? He supposed she was. "She's all right, I guess."

Chris raised an eyebrow at him. "Just 'all right'?"

"From her picture, I'd say she's too thin and too pouty-faced for my taste, but I suppose some would think her beautiful."

Chris felt the corners of her mouth twitch. Too thin? She'd seen Angela, though not up close, and she looked to be no thinner than she herself was. "You have to be quite slender to be model material, but you certainly have a right to your opinion." She bent to remove a file from her drawer. "What time is the luncheon appointment? I have Nancy coming in to go over some of the altered books in ten minutes."

"Not till twelve-thirty." He picked up the phone. "I'll make the arrangements for the typewriters to be checked before she arrives, then I think I'll run that note to headquarters. I've got some other things I have to check on as well."

"Just tell me where, and I'll meet you at twelve-thirty."

Paul mentioned a restaurant, and she nodded, already absorbed in some papers on her desk. He made his call, picked up the manila envelope and walked to the door. He didn't really have anything that needed checking on at the moment. He just needed to be up and about and gone for a while. He'd decided, after Sedona, that it would be best if they didn't spend too much time closeted alone together. "See you later."

Chris heard the door close behind him and leaned back with a sigh. The threatening note had frightened her more than she'd let on. For a moment, when Paul had walked in, she'd felt like rushing into his arms and staying there. She hated the weakness that brought out those feelings. She had no desire to reenter Paul Cameron's life on a personal basis, yet being around him constantly was playing havoc with her concentration. He was too damn attractive, too used to touching, too male. She'd have to be dead not to react to some of that. And she was discovering she was far from dead.

Maybe today, talking with Angela Knight, they'd discover some vital clue that would point to the embezzler, who, evidently was very aware she and Paul were there, checking and probing and questioning. They must be getting close, making someone jumpy enough to take a chance on a warning note.

Chris glanced up as Nancy came in, looking hesitant as usual, her arms full of ledgers. She smiled a greeting, trying to put out of her mind all that Dora had said about the complex accountant. She would set aside her worries about the note, too. She and Nancy had a lot of work to do before she met Paul and Angela for lunch.

TIMOTHY'S WAS THE PLACE to go for cool jazz and spicy Cajun food in North Phoenix. The intimate atmosphere lent itself to quiet conversation, and the blackened redfish was the best for miles around, two reasons why Paul had chosen the restaurant for their meeting. Arriving a few minutes before the appointed hour, he exchanged a few words with the owner before being told that one member of his party was already waiting at the bar.

Moving to the archway, he spotted the tall, leggy model twined around a bar stool as she sipped a Bloody Mary while her cool green eyes assessed the lunchtime crowd, consisting mostly of business people. Even from where he stood, Paul got the impression no one in her line of vision quite measured up. He strolled over.

"I hope you don't mind if I started without you," she said flashing him a perfect smile.

"Not at all," Paul told her, then leaned toward the bartender and ordered a tonic with a twist of lime. He looked her over again slowly, wondering if he'd missed something the first time since everyone raved about Angela's beauty.

He supposed she was an eyeful with thick chestnut hair and large eyes. But she was too heavily made up for his taste and too obvious for his comfort. Unbuttoning his jacket, he leaned on the back of the bar stool next to hers and smiled at her, anyway. "Been waiting long?"

"Long enough to need another drink." She waited patiently for the bartender, then took the drink from him without shifting her eyes from Paul.

A woman who reserved her smiles for the men who might possibly do her some good, he decided. More pragmatic than flirtatious. Little did she realize she was barking up the wrong tree this time, he thought as he sipped his drink.

"Your table's ready when you are, Paul," Timothy said from behind him.

"Thanks." He looked to Angela. "Chris should be along any minute. Shall we?"

She made a little ceremony out of getting off the stool, then slinked after the tall, bespectacled host, who settled them in a quiet corner as Paul had requested. He glanced at his watch, wondering if he should have checked on Chris before he'd left the station, then decided he was being silly. Leaning forward, he decided to get to know Angela Knight.

"How long have you been modeling for Lady Charm?" he began.

She took a long sip of her drink before answering. "Too long."

Another restless one like Steve. "Why do you say that?"

She took a cigarette from a gold case, stuck it into her mouth and waited for him to offer a light. Suppressing a smile, he reached for the table matches and did as she expected. Another good-size ego here. He watched her through a haze of smoke.

"It's small potatoes. You can't get anywhere modeling in Phoenix. I should be in New York."

"Why aren't you, then?"

Her green eyes narrowed with a quick flash of temper. "Because someone tied me up with an iron-clad contract that I haven't been able to break."

"And who might that be?"

"Diane Muldoon," Angela said through very white teeth clenched very tightly together.

"I'm so sorry I'm late," Chris said as she arrived at the table.

Paul stood. "I was getting worried about you." She smelled like a fresh breath of air in a sea of perfume and smoke. He held her chair for her.

"The traffic is horrendous. Nancy and I got involved, and I had to leave her in our office to finish." Chris smiled at the woman seated by the window and held out her hand. "Hello. I'm Chris Donovan. You must be Angela Knight. I'm happy to meet you."

Angela placed a cool, slender hand into Chris's for a brief moment and nodded wordlessly before taking another drag on her cigarette.

"Would you like something to drink?" Paul asked, noting Angela's disinterest in Chris. The model was clearly not interested in developing a friendship with another woman.

"Iced tea would be fine," Chris said. She'd easily picked up on Angela's indifference and decided to ignore it and let Paul ask the questions. She'd had to deal with haughty, self-centered women before.

"Shall we order first so we can talk uninterrupted?" Paul suggested, opening his menu.

"I never eat lunch," Angela murmured. "But I will have another Bloody Mary."

Three drinks in half an hour, Paul noted. Either alcohol would loosen her tongue and she'd say more than she intended, or she'd get fuzzy-brained and not be able to answer at all. Quickly they placed their order, and Paul turned to the model again. "So Diane Muldoon hired you?"

"Yes, nearly two years ago."

"How did that come about?"

"Steve had just invented a new perfume, and Diane named it Forbidden, trying to appeal to the young, single market. Most of Lady Charm's clientele up to that point were over thirty-five. More Maggie's crowd. But Diane has big plans, for the company and for herself."

Seated this near Angela, Paul decided she was every day of thirty and would soon look even older if she kept belting down the booze. "Since Diane's in charge of marketing, I suppose it's only natural she have plans for the company. Do you disagree with some of her ideas?"

The laugh was low, throaty. "Not some, most. She may know marketing but she doesn't know anything about modeling. I told her the ads she set up for me were all wrong. They're too subtle, too old-fashioned. Today's single woman is chic, savvy, with it. But Diane's word is law at Lady Charm. Now, Forbidden's not selling well, and she blames me. You can't win with that woman."

"Have you talked this over with anyone else at the company?" Chris interjected.

Angela's green eyes shifted to Chris. "Who, that mealy-mouthed husband of hers? He wouldn't know a good idea if it hit him right on his balding little noggin. And Maggie is too busy playing Bride of the Year." She shook her dark head. "No, there's no one. That's why I'm moving on. I'm tired of working with amateurs for peanuts."

Two specialty lunches arrived then and halted conversation for the moment. Chris inhaled the spicy fish scent hungrily, grateful for the interruption. She wondered if she could digest her lunch with this supercilious woman spewing complaints left and right. "Where are you planning to move?" Chris inquired when at last the waiter withdrew.

Angela tasted her fresh drink. "New York. There's no place like the Big Apple for models."

"I understand you worked for Four Seasons Modeling Agency before signing on with Lady Charm," Paul said as he buttered a roll. "Why did you leave there?"

"Things were slow, assignments were few and a change seemed like a good idea at the time." She ground out her cigarette. "What a mistake."

"Do you ever date anyone from Lady Charm?" he asked, hoping to lead her a bit.

"Certainly not." She managed to sound truly offended at the very thought.

Listening, Chris almost laughed out loud at the woman's indignation, as if every man there was beneath her. She raised her eyes to Angela's. "You're undoubtedly aware of the embezzlement. Can you think of anyone who might be responsible?"

"Not really, unless maybe Diane. I wouldn't put *anything* past that woman."

"Would she really need to embezzle, since she's married the man who's going to inherit the company one day?" Chris asked. "Wouldn't that be a little like stealing from yourself?" It had been a while since she'd questioned anyone who harbored so much accumulated jealousy and anger.

"Maybe she doesn't intend to wait around for little Teddy to inherit the company."

Something to consider, Paul thought as he finished his redfish. Angela might not be the sweetest lady around, but she wasn't stupid, either. She'd certainly given them an interesting viewpoint. It wouldn't hurt to check into her past, especially the company she'd modeled for.

"If you plan to move on to New York, how are you going to get out of your present contract with Lady Charm?" Chris asked.

"Honey," Angela said in an exaggerated drawl, "if you want something badly enough, you find a way."

"I'm sorry to interrupt, Paul," the host said coming up to the table. "There's a call for you."

"Thanks." Paul rose. "Excuse me, ladies."

Small talk was probably not Angela's forte, Chris thought as she sipped her tea. She noticed a large amethyst ring on the woman's right hand and hoped she would have a story about that. "What a beautiful ring," Chris said, leaning forward for a better look.

Angela gave her a smile at last, held up her hand for inspection and launched into a breathy story of a fascinating man who had gifted her with the ring. It was just ending when she saw Paul hurrying toward them.

"We have to go. Sorry to leave you like this, Angela, but something's come up that requires our attention." Taking Chris's elbow, he helped her to her feet. "Thanks for meeting with us. I've already signed the tab, but stay and have coffee, if you like."

Angela wrinkled her perfect nose. "Not coffee. I will have another drink, though."

"Fine. We may want to talk with you again later."

"Just call me."

Nodding, Paul ushered Chris through the crowd toward the door and into his car, which was already waiting outside. "I'll send someone back for your car. We need to get going." He shifted into gear.

"Will you tell me what's going on?"

"Nancy collapsed in our office. Ginny found her. They've taken her to Phoenix General Hospital." He eased out into midday traffic. "Preliminary reports seem to indicate she's been poisoned."

Chapter Five

"No, not food poisoning," Dr. Andrews said as he removed his rimless glasses. "Not the same symptoms at all." He rubbed the bridge of his nose tiredly before bringing his gaze back to Paul. "It's not as if she ate something definitely poisonous, either, or she'd have had a much more violent reaction." Thoughtfully he put his glasses back on. "It's more like something she ingested was tainted with a mild, herbal poison. Of course, we've run tests, and we'll be able to tell you more once the results are available."

"You say herbal poison?" Paul asked.

Dr. Andrews stuck both hands into his lab coat. "A general term. A poisonous plant, leaf, bush, flower, something from the dogbane family of growing things, most likely. That type causes abdominal pain, sometimes vomiting, even temporary blackouts or disorientation, but is seldom strong enough to kill or even seriously injure an adult. A small child or perhaps a cat might suffer irreversible damage, but not a grown woman."

"Doctor," Chris said, "you used the term 'tainted with.' I'm not sure I understand. Do you mean that some kind of poison was added to Nancy's food?"

The doctor frowned. "Quite possibly. In powder form or liquid. Most likely plant extract or juices. She could have ingested it in her food, in her coffee or tea. This isn't necessarily a police matter, you see. Perhaps she had something in the house, some concoction she used on her plants, let's say. And accidentally, she sprinkled it onto her food, thinking it a spice or herb or sweetener. Most poisonings are accidental, we find. And the amount we found in Miss Evans was a mere trace. If someone wanted to do her in using this method, they'd have to be very patient. It would take much larger doses and a great deal more time."

"Then she's going to be all right?" Chris asked.

"Definitely. She's resting comfortably now. We'd like to observe her for twenty-four hours, just as a precaution." He reached for the chart he'd set down on the counter. "I believe she lives alone, but her brother's been called and he's on his way."

Paul offered his hand. "Thank you, doctor, for your time. We appreciate it."

"Certainly." He shook hands with both of them.

"May I go in for just a minute to see her?" Chris asked him as he was about to hurry away.

"Yes, of course. Room 622. Be aware she may exhibit some mental confusion."

Nodding her thanks, Chris turned back to Paul. "What do you make of it?"

Paul led her to the small alcove that served as a waiting room on the sixth floor and drew her down beside him on the vinyl couch. "I'm not sure I agree that this was purely accidental. I think Nancy's a little scattered, but to think she sprinkled poison on her scrambled eggs instead of pepper seems farfetched."

"I don't even think she'd keep something poisonous around," Chris added.

"We need to find out who she's been eating with lately. Maybe this fiancé of hers...."

Chris crossed her legs and leaned back. "We have a quiet, shy bookkeeper and someone asks her to lunch and sprinkles poison in her salad while she goes to the restroom?'' She shook her head. ''That's bizarre.''

''Let's keep in mind that this quiet, shy bookkeeper may know who embezzled four hundred thousand dollars. She's working closely with us and may have some knowledge that even she's not aware she has. The thief might be getting worried.''

''And so he's trying to kill her?''

''Not necessarily. He's trying to put her out of commission for a while, or frighten her—or us.''

Chris let out a deep breath. ''I hadn't thought of that.''

''It seems too much of a coincidence to me to not have some connection to our investigation.''

''I thought you said white collar embezzlers aren't dangerous?''

''He wasn't trying to kill, just give a warning.''

''Somehow I don't find that very comforting.''

''I don't want to frighten Nancy further by both of us appearing at her bedside. Why don't you go in and see what you can learn?'' He smiled at her. ''In your gentle, nonthreatening manner.''

''Flattery will get you nowhere.'' She rose and walked down the hall.

The pale woman lying in the hospital bed seemed to fade into the white sheets. Chris walked closer and saw Nancy's eyes flutter open as she uttered a soft moan.

Chris pulled up a chair and sat down. ''How are you feeling, Nancy?''

She licked her dry lips, moved her hand to her stomach and pulled up her knees. ''Still hurts.''

Ginny had told Chris she'd heard Nancy fall from her chair and had found her doubled over and grasping her stomach in pain. She hadn't been able to walk or to straighten up. Chris patted her other hand, finding it cold and clammy. "I'm sure you'll be feeling better soon. Did they give you something for the pain?"

"I think so."

She wasn't sure how much Nancy knew about what had happened to her. "Did you eat something that disagreed with you, do you think?"

Nancy shook her head. "I didn't eat anything today. Just coffee and water." She moaned again. "Awful cramps."

"Did you go out to dinner last night?"

"No. I made some spaghetti at home. Sorry I didn't finish the books."

"Don't worry about that. I'll bet you're a good cook. Did you have someone over last night?" She wondered just how far she should question her, but it was important to know if she'd been with anyone.

Nancy shook her head. "Just my cat and me." She closed her eyes.

Chris got up. "I'll let you get some rest. Do you want me to call anyone for you?"

"My brother's been notified. Thanks for coming."

"Sure. I'll talk with you tomorrow." Halfway to the door, Chris had a thought. Where was Steve, the great love of her life? "What about your fiancé?"

"No. I—I'll talk with him later."

Why wouldn't she want someone she was so crazy about here with her? Puzzling. Quietly Chris left the room. As she neared the alcove where she'd left Paul, she saw him standing and talking with a familiar, broad-shouldered figure. "Mike, hello."

Mike turned as Chris joined them and smiled at his sister. "Hi, there. How'd you find our little victim?"

Victim. That was a good word for Nancy Evans. "A little groggy and still experiencing quite a bit of stomach pain." She looked up at Paul. "She hasn't had anything today except coffee, and she ate home alone last night."

"That still doesn't rule out accidental ingestion." Paul narrowed his eyes thoughtfully. "Do you think Nancy's careless or absentminded enough to have grabbed something by mistake?"

"No, I don't."

"Neither do I." Paul ran a hand through his unruly hair. "I'm going back to my original thought."

Mike's gray eyes studied Paul's expression. "And what's that?"

"That this is connected somehow to our investigation. Chris, you said all she's had today was coffee. Did she drink it in the office? And who else had some?"

Chris wrinkled her brow. "Nancy didn't drink coffee while she was with me. Ginny brought me a cup, but Nancy didn't want anything hot so she had water instead."

Paul's interest picked up. "Water from our cooler?"

"Yes. You know how she's always drinking. But that can't be it. I drink from that cooler every day."

"But did you today? Try to remember."

"Mmm, I might have. No, come to think of it, I didn't."

"Then, it's a possibility," Paul said. "I'll get a sample and send it to the lab."

"Someone's definitely getting jittery at Lady Charm," Mike commented. "First the note, and now the water, if it is that. It seems you two might be getting close."

"I certainly hope so," Paul commented.

"If we find that the water's been poisoned," Chris said, realizing her voice wasn't quite as strong as before, "I don't think Nancy was the intended victim." Her eyes were filled with worry.

Paul moved closer and slid his arm around her waist. "You heard the doctor. It wasn't a deadly dosage. He told us it would take gallons to harm an adult."

She looked up at him. "Another warning then?"

"Possibly."

"Let's not panic till we have the water analyzed," Mike said in his strong, soothing voice. "We could be on the wrong track." He reached into his pocket, brought out an envelope and handed it to Paul. "I have something here that will take both your minds off things for a while."

Paul pulled out two tickets, then frowned as he recognized them. "Oh, no. I don't want to go to this."

"What is it?" Chris asked.

"The annual Policeman's Benefit Dance."

Mike patted her shoulder. "It's just what the doctor ordered. Dress up, dance a little, forget the case for one night. Besides, it's for a good cause."

"This is quite a day," Chris acknowledged. "A threatening note, someone's possibly poisoning our drinking water, and you want us to go to a party. Honestly, Mike."

"I'm not crazy about going, either, but it's more or less a command performance. A lot of important people will be there, and it's handshaking time." He zeroed in on Paul. "I think you should be there."

"Is that an order, Captain?" Paul knew he sounded edgy, which is how he felt. Sometimes Mike pushed too hard.

"It's a request." He turned to Chris. "Unless you don't think you can handle the heat."

Mike was challenging her, Chris thought, wanting her to prove she could manage a social evening with Paul again. He certainly knew how to pull her strings. All right, she'd go and show them both. No more running away, as Paul had accused her of doing.

"I can if Paul can," she said, issuing her own challenge.

Paul dropped his arm. When the Donovans ganged up, they were a formidable pair. He could refuse. But if he didn't go now, it would appear as if he couldn't deal with that part of his job, and it would look as if he couldn't handle a simple evening with Chris. They had him.

"I'll pick you up at seven," he told Chris and saw her nod.

"Great," Mike said. "How'd the interview with Angela Knight go?"

Chris listened to Paul recount their conversation with the model. It seemed as if Mike knew every facet of the investigation. Did Paul run to the precinct every night and report dutifully every word that was said? Did that include their personal conversations as well? She took a deep breath. That was uncharitable of her. Of course, Mike probably drove Paul crazy asking questions. Maggie was his concern also. Chris waited until Paul finished before she interjected her own question.

"How is it you're here, Mike? Did someone phone you about Nancy?"

"No, I was here on another police matter. I was walking by when I spotted Paul waiting for you."

"I see." Why was it she doubted him suddenly? Because she knew her brother well and knew he liked to be in on everything.

"I've got to run," Mike said with a glance at his watch. "See you both tonight."

Paul watched him hurry down the corridor, then turned to see Chris studying him.

"Not an easy man to work for, is he?" she asked.

"Not always," he agreed. "But he's honest and fair."

"Yes, he is that. And he cares about you."

His hand at her back, Paul moved her toward the elevators. "The feeling's mutual. Well, it looks like we're going dancing."

Chris's sigh was exaggerated. "That's about the last thing I thought I'd be doing tonight."

"You and I both." He punched the elevator button. "Come on. I'll drive you back to your car. You might as well take the rest of the day off."

"What about you?"

"I'm going to personally get the water sample and take it over to the lab."

Chris felt a shiver trickle down her spine. As she stepped into the elevator, she fervently wished the water would test negative. "How dressy is this affair tonight?"

"Your best bib and tucker, babe. When cops decide to dress up, they really go at it."

The doors wheezed shut as she looked up at him. "You mean you're going to put on a tux, you who only wear ties to weddings and funerals?" She laughed at the pained look on his face. Maybe the evening wouldn't be so terrible, after all.

LOOKING AROUND THE crowded ballroom at the Hyatt Regency, Paul remembered why he hated these formal affairs, and wearing a tie was the least of it. Overdone beef and overblown speeches. Plastic smiles and polite handshakes. Phony friendliness and prudent politicking. The only thing that made it bearable this time was the woman he held in his arms as they moved around the dance floor.

Why'd she have to be so beautiful? he wondered. Why hadn't the sun wrinkled her skin and time hardened the blue of her eyes? Would it make any difference, since it wasn't only her outer beauty that attracted him? Christine Donovan was bright, quick, spirited, caring and, though she had a penchant for propriety, she also had a great sense of humor when she let herself relax. She seemed relaxed tonight, even though she hadn't wanted to attend this shindig any more than he had.

When they'd arrived, Paul had escorted her around, introducing her to dignitaries and officials under Mike's approving eye. The unpleasant task was made almost enjoyable by having her on his arm, he had to admit. She'd smiled, shaken hands, said the right things and had undoubtedly made a good impression. Last year, he'd brought Susan to this event, and he'd been bored out of his mind. He was not pleased at the realization.

"Enjoying yourself?" he asked as he reluctantly drew back a little from the fragrance of her hair so he could see her face.

"Mmm."

"Such enthusiasm."

"Well, the food was adequate at best, the service a bit harried, the people at our table a shade on the boring side and the speeches interminable." She smiled into his eyes. "But the band's not bad, and the man I'm dancing with hasn't stepped on my feet yet."

"Careful there, you'll turn my head with all those compliments."

"I sure wouldn't want to puff up your hat size any more than that woman with the plunging neckline seated next to you at dinner did. I thought she was going to crawl into your lap and start cutting your meat for a while there."

He laughed. "Jealous?"

"No, empathetic. The poor soul is evidently starved for male attention."

He maneuvered her toward the edge of the crowd. "Are you saying I only appeal to desperate women?"

"Hardly." To her eyes, Paul was by far the most attractive man in the room. She glanced around the floor. Mike cut a very handsome figure in formal clothes. And Phoenix's tall, distinguished mayor was awfully good looking. But Paul still outshone them all. Or was she still as prejudiced as she'd once been? No, facts were facts. His blond hair contrasting with his tanned skin and the white of his dress shirt was enough to make any woman look twice. She looked into his dark eyes. "You appeal to all manner of women. There, I said it. Does that make you happy?"

She made him happy. And Paul fervently wished she didn't. It was time to change the focus of the conversation. "Would you like to know what I found out at our lab today?"

"They couldn't have analyzed that water sample that quickly?"

"It's not complete yet, but I asked the technician a few questions, and he gave me some interesting answers. Do you know that one of the most common plants from the poisonous dogbane grouping found prevalently in Arizona is the oleander? And did you know what the fragrance basis for Forbidden is?"

"Not oleander?"

"The one and only. Oleander extract. And who invented Forbidden, a chemist who would know all about poisons?"

Chris's eyes widened. "Steve Thorn? Why would he try to poison Nancy Evans? Is he her fiancé?"

"I don't know. He denies being anyone's. And we haven't asked Nancy. She doesn't realize she was poisoned, and we still can't be sure it was the water that caused it. So, for now, I'm just speculating."

"Interesting speculation. As chief chemist, Steve would certainly know what to put in the water that would make a person uncomfortably ill yet not kill them. He could also be anywhere in the building and his presence not be questioned, so he could easily have slipped the note into our typewriter. But I still don't believe Nancy was supposed to be in that hospital bed. You or I were meant to drink that water, possibly both of us."

"Ah, but the embezzler's been awfully smart and quite patient for nearly two years. If he poisoned our water and we both became ill, he knows I'd surely have the water analyzed. And who's the first man we'd suspect if it's a chemical concoction but the head chemist, right?" Paul shook his head. "Too pat. Steve Thorn's obnoxious and egotistical, but he doesn't strike me as stupid."

Chris agreed. "Nor I. If not Steve, then who?"

The song drew to an end, but they were so engrossed in their conversation that they didn't move out of their embrace. "Let's try this on for size. Suppose Steve had only just been nice to Nancy and she's fantasized all that romantic stuff about him. Suppose Steve is interested in someone else at Lady Charm, someone who is cool and unemotional and probably manipulative as well. Someone married to a nonaggressive, wimpy type."

"Diane? Why would she need to steal money?"

"Like Angela said, maybe she doesn't want to wait around for Teddy to inherit the pot of gold. Or maybe Angela stole the money and set Diane up as the likely candidate. She certainly can't stand her."

Chris shook her head. "Angela doesn't strike me as being clever enough to alter those complicated ledgers and not be exposed for two years."

His hand on her elbow, Paul guided Chris toward the double doors leading to the terrace. "Really? Did you read her file? She graduated from UCLA, and her major was math."

"Now, that's a surprise. I would have thought she majored in men." Looking up, she stopped. "Where are we going?"

"Outside for a little air. I just noticed Mike slowly making his way toward us with the mayor and a couple of other bigwigs in tow. If I have to smile and shake just one more hand tonight, I'm going to turn real surly."

"We certainly can't have that," Chris said as they stepped out onto the deserted balcony. The night air was warm and heavy with the scent of honeysuckle. She walked to the railing and gazed out at the lights of Phoenix winking all around them and Camelback Mountain looming in the distance like a majestic guardian. She'd always loved the many and varied views of her favorite city. She turned to Paul, who was watching her and not the scenery. "I'm surprised your father isn't here tonight?"

"Who knows, he may pop in yet. He often hits two or three of these events in one evening. I don't know how he stands the pace."

John Cameron made the rounds regularly because he loved the praise and the power, Chris thought. If Paul couldn't see that, she certainly wasn't going to point it out to him, at least not now. Tonight they were managing to keep things friendly between them. Talking about the case kept things impersonal. "So you suspect even Angela?"

Paul didn't really want to talk about the case anymore but she kept bringing it up. The moonlight danced in her hair, and the long yellow dress she wore draped softly around her curves then exploded in a billowy rush of pleats at the bottom. He was having trouble concentrating. "Yes. I'm looking into her background, checking out the modeling agency where she worked previously and looking into her personal life."

"Personal life?" She leaned against the railing and looked up at him. "Is that ethical? I mean, she hasn't done anything."

"That we know of. Is it ethical for someone to steal from Maggie? We're not investigating hurt feelings here, you know. It may shock you to realize I'm also checking into Jeremiah's background."

"No, I'm kind of glad you are. He seems genuine enough, but so much about him worries me."

"Me, too. And Maggie's too much in love to be objective about him. It's the smart thing to do, to research everyone, but I sure hope it turns out to be someone other than Jeremiah."

Paul came a step closer and blocked out the moonlight behind him so she could see only him. He gave every indication of being so strong, so sure of himself. Was he really? "Do you ever get tired of doing the smart thing all the time, of being there for everyone, of pleasing your father, Mike and the world in general? Do you ever want to just do something for the hell of it, for yourself?"

"Yeah, I do. Right now." His arm slid around her, and she had no place to go.

She saw the kiss coming and did nothing. Later on she might berate herself for it, but when his head lowered, she opened her mouth and let time melt away.

If her mind had lapses of memory, her body did not. As his arms pulled her closer, every part of her sang a welcome. He had always been able to weaken her with his kisses, from the first one on Maggie's porch to the last at his hospital bedside. For a man with a hard, unforgiving occupation, he showed such sensitivity in a kiss that it nearly brought tears to her eyes.

It had been so long. The thought skittered through her mind as other sensations took precedence. His mouth, full and demanding, his taste, heady and exciting, his body showing her his need. She even found herself enjoying the unfamiliar bristly feel of his mustache on her skin. She clung to him, wanting to know again the passion that only he had been able to arouse in her. On a soft moan, she pressed against him, hungry to share again the magic they'd had together.

Paul had kissed her almost on a dare, a challenge he couldn't refuse. But in moments that had all been forgotten. The contrasts of her had always fascinated him—the cool executive in the business suit and the hot-blooded woman she could become in his arms. His body pulsed in total recall of those moments. She was everything he'd ever wanted, and he'd done without so long. He wound his arms around her and took his fill.

Or could he ever get enough of this one woman? As he tasted her quick desire, he thought not. What man didn't want to tame the rage of the storm? What man could discipline himself not to touch fire of this magnitude? He had once and should never have touched her again.

Paul drew back and saw her eyes, huge and dark and shaken by needs she'd thought she'd buried. At least he'd been honest with himself. She was all wrong for him and would hurt him again, but he'd never quite gotten over her. He stepped away so they were no longer touching.

"It's time I took you home," he said quietly.

No, Chris thought moving slowly toward the doors. It was past time.

"CHRIS, COME OUTSIDE WITH ME," Maggie called, her voice full of excitement.

Chris came down the stairway fastening her gold hair clip at the back of her head. "What's going on?"

"Jeremiah should be here any second," Maggie said, walking to the double doors. "He said for me to be out front at two because he had a surprise for me. I want you to come with me."

Her aunt's happiness was contagious. Linking her arm with Maggie's, Chris smiled and went out into the sunshine with her. It was a lovely day, and Chris was looking forward to an interesting Saturday afternoon. "He's not here yet," she commented as she craned her neck toward the winding driveway that led up to Maggie's place.

"No, but he'll be along soon."

"So will your other guests. I think it'll be a fascinating gathering, but what prompted you to invite all these people to your home today?"

"I was having a talk with Paul a couple of days ago. It was his idea." Maggie went on tiptoe as she searched the path.

"Paul thought you ought to invite half your office staff here? Whatever for?"

"I believe he said that by observing people when they're relaxed you can often get real insight into them, better than quizzing them endlessly. And it's not half my staff, it's only a few. However, I really don't think any of the ones he wanted to be here are at fault in this messy business."

"Who's coming?"

"Well, Teddy and Diane, of course, and Steve Thorn. And Jeremiah and I and you and Paul. Oh, and that model, Angela something. Yes, eight of us altogether." She frowned as she looked around. "Where is that man?"

"Angela Knight? Quite a list. I'm a little surprised."

"Are you, dear? Well, I imagine Paul has his reasons." A car approaching had her head turning and her feet moving to greet the new arrival. "Who is that? Oh, I can't believe it. Jeremiah?"

Chris watched a low, sleek, silver Jaguar with its top down slowly inch around the curve and stop on the drive in front of them. Jeremiah unfolded his tall frame from the car, smiling through the ever-present cigar stuck in his mouth. Maggie scooted around and hugged him excitedly.

"You did it!" she squealed in her throaty voice. "You chose the one I liked. Oh, darling, it's beautiful."

"Drives like a dream, Maggie," he told her. "Come on, I'll take you for a spin."

"Oh, I can't right now. Our guests will be here any minute." She reached up and kissed his cheek. "I'm so glad you got it. Now Chris can use my Mercedes while she's here." She turned to her niece. "Isn't this something?"

Yes, something very expensive, Chris couldn't help thinking. Walking nearer, she smiled at both of them. "It's quite a car."

Jeremiah beamed his acknowledgement, then looked at Maggie. "I've got another surprise, for later."

"You aren't going to tell me?" she pouted.

"You'll see soon enough. It's a little entertainment I cooked up for everyone. I arranged it with Mendosa's help. That woman's wonderful."

"Yes, she is," Maggie said, "but she's going to be quite annoyed if I don't get in there and finish discussing the dinner arrangements." She squeezed Jeremiah's hand. "I'll just be a minute." And she dashed off through the front door.

Jeremiah threw his unlit stub of a cigar into the shrubs and turned to Chris. "You really like it?"

She ran her fingers along the smooth chrome edging the door. "Oh, it's not important if I like it, just if you two do."

"I suppose you think I'm somewhat foolish, getting a sports car—a convertible, at that—at my age."

She looked into his light blue eyes, thinking they weren't quite as guileless as she'd originally thought. "I think age is a state of mind. As long as you make Maggie happy, I don't care how old you are or what kind of car you get."

Thoughtfully Jeremiah stuck both hands into the pockets of his finely-creased linen slacks. "I want nothing more than to make Maggie happy." He walked slowly around the front of the car and stopped by her. "And I'd like to get to know you better. We're going to be family soon."

"Yes. Speaking of family, are some members of yours coming to the wedding?"

"No."

"That's a shame. Maybe if Maggie called—"

"No." His voice was louder this time and, as if realizing it, he softened his eyes. "I left all that behind me. I don't want them involved in my new life. They...they're not very happy with me."

"I see," Chris said, not seeing at all. "Well, Maggie has so many friends that I'm sure we'll still have a good crowd at the wedding."

"Yes. Maggie's so good it's small wonder everyone loves her. A little too good, I sometimes think. But, no matter. I certainly love her."

Chris found a smile. "I'm glad to hear that. I'm going inside. Coming?"

"I think I might put the top up. Dust, you know."

With a wave at him, Chris went inside, wondering if Paul had started poking around in Jeremiah's past yet. She'd ask him as soon as she could. She felt a little guilty suspecting Jeremiah's motives, but they owed it to her aunt to check everyone out. She decided to search out Maggie and Mendosa before the guests arrived.

"I CAN'T BELIEVE JEREMIAH has such a high bank balance," Chris said. "No wonder he can afford to buy a Jaguar."

Paul outstretched his hand to help her up the steep incline of the rocky path. "But that's not the only odd thing. He opened the account about a year and a half ago when he came to Phoenix. Since then, he's had sporadic deposits totaling well over two hundred thousand."

Chris stopped as she reached his side. "That's a very good salary for doing 'this and that' at Lady Charm, which is what Maggie said he does." She squinted up at the sun, low in the blue sky. "I don't know what to make of it."

"I don't, either," Paul said as he leaned against the stone ledge, a guardrail formed by nature along the edge of the cliff. Below them, the city of Phoenix spread as far as the eye could see.

Chris took a deep, cleansing breath of the fresh mountain air. It was late afternoon, and she and Paul had gone for a walk away from the others, who were involved in learning skeet shooting, Jeremiah's second surprise. With Mendosa's help, he'd lined up a twelve-gauge shotgun for everyone and enough clay pigeons to keep them all happily busy trying their hands at a new sport.

Chris and Paul had stood watching for a while as the novices had lined up in a semicircle on a rocky hill behind Maggie's place. Like a patient host, Jeremiah had explained the old Scandinavian pastime, showed everyone how to hold the gun, then demonstrated as he released the clay targets in such a way as to simulate the angle of a bird in flight. The whole group had cheered as his first shot shattered the clay target. Even now, they could hear them taking turns, laughing at one another's ineptitude, the better shooters giving hints to the others.

While they'd observed, the only person who'd scored a hit other than Jeremiah had been Diane, a fact that seemed to surprise even her. She'd shared one of her rare smiles. Teddy looked awkward with the rifle in his hand, Maggie seemed pleased as punch at everything her fiancé did, Steve appeared bored, and Angela frowned at the wind mussing her perfect hair. After the second round, Paul had taken Chris's hand and had suggested they take a break and check out the neighboring redrock hill. She'd been more than ready to leave. Spying on invited guests didn't sit too well with her.

Paul continued to puzzle through Jeremiah's finances. "I don't think the deposits are his salary or his retirement checks. It might be from insurance policies he had on his wife. I've made some calls to the East Coast asking for copies of those plus her death certificate."

"What did Jeremiah's wife die of, do you know?"

"We'll soon find out."

Chris sat down on the ledge and leaned her back against the rock wall. "I talked with Jeremiah shortly before you arrived. He's very adamant about not asking any members of his family to the wedding. He said they're not very happy with him these days."

"I don't doubt that. If they didn't want Jeremiah to marry Maggie years ago, they probably haven't changed their minds."

"But the man's in his sixties now. His parents are probably dead. Who could still object?"

"Hard to say."

"His background is baffling, to say the least. I hope we get some answers soon. I'm so afraid Maggie's going to get hurt. She cares too much."

Paul shifted away from her so he could see her eyes. "Can we care too much for someone?"

Chris got the feeling they were no longer discussing Maggie and Jeremiah. They hadn't talked since last night when he'd brought her home from the dance and again left her at Maggie's door, looking as stunned as she'd felt after the powerful kiss they'd shared on the terrace. She knew one of her shortcomings was running away from her feelings, yet it seemed conversations with Paul inevitably led to that. Sighing, she looked up at him.

"Yes. It makes us vulnerable, careless and blind to their weaknesses."

"That doesn't apply to you, does it, Chris? You're very careful, very aware of a man's weaknesses, and very quick to run so you won't become vulnerable—to anyone."

"Is that how you see me?"

His dark eyes were challenging. "Tell me where I'm wrong."

"I don't feel I have to... oh!" She ducked swiftly as she felt more than heard something whiz by her ear, something that set her heart pounding. From her crouched position, she felt a spray of splintered rock fall on her head as Paul pulled her against him.

"What was that?" she asked against his chest, her voice breathy with fear.

He stared at the black mark where the shotgun blast had hit the stone, and he clenched his jaw. An accident or...? He drew back to look at Chris. "Are you all right?"

"Yes, fine. A little shaken." It had all happened so fast. She stared at the spot and couldn't prevent a shudder. "Someone down there is really a bad shot."

Or maybe not. "Stay low and follow me, quickly." Paul took her hand and pulled her along the narrow path.

"Where are we going?"

"Back to the others."

It was a short run down the crooked path for two people in good shape. Paul arrived at the clearing where the skeet shooters stood, Chris right behind him. He estimated that less than two minutes had passed since the shot had sailed within an inch of Chris's head.

All six of them looked up, each one holding a shotgun in their hands. From where he stood, Paul glanced upward and could see through a crevice in the adjacent hillside the approximate spot where they'd stood. Could one of these people have shot that far off target accidentally? Or had someone dropped back and aimed very carefully at a target that wasn't clay?

"Is anything the matter?" Maggie asked, looking concerned at his expression. She peered around Paul and noticed Chris's white-faced expression. "Are you all right, dear?"

There would be no point in revealing his anxiety to the shooter and no reason to needlessly alarm the others. Paul tired to look casual. "Nothing's wrong. We're heading back to the house. Go ahead and enjoy yourself."

Maggie frowned. "I'm the only one who hasn't hit a pigeon yet, I'm afraid. I'm not very good with guns."

Someone was, Paul thought wearily. Was he reading too much into minor incidents? No. He'd been looking at Chris when the pellets had sped by, narrowly missing her ear. It had come from this direction. Who else was out here in Maggie's mountains with a gun? Was the embezzler one of these six people before him? If so, he or she was getting bolder, more impatient and definitely nervous.

"We won't be much longer," Maggie said as Steve got into firing position while Jeremiah released another pigeon.

Chris shuddered, and Paul pulled her close as the clay bird in the sky split, making a popping sound. Steve turned around with a satisfied smirk.

"Not bad for a man who's never even held a gun before today, right, Sergeant?" Steve asked with his characteristic conceit.

Was that the truth, or was he going on record with that comment? The man was certainly capable of shading the truth, Paul suspected. "Yeah, nice shot. See you later." He turned Chris, and they headed down the winding path.

As they moved around the next bend, he felt her tremble, and he stopped. "Are you okay?"

"Just hold me, please," she whispered. "Just for a minute." Her arms went around him, and she placed her head against his chest.

Paul angled them into a secluded niche and held on. He should have known she might have a delayed reaction. It was no laughing matter to realize you might have had a shotgun aimed at you. He put his hand on her hair and gently smoothed it back from her face.

Chris breathed in the clean, male scent of him and was comforted by the steady rhythm of his heart beneath her ear. She concentrated on those things and on the way his hard hands were rubbing her back and the feel of his warm breath as he bent his face into her hair. Finally the panic began to leave her. So stupid to be so afraid, yet she hadn't been able to stop the shivering. Paul must think her a child.

She raised her head. "I'm sorry. I know it's irrational to be afraid *after* the incident, but—"

"It's a perfectly normal reaction."

"Do you think one of them...?" She couldn't quite complete the thought.

He shook his head. "If that blast came from down there, it was either a wild shot or someone's one hell of an actor."

She nodded vaguely, then moved back into his embrace. She didn't want to think about any of that right now. She just wanted to hold and be held until the fear went away.

Paul's arms encircled her in a loose embrace, and he felt her breathing gradually calm. There was nothing sensual in the way he held her, yet it evoked feelings almost more powerful. For this moment in time, she needed him, and he was anxious to give to her. She was so independent most of the time, so intent on going it alone, that it pleased him to have her lean on him, even if briefly.

"Uh, excuse me," Teddy said behind them, and Paul whirled about, his body instinctively shielding Chris.

Teddy looked chagrined. "I'm sorry to interrupt. You weren't down below so Maggie sent me to find you. She said to tell you that dinner will be served in half an hour."

The man had to walk on cat feet, Paul thought as he noticed Teddy's rubber-soled shoes. He cleared his throat and nodded. "We'll be right there. Thanks."

Teddy nodded uncomfortably and retraced his steps.

Paul turned back to Chris. "Feeling better?"

She refastened her hair clip with fingers once more steady. "Yes. Thanks for letting me sniffle all over you."

"You weren't sniffling." He held out his hand. "Come on. Last one down the mountain's a rotten egg. Fair warning, I'm fast."

"Fair warning, I cheat," she said through a forced smile, then dodged around him and went racing downward, anxious to be off the hill.

THE EVENING WAS GOING to be a bust as far as learning anything new, Paul decided as he listened to the conversation around the table. He'd told Maggie that in a dinner setting you could often catch an unplanned remark or a telling gesture, but tonight wasn't panning out. Everyone seemed relaxed enough, loosened by Maggie's wine and Jeremiah's terribly outdated jokes. Even Steve was almost pleasant, and Angela managed to keep a lid on both her drinking and her temper.

Diane, on the other hand, smoked almost nonstop, even between each elaborate course, holding her cigarette holder almost in Teddy's face, reminding him to offer a light. Maggie was particularly attentive to Teddy, talking steadily with him, looking at him with warmth and affection. Was that because of Diane's disdain? Paul wondered.

He couldn't help but notice that though Jeremiah had made several efforts at conversation with Teddy, Maggie's son had cut each attempt short. Since Teddy was hardly effusive, that wasn't exactly surprising.

Chris, looking lovely in a pale blue halter dress, had managed to put the shooting incident out of her mind as she chatted with the guests. The conversation ebbed and flowed, airy and meaningless. No, not much here, Paul realized with disappointment.

When the doorbell rang, Paul looked up with interest, hoping that Mike had decided to drop in. Instead, Mendosa stood in the archway and beckoned to Chris. He watched her walk over, then saw a dark, curly-haired man join them and immediately pull her into a quick, hard embrace. The man stepped back, and Paul got a look at his face.

What in the hell was Mark Emery doing in Phoenix? he wondered.

Chapter Six

He didn't give a damn who Chris hugged, Paul told himself as he drained his wineglass, his eye on the foyer. Mark was professional perfection in a three-piece suit, his tie just so, every curly hair in place. No one dressed that formally for a casual evening in the Southwest, but this guy did. Well, why should he care what the man wore or what Chris possibly saw in him? It was her life and her business.

Deliberately, he turned to Diane, who was seated on his right, and began an innocuous conversation with her. From the corner of his eye, he saw Chris quietly talking with Mark. By turning his head just a bit, he knew he could keep them peripherally in sight. He prided himself that he kept his eyes trained on Diane Muldoon's silky smooth features instead.

In the foyer, Chris was trying to keep the annoyance from her voice. "You didn't mention you might be coming to Phoenix." Was Mark checking up on her? she wondered. His almost daily phone calls should have been enough. He'd never been this concerned on any other assignment she'd had.

"It was a spur of the moment trip." He glanced in at the others still seated around the dining-room table. "Please, don't let me interrupt your dinner."

"I've finished. Have you eaten? We could set another plate..."

"No, thank you."

Chris glanced in and saw Paul's fleeting scowl. "Let's go out on the terrace," she said, taking his arm. At the waist-high brick wall, she turned to face him. "You flew in for a meeting, you were saying?"

"Yes, at the Biltmore. I usually send Freda Jones to these regional things, but I wanted to see you."

"Well, that's awfully nice," Chris said, wishing she felt genuinely pleased to see him. They hadn't talked about drop-in visits. She'd just assumed he wouldn't. "We do talk on the phone nearly every day. There simply isn't that much happening in the case just yet beyond what I've already told you."

Mark stepped closer. "I'm interested in the case, of course, but I wanted to see how you personally were doing."

He was such a nice man, always concerned about her, always interested. Maybe too nice—and his attention was a bit stifling. "I'm fine." She glanced through the arch and across the foyer. Everyone was still at the table. Paul was listening intently to Diane, who had turned her back to her husband and was evidently telling a fascinating tale, if Chris were to judge by the look on Paul's face. Not that it mattered to her. "I'd like you to meet Maggie and..."

Mark touched her arm. "In a minute. How's it feel to be back? Are you having any problems?"

Now she understood. He was referring to Paul. Mark knew that she and Paul had dated each other. But he didn't know just how close they'd been, and he didn't know exactly why she'd left Phoenix. And she wanted to keep it that way. "Not really."

She thought it best to skirt the issue and return to the case under investigation. "It's not easy to pinpoint any one person, as I mentioned to you on the phone last Friday. Then there's this mysterious business about the head bookkeeper's sudden illness.''

As she related what had happened to Nancy and their suspicions about the case, she saw the patient look Mark wore and knew he'd figured out that she was going on in an attempt to divert his attention from his veiled reference to Paul.

Mark took her hand, stopping her dissertation. "I worry about you. If that water in your cooler turns out to have been tampered with, perhaps we ought to consider taking you off the case. Maybe your personal involvement in this case is making the embezzler take additional risks. If anything happened to you, I wouldn't be able to forgive myself.''

Why couldn't she care about this man, as he so badly wanted her to? Chris asked herself, not for the first time. Evening shadows dappled his strong face, and a splash of moonlight danced in his warm eyes. He was some woman's dream, but she wasn't that person. Often, she felt guilty that she couldn't be all that Mark wanted her to be. "Nothing's going to happen to me. I'm being careful." Yet it hadn't been enough to prevent someone from taking a shot at her just hours ago. She felt a shiver race down her spine at the memory.

Mark reached up and cupped her chin, forcing her to meet his dark eyes. "Come home with me, Chris. Let me put someone else on this case. I miss you." As if to emphasize his point, he bent his head and touched his lips to hers.

As she felt the gentle pressure of his mouth on hers, several thoughts skittered through her mind. A very private person, she wasn't pleased to be kissed in full view of any number of people who had only to glance around to see them. Mark had kissed her before, and then, like now, she'd tried to respond and had grown annoyed with herself that she felt so little. And finally the potent memory of the effect Paul's kiss last night had had on her made this seem like a brotherly peck. Irritated with her inflexibility, she stepped back from him.

"I can't leave, for Maggie's sake. Please try to understand."

Mark averted his gaze. "They're putting some pressure on me from the home office about this case. We need to see some action soon."

"What do you mean?"

"Just that. If I don't see some results in, say the next two weeks, I may be forced to put someone else on it."

He still hadn't looked her in the eye. Something fishy here, Chris decided. She had a dark suspicion as to just who would want her off the case and out of Phoenix. "You wouldn't have received a phone call from Senator Cameron by any chance?"

Mark sighed. "Not me personally. The senator's a good friend of our regional manager. And a big stockholder."

The barracuda. "I see." She wasn't going to allow him to interfere this time. She hadn't returned to Phoenix to try to snare his precious son, and she'd be damned if she'd let him maneuver her. She looked into Mark's eyes and knew he felt helpless. He had a job to protect. She gave him a smile. "Don't worry. Something will break soon."

He nodded unhappily. "All right, but I hope it breaks wide open, and fast. San Diego's not the same without you."

Chris heard the group straggling out of the dining room, the only one still at the table was Paul, his hooded eyes on her, his face dark and brooding. How much had he seen? she wondered. And what was he reading into Mark's gentle kiss? Chris squared her shoulders. It was none of his concern who she chose to kiss.

Mark glanced at his watch and spoke with regret. "I've got to catch a late plane and turn in my rented car." He took her arm. "Walk me to the door?"

"Sure. Let's find Maggie and Jeremiah." As she headed for the double doors with him, she saw Paul rise and watch their progress. She pretended not to notice as she hailed Maggie.

Paul lingered in the dining room, ostensibly to say a few words to Mendosa about the wonderful menu, but really to buy a little time. From the doorway, he saw Chris, looking a shade too animated, introducing Mark to her aunt and cousin.

He'd seen the man kiss her, had watched as she'd not really participated in the kiss wholeheartedly, yet hadn't pulled away, either. She didn't seem exactly crazy about the guy. Mark, on the other hand, had probably made up some excuse to fly to Phoenix to see her. Paul leaned against the arch, wondering why it should matter to him, why he should care who Chris kissed?

"She looks nice in blue, doesn't she?" Mendosa said, standing beside him and following his gaze.

Paul took in a deep breath. "She looks good in any color, Mendosa." He braced one hand against the wall and looked at the woman who'd been far more than a housekeeper in Maggie's house. All the months he'd dated Chris, she'd been his ally, approval of him apparent in her eyes and in her words. He also knew she'd always seen through him. "You caught me."

"Yeah, I caught you," she said, wiping her hands in her apron. "Long time ago, I caught you watching her. The look on your face is the same."

He shrugged, hoping he looked nonchalant. "Some things change, some never do."

She smiled sympathetically. "That's a fact."

Paul waited until nearly everyone had left before he sauntered outside. He watched Jeremiah help Maggie into his new Jaguar, about to take her for a spin, as Chris stood looking on. When they pulled away, he stepped out of the shadows.

"Your boyfriend didn't stay long," he said.

Chris turned to him and folded her arms across her chest as she looked up. "'Boyfriend' is something of a teenage term, don't you think? Mark is the manager of the company I work for. Nothing more, nothing less. Not that it's any of your business."

"A friendly sort of guy, isn't he? Does he kiss all the hired help?" He saw her eyes quickly flare as he fished his keys out of his pocket, but she didn't answer. Her silence grated on his nerves.

"He's quite the junior executive in his neat little suit and his paisley tie. I've never seen him even unbutton his vest. Tell me, does he sleep in that getup?"

Chris had had it. She put on a devilish smile. "Actually, no. He sleeps in the nude. Anything else?" She saw his mouth thin to a narrow line as he struggled with that bombshell. "Just what has you so upset?"

"Me, upset?" He gave a short laugh. "You must be mixed up." He glanced up at the near-full moon. "I'm not in the least bothered. It's only nine o'clock on a beautiful evening and I've got a date. See you later." Whistling, he walked toward his car.

As he climbed in, he hoped he looked devil-may-care. He saw Chris lean against the trellis, her expression amused. He'd show her. He'd stop at the nearest phone booth and call Susan, take her out somewhere. To a quiet place where they had a piano bar maybe. Susan could always be counted on for interesting conversation and a few laughs.

Putting the car into gear, Paul sent gravel flying as he turned and shot down the winding driveway.

IT WAS LATE TUESDAY AFTERNOON before the lab had the official report on the water-cooler sample. Paul picked it up and read that minute tracings of poisonous oleander extract had been found, just as the technician had predicted after his preliminary studies. Arriving at their office, he handed the report to Chris and watched her face as she read it. A small muscle twitched under her eye, but otherwise she handled the news well.

"Are you going to tell Nancy?" she asked.

"Eventually. She's taking a few days off, so I think I'll let it go till later. I don't want to scare her off, maybe have her quit on us before our investigation's over."

Chris chewed on her lower lip thoughtfully. "Who but you and I knew that she was spending a good deal of time in our office and that she drinks a lot of water?" She shook her head. "The attempt was on us, not Nancy."

"You're probably right," Paul admitted. "How do you feel about that?"

"How? Terrific! I love it when people try to poison me." She jumped to her feet and went to stand by the window. "Maybe you're used to this, I'm not." She stood looking out toward the parking lot, rubbing a knot of tension at the back of her neck. It was quitting time, she realized as several hundred men and women poured out of both factory and office doors. Suddenly Chris wished she were safely back home in her cozy apartment by the sea, away from threats and problems.

Paul walked over to her. "You want off the case?"

"No."

Standing behind her, he placed his hands on her shoulders and began to knead the tight muscles. Surprisingly, she let him. He hadn't touched her, had barely spoken a personal word with her, since he'd sped from Maggie's Saturday night, behaving like a jerk. "I know this is hard on you, especially with your personal interest. But we *are* making progress.''

"I wish I could see it."

"I learned something yesterday that may or may not be significant. Steve Thorn *is* the man Nancy's involved with.''

Chris turned to face him. "How'd you find out?''

"After she checked out of the hospital, I asked for a copy of her phone bill. It included six calls to the same number. Steve Thorn's unlisted one.''

"Well, I'll be!" Being a police officer came in handy in obtaining the cooperation of the phone company, Chris thought. "Is Steve the one who picked her up and took her home?''

"No. Her brother came for her. Other than us, he was the only visitor Nancy had. Steve never showed up, nor did she get any incoming calls.''

Chris pondered the possibilities. "Yet she called him six times. And he denies dating anyone in the company or having wedding plans. Do you suppose Nancy made up all those wildly personal things she told Dora Phillips about her romance?''

"Could be, I suppose. Or maybe they really happened but, for reasons of his own, Steve doesn't want his relationship with Nancy known. Maybe they've broken up, and she refuses to let go.''

Chris nodded in agreement. "But is any of it relevant to our case?''

"I wish I knew." He turned her toward the window and went back to massaging her shoulders. "Feel good?''

She let her head drop forward loosely. "Mmm, yes." His touch was lazy and impersonal, and she was glad of it. After the way he'd zoomed off in a cloud of dust Saturday night, she'd thought things would be strained between them again. But evidently, he'd thought things over, because when he'd come into the office Monday, he'd acted as if the incident hadn't occurred and was once more his business-like self. She much preferred that over the tension that Mark's visit had brought about.

"I've arranged a trip for us," Paul said matter-of-factly. "A working trip, but it'll get us out of this atmosphere for a while."

She stopped the progress of his hands and turned, her eyes immediately wary. "What kind of working trip, and where to?"

"Tucson, to visit the cosmetics company where Steve Thorn worked before coming to Lady Charm. I've got an interview set up with the president, day after tomorrow."

"I see." She walked back and sat down at her desk. "So we'll fly in Thursday..."

He came over and placed a lean hip on the edge of her desk. "No, we'll drive down tomorrow afternoon. It's only two hours. I have a personal favor to ask you. Actually, it's a request from someone else that I've been asked to convey to you."

Suddenly suspicious, Chris wrinkled a brow at him. "Whose request?"

"My father. He called Sunday to say he was sorry he missed us at the dance. He did stop in after we'd left. There's a dinner tomorrow evening for him in Tucson, a fund-raiser for his reelection. He's also slated to receive some sort of civic award, and he specifically asked me to invite you. He's always admired you."

Chris had known for a long while that Paul had a blind spot when it came to his father. She certainly didn't want to be the one to enlighten him. Yes, John Cameron admired her looks—and thought her empty-headed and easily manipulated. She'd never bothered to correct his impression.

Paul decided she was too quiet too long. "I rarely attend these things, but once in a while I feel I owe it to him.

Even my brother will be there. I just thought, since we need to check on Steve anyway, we could kill two birds with one stone. What do you say?''

She certainly didn't feel as though *she* owed John Cameron one single thing. But she was curious why he'd specifically invited her after all, but demanded that Mark pull her off the case. It might be interesting. She turned her gaze to Paul and found him looking studiously indifferent, as if it didn't matter to him if she went or not. Yet she'd picked up on a bit of anxiety in his voice. "All right, I'll go."

"Great."

Chris watched him try to hide the flicker of pleasure from his face. Reaching for her briefcase, she hoped she hadn't made a mistake.

THE EL CONQUISTADOR HOTEL, snuggled into a rocky hillside northeast of Tucson, had pulled out all the stops in decorating their ballroom for the dinner honoring Senator John C. Cameron. The mirrored ball high above the patrons' heads reflected the candles that flickered on over one hundred tables, each seating ten expensively attired voters. Looking around, Paul flinched at the sight, wondering how any one of them could honestly enjoy this extravaganza.

Watching his face, Chris caught the look and touched his sleeve. "Not exactly your cup of tea?" she asked gently.

He ran a finger under the collar of his formal shirt, realizing he'd somehow been conned into wearing his monkey suit twice in less than two weeks. "No, it isn't. I'd rather be on my own patio with a six-pack." He swung his gaze to her, took her hand and laced his fingers with hers. "Not necessarily alone. Have I told you lately that you're beautiful, *the* most gorgeous woman here?"

No, he hadn't, but his eyes had ever since he'd come to her room to escort her to the dinner. He'd schooled himself to hide his emotions, when the need arose, behind an almost-bored facial expression. But his eyes, the warm color of pecans, spoke volumes. Keep it light, she warned herself. "Have you checked out all the other women in this room?"

"Yes. You win, hands down." With her black hair and golden skin, she was made to wear white. The dress was high-necked, long-sleeved, very simple, with a long row of tiny buttons up the back. It was made of something very soft, subtly outlining every feminine curve, almost Victorian in style, yet sexier than anything else in the room. Yeah, no contest among all the overstuffed frilly outfits with bulging cleavages and too much skin showing. The lady knew how to make an impression. He let go of her hand and shifted his gaze, knowing he couldn't look at her much longer without wanting to touch more. And that would be a mistake.

"I wonder where Pete is," he said, craning his neck. They were seated at one of the front tables, facing the dais where the dignitaries would sit.

Chris watched the room fill up, the tuxedoed men hailing one another with jolly claps on the back as they found their chairs, followed by their bejeweled women, smiling gaily. Chris wished they'd get on with it so the speeches could begin and the evening could end.

The drive down had been pleasant, a relaxed Paul chatting most of the way, avoiding touchy topics. They'd arrived late afternoon and checked into adjoining casitas, private rooms away from the main structure of the hotel, filtering down the hillside in strings of six or eight, each affording a magnificent view. Motorized carts had carried them back up to the lobby where swarms of people flowed toward a variety of events. Chris took a sip of the champagne Paul had brought her and noticed her hand wasn't quite steady.

Her mind drifted back to another such evening, a fund-raising dinner-dance she and Paul had attended. It had been held at a hotel in Phoenix, and John Cameron had been the featured speaker then, too. The looks he'd sent her as Paul had whirled her around the dance floor had been cool and disdainful, but she'd hardly noticed. She'd been in the first flush of love. Afterward, Paul had reached into his pocket and brought out a key to a room at the hotel, in his eyes a question. Wordlessly, she'd taken his hand and moved toward the elevators. It had been the first of many beautiful nights.

Chris set down her glass and wished she could set aside her feelings as easily. The last two weeks, hours spent with him almost daily, had resurrected too many memories. Try as she would, she couldn't make them go away. Awareness crackled between them at the slightest touch, though she could see he fought it as valiantly as she. Perhaps she'd been foolish to agree to come on this trip. Spending business hours with him was bad enough, but it was the leisure times like now that started her mind floating back. Behind her, she heard a man speak Paul's name, and she turned, grateful for the distraction.

"Pete!" Paul stood and shook hands with his brother, then pulled him into a quick hug. "Glad you could make it."

"Me, too." He stepped back as Chris stood.

Odd that their paths had never crossed during all the months she'd dated Paul. But that had been back in Pete's vagabond days. She saw now that the family resemblance was unmistakable. Paul's brother was a couple of inches shorter, his shoulders not quite as broad, but he had the same lean, athletic look. The difference was in the eyes. Pete's were a little world-weary, as if he'd seen a lot of unhappiness in his life. Though he was two years younger than Paul's thirty-two, his face looked older, with deep lines etched into his tan skin. Yet his handshake was warm and friendly as Paul introduced them. "My brother's taste has definitely improved. It's good to finally meet you, Chris."

"Thank you. I understand you've just taken the bar exam."

Pete ran a hand through his fresh haircut. "Yeah, and am I glad that's over." Noticing a waiter passing with a full tray, he grabbed a glass of champagne. His eyes darted around the vast room as he took a healthy swallow. "The old man's not here yet?"

Paul noticed that the head table was almost complete. "Any minute now." He looked pointedly at Pete's glass. "Do you think you ought to?"

With a careless wave of his hand, he dismissed Paul's comment. "Relax, big brother. I promise not to embarrass you." He held Chris's chair for her. "Sit down, and let's get acquainted."

Someone in the aisle began a conversation with Paul just then, so Chris sat down as Pete motioned for the waiter to bring him more champagne. Did he need some liquid courage to face one of these affairs? Chris wondered. Or was it the imminent arrival of his father that had him a little jumpy?

"So, why'd you come back?" he asked, leaning forward, his elbows propped on the table, his eyes trained on her face.

She frowned in annoyance, wondering if Paul had discussed their relationship with his brother. Unlikely, she decided. "I'm working on a case. I'm an insurance investigator."

"Mmm-hmm." Pete sipped slowly from his second glass of champagne. "Let's try another angle. Why'd you leave?"

She frowned. "Are you always this nosy?"

He laughed, and it softened the harsh lines of his face, making him look momentarily as attractive as his brother. "Yeah, I'm the outspoken Cameron, haven't you heard? The blunt black sheep. Are you going to answer me?"

"No."

"All right, then I'll tell you why." He moved closer and lowered his voice. "My father didn't think you were the kind of woman his favorite son should marry so he found a way to pressure you to leave town." He watched the surprise register on her face, saw her eyes widen with shock. "Bingo." He swallowed more champagne.

Chris's recovery was slow. She glanced behind her and saw that Paul was listening intently to the man who'd stopped him. She returned her gaze to Pete, who was watching her with a sardonic smile. She'd told no one about that disturbing conversation with John Cameron and had been reasonably certain he hadn't mentioned it to anyone, either. Still . . .

"Pretty sure of yourself, aren't you?" she asked.

"Not until just now I wasn't. Don't worry, your secret's safe with me, though why you'd want to protect my father is beyond me."

"I don't. I didn't want Paul hurt. He seems to admire his father."

"Yeah, he does. My brother's a great guy, but he's been programmed."

"I don't understand."

"It's a long story, and not a very pretty one."

"I've got all evening."

Pete rubbed his forehead briefly before stretching his arm along the back of her chair as he leaned closer. "My father's into control—with everyone. Let me tell you a little story. We grew up with plenty of money, and Paul and I had this governess. Her name was Sarah. She was my first crush. I was nine or ten when I saved up my allowance and bought her this bouquet of flowers. Don't laugh, okay?''

''I'm not.'' But she did smile.

''I went to her room and knocked, but she didn't answer so I sat down in the hallway to wait. A little while later, the door opened, and Dad came out. He just looked at me, then walked away without a word. He knew I wouldn't say anything. He knew I was already under his control.''

''And your mother was . . .''

''Still alive then, yes. I told you it wasn't a pretty story. Dad always thinks he's doing what's good for us, but what he's doing is trying to control us so we'll do what's good for him. He's still trying.''

''Only you rebelled.''

Pete shrugged and took another sip. ''It was the only way I could get out from under. He thinks because I never stayed in one place that I'm shiftless. I didn't come back to Phoenix until I thought I was strong enough to stand up to him. I'm still not sure I am.''

''Did you ever tell Paul that story?''

He shook his head. ''Never. He wouldn't have believed me if I had.''

''Why do you think Paul's so blind to his father's faults?''

''Dad's told us all these stories about his youth, his father failing him, his mother letting him down. Paul hates to disappoint anyone, so he's the model son.''

She took a deep breath. ''Just for your information, John Cameron isn't the reason I left.''

''Then what is?''

''That, too, is a long story.''

Suddenly, there was a commotion at the front of the room, then the sound of applause as people got to their feet. The man of the hour had arrived and was being ushered to the seat of honor at the dais.

He hadn't changed, Chris thought as she reluctantly stood. John Cameron was a man with a presence. Nearing sixty, he could easily have shaved ten years off that figure. He was tan and fit, his blond hair showing the merest trace of white at his sideburns. He smiled easily as he shook hands and accepted his due. She used to wonder if she was the only one who saw through the phony facade. After her conversation with Pete, she thought perhaps his youngest son had also glimpsed the man behind the practiced smile and found him wanting.

Paul rejoined them as the applause died down and the master of ceremonies invited everyone to enjoy their dinner before the speeches began. Watching him closely, Chris saw John nod to his two sons, then train his eyes on her for a long moment. They were the same cold blue she remembered. Fighting a chill, she picked up her fork.

Seated between the two brothers, Chris listened with half an ear to the table conversation around her as she pretended an interest in her dinner. Her glances and her thoughts kept returning to John Cameron as she wondered just why he'd wanted her here tonight.

As coffee was served, the MC rose to present a civic award to the senior senator from Arizona, rambling on for twenty minutes as he extolled the virtues of the recipient. Fleetingly, Chris wondered if John himself had written the man's speech. Finally, the senator stepped to the microphone and tried to put on a modest smile as applause once again rocked the room. An accomplished public speaker, his voice had a rich timbre, his hands given to eloquent gestures. Chris tried to tune him out as she stared into her coffee cup.

At last it was over and people started milling about, many surging forward to shake John Cameron's hand, others moving to the already crowded dance floor as the band swung into a medley of popular tunes. She felt Paul lean toward her.

"You're a little quiet tonight," he said into her ear in an effort to be heard over the noisy room.

"Just a little tired," she said, thinking that if she feigned fatigue, they could make an early night of it and she wouldn't have to spend more than a few minutes with his father. As she looked up, she saw the eminent guest of honor making his way toward them and braced herself.

Paul, Chris and Pete rose as he came up to them. Chris watched as he shook hands with Pete, his eyes cool and assessing. But he clasped Paul's hand warmly and pulled him into a fatherly hug before turning to her.

"You look wonderful, Christine," he said, holding on to her hand. "California living agrees with you."

And therein lies the point, she thought. Looking into his eyes, she was certain he'd insisted on seeing her to shore up his argument that she should stay out of his son's life. She straightened her spine defiantly. "Thank you, Mr. Cameron."

"Call me John, please."

Paul said something innocuous, and she heard herself answer in kind. From the corner of her eye, she saw Pete drain his wineglass and saw the quick flash of disapproval cross his father's face. She wished he'd move on so she could stop smiling.

"We've got an early day tomorrow, Dad," Paul said at last. "I think we're going to turn in."

Chris could have kissed him. But his father was not to be thwarted.

"In a moment." The senator took Chris's hand. "Allow me the pleasure of one quick dance, won't you, please?"

She should have known. The sea of people parted as they made their way to the wooden floor. Expertly, he led her into an easy fox-trot. She'd expected he'd be an accomplished dancer, and he was. The elder Mr. Cameron had mastered all the social niceties, save one. He'd begun to believe his powerful position no longer required the human touch.

"How is the investigation going?" he began.

She'd prepared herself. "As well as can be expected."

"Do you think it's wise, your working on a case where your closest relative is involved? There are those who might say you're biased."

"They'd be wrong," she said as sweetly as she could manage through her building anger.

"I spoke with Mark Emery last weekend. I believe he agrees with me."

Chris leaned back to look into his cool blue eyes. "And you made sure by twisting a few arms, putting a little pressure on him so he'd put a little on me." She felt the heat rise. "Why don't we quit beating around the bush, Senator? Just what is it you want from me?"

"The same thing I've always wanted. Paul's up for another promotion, lieutenant this time. I'm running for re-election, and I'll win. My son's got a law degree, you know, though he's never used it. I want him to become our next district attorney. In Washington I'm cutting a path he'll have no trouble following." Without missing a beat, he smiled at a robust friend on the sidelines as he maneuvered Chris around the edge of the crowd. "I thought we had an understanding. Your coming back is not good for either of you."

She let that go for now. "It seems as though you've got Paul's future nicely mapped out. And I suppose you'll begin grooming Pete, too, once he passes the bar."

John shook his head in dismay. "Even if Pete passes, I doubt that he can catch up. He's frittered away too many years of his life on fun and games and frivolous women. It's too late for him, but not Paul. He's made all the right moves, and I intend to see that he gets to the top.''

"Is that what Paul wants?"

"He will when the time comes. He'll also want a wife that can boost him up the ladder, a woman well-connected, an asset, not a liability.''

Chris felt a sense of déjà vu. Hadn't they had almost this exact conversation just two years ago? She'd grown angry then, and she was even madder now. "And as before, you consider me a liability.''

He gave her his best persuasive smile. "Christine, you're easily the most attractive woman in this room. I'm sure you're extremely bright and very capable as well. But you're wrong for my son. I want you to stay away from Paul because you weaken him. When I think how far I could be by now if I'd have married a woman from a well-known, powerful family, instead of a— But that's in the past. We can't change it, but we can control the future.''

There was that word again—*control*. Chris doubted seriously if Paul could be coaxed into a political career any more than he could be pushed into a loveless marriage. But this shortsighted man, who didn't know his son at all, couldn't see that. He saw only his own ambitions. At that moment, however briefly, she felt sorry for him. If Paul decided to listen to his father, he deserved all he got.

"We need to set the record straight, Mr. Cameron. I didn't leave Paul two years ago because you asked me to. I left because I couldn't see myself sharing a future with a man who thrived on danger, one whose job called for daily risk taking.''

She knew of only one way to remove that smug, self-assured look from his face. She gave him a pleased smile. "But I *am* grateful you clarified things. Now that I know Paul will be leaving police work soon for the life of a politician, I think I'll just change my mind and transfer back to Phoenix. I believe we can work out our differences, after all.'' She dropped her hands and stepped back from him. ''Thanks for the dance, and for helping me decide.''

It was all she could do not to laugh at the stunned look on his face as she turned and left him in the center of the dance floor. She needed to do one more thing to convince John Cameron he'd really fouled up for once in his scheming life. Taking a deep breath, she walked over to where Paul was talking with his brother.

With a quick glance of apology to Pete for interrupting, she went up on tiptoe and whispered into Paul's ear. ''Could we leave now? I'm not so much tired as bored with all this, and I'd love nothing more than to be alone with you. Maybe you could find a bottle of champagne and bring it to my room...'' She let her voice drop off seductively, seeing the shiver her warm breath in his ear had caused. Easing back from him, she waited.

She was up to something, Paul knew, and it wasn't necessarily seduction, as she wanted him to believe. Did it have something to do with the dance she'd shared with his father? What could he have said to her? She stood there, trying to look deliberately enticing, a side of her he'd never seen. What the hell! Maybe it was time he found out.

''Why not?'' With a crooked grin, he grabbed a bottle of champagne from the adjacent table and took her hand. ''Let's go.''

Pete flashed her a broad wink and was rewarded with a smile. As she followed Paul through the maze of people, Chris glanced over her shoulder and caught John Cameron's narrowed-eyed look of fury. Feeling triumphant, she left the ballroom.

Chapter Seven

"I didn't mean it the way it sounded," Chris said as she stood outside the door of her casita.

Paul paused with the key halfway to the lock. "You mean you *wouldn't* rather be alone with me than back in that crowded ballroom?"

"Of course, I would. I just didn't mean the invitation to sound quite so...intimate." Chris threw a quick glance at the dark, shifting clouds and felt the first raindrops fall. By the looks of the turbulent sky, they were in for a beaut of a storm. Perhaps inside her room as well as outside, if she couldn't explain away her impulsive remark.

"This key doesn't work," Paul muttered as he tried every which way to insert it.

The shower was quickly turning into a downpour. "Here, let me try." Moving closer to the door to avoid getting soaked, Chris tried gently easing the key into the lock. It would only go so far. Frustrated, she shoved again to no avail.

"Hey," Paul yelled, trying to get the attention of one of the cart drivers pulling in a few doors down. "Could you help us?"

The boy delivered his passengers, then came to assist. Several times, he tried the key but it stubbornly refused to go in. "I think you've got the wrong key," he said, trying to make out the number in the dim light.

All three of them were huddled under a small overhang as the heavens opened up, dumping a steady stream of water on them.

"My dress is going to be ruined," Chris said somewhat resignedly.

"I'll have to go get another key," the cart driver told them.

Paul took her hand. "We'll be next door in my casita," he said before dragging her along the short walk. He opened the door on the first try. They hurried in as the cart pulled away.

"Good thing it's not cold," Paul commented as he turned on a light and grabbed a couple of towels. Handing one to Chris, he caught his breath as he looked at her. Her dress was wet, clinging and nearly transparent. He rubbed the towel vigorously over his hair. "I don't think that material was meant to be worn in the rain."

Chris glanced down, then plucked at the front of her dress. "No telling when that kid'll be back in this downpour. Do you have a robe I could borrow?"

Shrugging out of his wet jacket, Paul walked to the closet. "I don't travel with a robe. The best I can do is this." He reached in and handed her a long-sleeved blue shirt.

She didn't have much of a choice. Perhaps if she removed her dress carefully, the cleaners could save it. She took the shirt into the bathroom. But in moments, she was back. "These buttons—I can't seem to manage."

He'd taken off his damp shirt and had been standing watching the storm out the back patio door, the towel slung around his neck. He turned and walked to her. His hair fell in wet ringlets onto his forehead. Swallowing, she presented her back to him.

His large fingers had trouble with the small button-holes. "How did you ever fasten these by yourself?"

"It's not so difficult when it's dry." Her voice sounded hoarse, odd. She cleared her throat as he slowly made his way down her back. She could feel the warmth of his fingers, their slight trembling. The dress had a built-in bra, so her back was bare. She moved her hands to her chest to hold the material in place as he widened the opening. "I think I can take it from here."

"Just a few more." Paul recognized the huskiness in his voice. The heated fragrance of her drifted to him, and he drew in a deep breath. He wasn't sure how much more of this he could take, yet his fingers moved to the next button. Suddenly, he heard a soft sound escape from deep inside her, and he lost it.

With one swift movement, he slid his arms around her waist and pulled her close up against him as he lowered his lips to kiss the back of her neck. The breath trembled from her as he tightened his arms, inching his hands closer to her breasts.

When she stopped his forward movement, he lifted his head and turned her within his arms. Her eyes were huge and dark with desire. But she shook her head.

"No, I don't want this. I—"

He cut off the rest of her words with a kiss. She felt his tongue push into her mouth, felt her own resistance drop away like her forgotten dress. It had always been this way with Paul. The years apart had changed nothing. She could only defy him so long before her body betrayed her. Greedily, she reached for him.

Her fingers snaked through his thick, damp hair as the robust male scent of him captivated her senses. There was desperation in the movement of his hard, lean body against hers, a desperation she shared. A loud crash of thunder outside the room had the floors reverberating, yet she heard only the beat of her heart against his.

He pulled his mouth from hers only to bury his lips in the soft curve of her throat. His seeking hands pushed between them and tenderly closed over her breasts as he released a deep sigh. Like coming home, to touch her flesh again, to feel her respond avidly as she always had. She whispered his name, and his mouth found hers again. How beautifully they fit together, he thought as she curled into him.

She was sinking fast in a leaky boat she'd capsized herself. How had she thought she could prevent this? Chris asked herself as she felt the familiar passion building and melding with needs newly discovered. This man with his strong, clever hands, with his hungry, searching mouth, with his savage tenderness had turned her world upside down before. And would again.

Hands braced on his shoulders, she pushed back, touching her brow to his chin. "Please, Paul. I need some time."

In answer, he dipped his head and placed his mouth on her ear, breathing softly there. She shuddered involuntarily.

"Did I start it, or you?" he asked, his voice husky.

What difference did it make? She would take the blame, if there was any. She eased back, a little calmer now. "If I did, I didn't mean to."

In her eyes he saw vulnerability and lingering passion. Those huge blue eyes were always his undoing. Unhappily, he backed off and shoved his balled fists into his pants pockets as he turned to stare out the window.

Pulling the dress in front of her, Chris went into the bathroom and closed the door. When she came back out, a bellman had just dropped off her key. Paul flung it on the table and handed her a glass of bubbling champagne.

"I really don't need any more to drink," she said, though she took it from him.

She'd rolled up the sleeves of his shirt and buttoned even the top button, though it still drooped to her collarbone. The tail hung past the backs of her knees. How was it possible that she looked even more appealing in that ridiculous outfit than in her own dress? He nodded toward the small sofa that faced a stone fireplace. "Sit down."

"I'm not sure that's a good idea."

"I promise I won't touch you." He stood by the hearth opposite the couch.

She couldn't walk away, not while he had that haunted look in his eyes. Her feet bare, Chris walked over and sat down. She set her glass on the table as lightning lit up the sky for a fierce moment outside the window, followed by a vivid burst of thunder. She jerked her head toward the sight and sound, then eased back into the limited comfort of the couch. "I hate electrical storms."

"Are you afraid of them?"

"My mother was terrified of them. When Mike and I were little and it stormed, she shoved us under the kitchen table or in the hall closet and joined us until it eased. If we'd have had a basement, I'm sure we'd have been crouching down there. She was from the Midwest and had been through a tornado as a child. It left an indelible mark on her."

Paul walked over and pulled the drapes across the wide patio door, blocking out the storm. He came over to the couch and sat beside her, but in the far corner, angled to face her. "And so she passed her fears on to you."

Chris sighed, knowing where he was headed. "Don't pick on my mother. You didn't know her. She had her reasons for feeling the way she did."

He stared into his champagne bubbles for a long minute. "Does it ever seem to you that the problems between us are centered around our parents and their viewpoints more than on you and I and how we feel about things?''

She had thought that when she'd been dancing with John Cameron, listening to *his* plans for *his* son, without regard for Paul's own ideas on his future. Did he even know of his father's ambition for him? She decided to find out. "I understand you're up for another promotion soon. Lieutenant, is it?''

He wondered where this had come from, in the light of his own question to her. "Did Mike tell you that?''

"No, your father.''

He stretched his arm along the couch back. "Is that what you two discussed on the dance floor, my career in the department?''

"That and your political career.''

Paul frowned. "What political career?''

She'd thought as much. She pulled her knees up and adjusted the ends of the shirt more modestly as she searched his face for the truth. "He has big plans for you, first locally, then to Washington and all the way to the top. His words, not mine.''

Indulgently, Paul shook his head. "A father's dreams, not based in reality, not even based on my plans. But you can't blame him for his ambitions for his sons.''

"Not *sons*," she corrected. "He doesn't think Pete can catch up after all the wasted years.''

Paul set down his glass and stretched out his legs. "My father hates wasted potential more than anything. His own father was a brilliant attorney at one time, married to a wealthy woman. But he fell in love with a young widow, a seamstress. She was pretty, I understand, but penniless and came from a questionable background. None of that mattered to my grandfather. He walked away from his wife and son, his practice, all of it. The story goes that he and the seamstress bought a small farm and raised chickens and a houseful of kids. My father never forgave him for wasting his life, his potential.''

It was becoming clear. ''I think I'd have liked your grandfather.''

He touched the loose material of his own shirt gathered at her shoulder. He'd told her he wouldn't touch her, but he seemed unable to stop himself. ''Yeah, me, too. I've always been drawn to rebels.''

''Someone like Pete.''

''No, not Pete. He just runs away from situations and people he can't cope with. He thinks avoidance is the answer.''

Was he talking about his brother or her? ''Sometimes that's better than staying to fight a battle you can't win.''

''There are no battles you can't win—if you care enough.''

This was getting them nowhere. She stood. ''Caring enough was never the problem between us.'' She picked up her wet dress and her key. ''I'm going to my room.''

Paul rose and stood beside her. ''It's pouring out there. You'll be soaked.'' As if on cue, a clap of thunder echoed through the room, and he saw her flinch.

Chris squared her shoulders. ''I'll dry off.''

''Give me your key,'' Paul said. ''I'll run around, go inside and unlock the connecting door so you won't get wet.''

''What connecting door?''

''This one,'' he said as he walked to a door on the side wall, turned the lock and swung it open to reveal another door.

She hadn't even noticed the connecting doors. She ran a tired hand over her eyes. What difference did it make? She heard him open the front door and rush out, heard the rain pour from the tiled roof and splash heavily on the roadway and a small patch of grass. More rumblings in the distance hinted that the shower would not let up anytime soon.

She turned from the storm when she heard the connecting door open.

Paul stood in the doorway, barefoot, wearing only his black tuxedo pants, water dripping from the golden hairs on his chest, his wet hair plastered to his head. He looked oddly primitive and a little dangerous. Chris felt excitement churn inside her as she stared back into dark eyes alive with desire. She watched his chest heave with the effort to control his breathing. And still he stood there, not moving, waiting.

She knew what he was feeling, and also knew he was leaving it up to her. He'd gathered her to him earlier, but now it was her move. Chris felt her nerves jump as her stomach muscles tightened. Outside, the rain beat against the windows and thunder moaned a savage melody. The poise that usually carried her through most situations had abandoned her.

She wanted him. But the wanting included more than the physical. She wanted to sleep with him, to waken in his arms, to walk in the sunlight holding his hand, to share her feelings and ideas with him. She knew there were still many obstacles in the way, but even that thought couldn't change the basic fact. She wanted him.

He was watching her carefully. It would take only two steps and she'd be in his arms. In his embrace where she'd longed to be, not just these last few weeks, but all the lonely months without him. For two long years she'd dreamed of this, waited for this, though she'd buried her desire so deep she'd thought her love a thing of the past. If she reached for him, she'd be stepping over the line she herself had drawn. Foolishly, she'd erected barriers, but the first time he touched her, they'd tumbled down. She threw aside the dress she held and slowly walked to him, wrapped her arms possessively about him and lay her head against his shoulder.

With a soft moan, Paul bent his head to hers, closing the circle of his arms about her. He felt her tremble and realized she was as nervous now as the first time. Gently, he took her face in his hands and let her see in his eyes what he'd so long denied to himself. He saw her recognize the love she couldn't miss, saw her sweet smile as her lids fluttered down.

Without haste, he sent his lips on a journey to reacquaint himself with her face. He kissed each closed eyelid, the sleek line of her brow, the delicate spot at her temple, the satin of her cheeks. Her mouth beckoned him, and he gave in to the need to taste her more deeply. She gripped his arms as his tongue took possession of hers in a dance of remembrance.

His hands on her back pressed her into him, and Chris could feel his need swelling against her. He was wet and slippery and salty, and she didn't care. He was growing a little wild, a little crazy, and she didn't care. He was all wrong for her, and, at this moment, she didn't care.

"So long," she whispered breathlessly against his mouth, "it's been so long."

"Has it?" he asked as he rained kisses on her face, her throat.

She knew what he was asking. She brought her hands to his face, his eyes to hers. "Yes, a very long time. You were always the one—always. Just you."

He let out a ragged breath and clutched her to him. His hands pushed up the shirt so his fingers could touch the silk of her bare back. "It feels so good to hold you like this. I've had such empty arms without you."

Needing to see her, he led her to the bedside lamp. She watched his fumbling fingers unbutton the shirt that hung past her knees, then slowly slide it from her. With a shaky finger, he tugged the silken swatch of her panties lower, and she stepped free of it.

The soft light exposed the creamy white sections of skin not touched by the sun. Her breasts were firm and full and moving slightly as she breathed. "So beautiful," he whispered as his eyes devoured her. He'd dreamed of her like this, standing before him, anxious as he. She was no longer a dream, but a woman waiting for him to love her.

Restlessly, her gaze roamed his face and settled on his mouth. She leaned closer to nibble on his strong jaw, then shifted to the hollow of his throat before she pressed her lips to his. Impatient for the intimacy of his bare flesh, her fingers moved to the buttons of his pants and worked to free them. But he stopped her from touching him, needing more time. He knew if she touched him too soon, he would be out of control.

"Why are you in such a hurry?" he murmured against her hair. "We've waited two years. Let's enjoy."

Chris felt the mattress give under her weight as he pressed her downward, then felt him follow alongside. Her skin quivered with anticipation as she allowed him the freedom to explore her. And he did, lazily with lips that left a trail of fire wherever they touched, and they touched everywhere. She heard herself moan as her urgency grew, but still he would not be rushed.

She could no longer be still under the delicious onslaught of his rough tongue as he found the peak of one breast, then moved to the other. Passion, powerful and demanding, had her arching to meet his touch as he moved lower. Again, she brought her hands to the waistband of his pants and this time pulled them from him, no longer willing to wait.

Paul squirmed free of his clothes as she struggled to assist him. He loved her like this, wild and abandoned, unafraid to show him what she needed, unashamed of her desire for him. No other woman had ever excited him as Chris could, with her small hands that knew just how to touch him, her warm mouth that could delight him so effortlessly. Pushing the tangled sheets aside, she pulled him back to her.

Bracing himself with an arm on each side of her, he gazed into her eyes until she returned the look. He could smell her—the rain in her hair, the light, sexy scent she wore. He bent to touch his lips to hers, tasting the faint hint of wine, savoring the flavors that were hers alone. God, how he'd missed her.

He took a deep breath, then raised a questioning brow. "We can still stop."

Eyes steady on his, she shook her head. "It seems I can't stop wanting you. I've tried. I'm tired of fighting this."

Ever so subtly, she began moving beneath him—inviting him, daring him, seducing him. There could be no stopping now...didn't he know? Without him, she'd been empty, and she longed to be filled. Shifting, she urged him to her.

His head swimming, Paul entered her and took control. His mouth fastened on hers as she wrapped herself around him. Outside, thunder crashed and shook the earth. Inside, sensation spiraled and pleasure exploded as he drove them both. His blood pounding, he felt her climb with him. At last, he let himself join her, finding again the ecstasy he hadn't known since she'd left him.

Chris drifted back slowly. His weight on her was heavy, familiar, endearing. She trailed her hands along his back, over his neck and into his thick hair. His warm breathing on her neck slowed to a more normal pace. Slowly, he lifted his head, and she opened her eyes.

"How do you feel?" he asked, searching her face as he brushed aside a lock of hair from her cheek.

"Astonished at how well you know my body after so long."

"Did you think I'd forget?"

"I thought you wanted to."

"I did, for a while. Wanting doesn't always make something happen." He drew back a little. "I'm crushing you."

Her hands held him fast. "It's all right."

"You like being crushed?" he teased.

But she hadn't let go of her serious mood. "I love having you here, with me, in my bed." Her voice sounded resigned and not terribly pleased.

"Yet you're not happy that you want me." It wasn't a question.

Chris sighed as she watched her fingers thread through his hair. "Making love with you is wonderful. But it doesn't solve any of our problems."

Paul shifted, turning over onto his back, his arms keeping her body aligned with his. Still joined to her, he settled her atop him. "Do you know anything about humpback whales?"

Crossing her arms over his chest, she smiled down at him as she raised questioning brows. "Humpback whales? No, not much. Why?"

He laced his fingers together as they rested on her bare back. "I spent some time in Nantucket one year. Whale watching in season is a big deal around there. I learned quite a bit about them."

"No kidding?" This had to be the strangest pillow talk they'd ever shared, Chris thought, waiting for him to make his point. Which she was certain wasn't centered around whales. "Tell me what you learned about whales."

"If you insist. Humpback whales spend their entire lives searching the seas, looking for their one true mate. They never give up, and if they don't find that special one, they swim single. Did you know that?"

"I find I'm grossly uninformed about whales."

"Then I shall continue. A male whale may have trouble, once he finds the female whale of his choice, convincing her to be his mate for life. It seems female whales are as stubborn as female humans. Yet the male keeps at it until she finally agrees to swim alongside him as his forever choice."

"Fascinating."

It was his turn to grow serious. "I'm like one of those humpback whales, Chris. I'm not sure if I fell in love with you the first day we met, or the second. But I know it was right in there somewhere. Yes, we have a few problems, but I think we can work them out. I'm having a little difficulty convincing you to mate with me for life, but I'm not giving up. I let you go once, but I won't again. You are my only choice. Don't let me swim alone for the rest of my days."

"Oh, Paul," she moaned, then slid up to kiss him. It was a gentle kiss, offering a fragile hope. But her eyes, when she opened them to his, were not hopeful. "You know I want you just as much, that I love you deeply."

"No, I didn't know that. The last two years—"

"Have been miserable." She looked down at her fingers tangling in the curly hairs of his chest. "I even hate to admit to you *how* miserable. Not a day went by that I didn't think of you and remember times like this when I lay with you, when I thought our hearts beat in perfect time together. And now we've proved that physically we still fit together beautifully. But you're still a cop, and I still can't live with that. Maybe we'll both have to swim single."

"Maybe," he admitted with sadness. "Did I ever tell you that cops are very patient? You could change your mind. I'll wait. You're the one I want."

Again, she leaned down to kiss him. It started out sweetly, but heated up quickly. Chris felt him grow and stir inside her. They'd had enough conversation. "Speaking of wanting," she whispered huskily, "I want you again."

"Did you think once would be enough?" Paul asked, then rolled her over and took her mouth in a passionate kiss.

Chapter Eight

The ice cream was melting rapidly. Paul entered the executive office building of Lady Charm and hurried toward the office he shared with Chris. He'd gotten her her favorite treat, hoping to soften the blow of the report he carried in his coat pocket.

Though their personal relationship had improved since their trip to Tucson, the investigation wasn't exactly moving along by leaps and bounds. They'd awakened the next morning after lovemaking and, after a delicious delay while they'd shared a shower, had visited Eastbrooke Cosmetics, the company where Steve had worked. The president of the firm had told them that Steve was a highly respected chemist. However, they'd found him to have an arrogant attitude and a hair-trigger temper, confirming Paul's opinion. Yet, asked if he'd be hired again, the man had nodded yes. They'd driven home thinking that though Steve's personality was annoying, nothing in his past indicated he was a thief.

And now there was this disturbing news. He'd spend the morning at headquarters and had picked up several reports to show Chris. As much as Paul wanted to apprehend the embezzler, he really hoped the report on Jeremiah had a reasonable explanation. He opened the office door.

She was on the phone and glanced up, her eyes going wide when she saw what he had brought her. She motioned that she'd be with him in a minute. However, as the ice cream melted down the sides of the cone, Paul had no choice but to lick off some of the drips.

"I appreciate the information," Chris said into the phone. "Yes, if you could just drop all that in the mail to me, it would be most helpful." She recited the company's address and hung up. "Is that your cone or mine?" she asked as she came around the desk.

"Mmm, it started out yours, but it couldn't wait for you." He took one last swipe with his tongue. "Here. It's messy but delicious."

"Thanks." She took the cone from him and leaned in for a taste. "Coffee ice cream, my favorite." She gave him a delighted smile. "You remembered. Thanks."

Paul wiped his hands on a napkin. "Of course, I remembered, and you're welcome." He kissed the top of her head. "Anything new? Who was that on the phone?"

"That was Alicia Morgan, who owns the Four Seasons Modeling Agency," she said through a chilly bite. "I should say owned. It's no longer in business."

Paul leaned against her desk as he watched her work her way through the cone. She did it with gusto, as she did most everything. He noticed she wore her hair down today, loose and flowing, the way he liked it. He'd just happened to mention that small fact to her yesterday on the drive home. She had on a white skirt and turquoise blouse the exact shade of the jewels in the necklace she wore, the one he'd bought her in Sedona. It rested on her golden skin, then disappeared in the V of her blouse. It took some effort for him to drag his attention back to the subject at hand. "Isn't that the agency Angela Knight worked for before Lady Charm?"

Chris nodded as she swallowed. "The same. It closed down shortly after Angela left, and do you know why?"

"I'll bite. Why?"

"Someone absconded with some funds, about ten thousand dollars. They had nine people working there at the time, seven models, an office girl and Alicia. She was operating Four Seasons on a shoestring, so when that happened, she had to shut down. The guilty party's never been caught." She cocked her head at him. "What do you make of that?"

Paul's whistle was long and low. "Did Alicia report this to the police? Was there an investigation?"

"Oh, sure. You should be able to look it up in your records downtown. Angela was even called back and questioned, but there was no single piece of evidence pointing to any one person. The insurance claim was paid when the investigation wound up inconclusive." Chris finished the last of her cone with a satisfied smack of her lips. "That was delicious. Thanks, again."

"That was lunch. For you. Come here and give me mine." He took her hand, opened his knees and pulled her close to his body. Half sitting, he was at eye level with her as she stood within the circle of his arms. He tilted his head to kiss her. His tongue tasted ice cream and pleasure as he lingered over her lips. "Mmm, better than a three-course meal."

"This behavior isn't very businesslike." But she didn't step away. "So what do you think, could Angela be involved?"

"Doubtful. She wouldn't have the opportunity around Lady Charm. The shoots are done at a studio miles away." He shook his head. "She'd be noticed if she hung around the offices a lot. I think the missing money at Four Seasons is just a coincidence, but I'll order a check on Angela's bank accounts and assets, to be sure." He reached into his pocket and took out two folded sheets of paper. "This, however, is another story."

Chris opened the first document and found a death certificate, that of Jeremiah's wife, Annabelle S. Green. Stepping back, she frowned. "I'm not sure I understand this cause of death. Anaphylaxis. Isn't that—"

"A fatal reaction to a toxin, such as venom or drugs."

"Of course. I'm familiar with that. Are you sure?"

"Well, this is an official document. Maybe she took the wrong medicine, too much of it. Or perhaps a doctor gave her a wrong prescription. Or—and I know this is a little bizarre—perhaps she was a drug addict. Prescription drugs. It happens to the best of people."

Chris's mind was awhirl. Did Maggie know any of this? Were any of Paul's guesses right or . . . was Jeremiah responsible for the drug that entered his wife's body? How could they find out? She turned worried eyes to Paul. "He looks like such a nice man. There are things about him that bother me, but I can't believe he would actually harm his own wife."

"We need to keep an open mind."

Nodding, she opened the second sheet and almost groaned aloud as she read it. "Jeremiah declared bankruptcy just months before he came to Phoenix? And now he's got—what did you tell me?—two hundred thousand in his bank account." Chris walked to the window and stood looking out, trying to collect her scattered thoughts.

"Annabelle had only enough insurance to bury her, so there's no motive there. I've got a call in to the doctor who signed the death certificate." Paul moved to her side. "Maybe he can shed some light. I don't want to question Jeremiah's relatives unless I have something concrete." Her back was ramrod stiff, but she didn't comment. "You wouldn't know if Maggie might have drawn up a prenuptial agreement between them, would you?"

Turning, Chris sighed. "I doubt it. Her mind doesn't work that way. She trusts everyone, especially people she loves."

"Then I don't suppose she would have checked him out when he suddenly appeared on her doorstep, either." He traced his fingertips along her cheek. "Try not to worry. There could be a reasonable explanation for all this. And if there isn't, we can still prevent Maggie from getting seriously hurt."

"Jeremiah's a little evasive, but I can't imagine a small-town professor knowing enough about corporate books to be able to embezzle so much money without anyone becoming suspicious."

"You're right. He's an unlikely suspect." He slid his arms about her and held her a long moment. "Let's put it aside until we know more. I hated telling you, but I thought you should know."

She leaned back from him. "Of course, I should know. I don't want you to shield me from things. I'm not as fragile as you seem to think."

Paul nodded, wondering if she was trying to convince him or herself. "Where's Jeremiah's file? I want to go over it."

"I locked it in my top drawer when I left for Tucson," she said, going to her desk. She found her keys quickly. "I didn't want to leave it where someone might see it." Sliding the drawer open, she raised her hand to reach in. "Here, it . . ." She hesitated, looking taken aback.

"What's wrong?" Paul asked, going over. Peering over her shoulder, he saw what had stopped her. Another note placed on top of the file folder. The message was crudely printed in red ink, all the more chilling: LAST WARNING—BE GONE BY MONDAY—OR ELSE. Paul swore under his breath.

"How could they have gotten into this drawer?" Chris asked, studying her key. "Do all the keys fit all the drawers?"

"They shouldn't. This one's written with a fine-line red pen instead of the typewriter. I just picked up the report on the first note this morning. It was typed on a machine that's located in an office on the fourth floor. Now this." He reached for an envelope and slid the note inside. "I'll send this to the lab."

"That's the kind of pen they use in accounting," Chris commented. "On ledger books."

Paul sealed the envelope. "True, and a lot of other things. There must be a hundred throughout the building."

Chris leaned back wearily. "So that's probably not traceable. Was the lab able to pick up any fingerprints on the first note?"

"Not a one, but I'd expected that. The lab report indicates that the first message was typed on a manual machine by someone who isn't a good typist, someone who uses the hunt-and-peck method. Some of the letters were very faint, some darker, some with strikeovers. That's interesting but not awfully helpful since most of our suspects aren't typists. The typewriter used is in an office that's seldom occupied. It belongs to one of the traveling salesmen, Don Léonard. I understand he's in one day a week at the most."

"If that office is empty a lot, our embezzler could easily have gone in there unseen and typed the note. I wonder why he didn't go back and use that machine for the second note?"

Paul shrugged. "Could be that word got out that we were checking all the typewriters. I didn't keep it under wraps because I wanted the person to get nervous, to push him or her into some other action."

Of course, he did. Paul wanted action. He probably wouldn't mind a shoot-out in the hallways, anything to get his man. Chris rubbed the back of her neck. That had been most unkind and unfair. All these suspicions and threats were getting to her, she supposed. "Well, it worked. We got a second note. I wonder if the person who left it there also read Jeremiah's file in the same drawer."

Paul reached for the file and opened it. "Is there anything incriminating in it?"

"Just background information so far. But I didn't especially want Maggie to know we were also investigating the man she loves."

"I don't suppose the embezzler's going to run in and tell her, do you?"

"I don't know what that person is going to do next. I just wish this would end." She frowned, remembering the message. "Why do you suppose he or she wants us gone by Monday?" She saw Paul shake his head absently. "You are coming to the prenuptial dinner at Maggie's tomorrow night?"

He closed the file, deciding its contents were too bland to have revealed anything. "Yeah, Maggie left a message on my answering machine at home. Maybe we'll learn something watching some of these people at play."

"We didn't at the last dinner party."

"You were a little busy kissing Mark Emery to pay much attention." He pulled her up into his arms, as much to distract her from the harsh realities of the case as anything. He tilted her chin up so he could see her face. "Does he kiss well?"

Mischief moved into her eyes. "Does he ever! Mark is a marvelous kisser, the best I've ever sampled. He's vastly experienced, totally seductive, very erotic. He—"

Paul's mouth covered hers, and his arms pulled her tight as she swallowed a giggle. Immediately she forgot her teas-

ing as he molded her to his hard body while excitement sped
into her. In moments she became as aggressive as he,
meeting his hungry needs with her own. Would it always be
like this? The smoldering desire just under the surface,
bursting into hot fury the moment he touched her. His taste
filled her and, with a soft sound, she let herself enjoy.

After what seemed like a split second but had probably
been much longer, Paul pulled back, then dropped his face
into her hair as he took a steadying breath. He needed a
minute to get hold of himself. He had to remember where
they were before he lowered her to the plush carpeting. He
hung on to her while the ripples of passion aroused coursed
through him. Yes, a long minute.

Chris smiled, resting her head on his shoulder. "You
wanted to make me crazy, didn't you?"

He looked into her eyes. "I wanted to erase every memory of Mark from your mind. I want no other man to kiss
you, to know you." He couldn't put it any plainer than
that.

He'd done that already, spoiled her for any other man.
But she shied away from letting him know all of it. "Mark
who?" she asked, giving him a smile.

"That's better. I—"

The quick knock on the door had Chris jolting free from
his embrace as he gave her an amused look. Didn't she
know how thoroughly kissed she looked? He turned to the
door as a small woman wearing a full apron hesitantly
peeked in.

"Yes, can we help you?" Paul asked as he ran a hand
through his tousled hair.

"I was told a Sergeant Cameron wanted to see me," the
woman said as she entered. "I'm Bertha Nabors, the
cleaning lady from the fourth floor."

"I'm Sergeant Cameron, Bertha," Paul said ushering her
to the chair alongside his desk while Chris resumed her seat.

"And this is Christine Donovan. I understand you clean Don Leonard's office."

"Yes, I do. The whole fourth floor. I've been with the company for five years." The woman looked apprehensive.

"Then you've probably run into him, haven't you?"

"Yes. Mr. Leonard travels a lot, being a salesman, but when he's in town, he occasionally works late. I came in early this afternoon because they said you wanted to see me. Usually my shift doesn't start till six. Most everybody's gone home by then. His office only needs light dusting most of the time. Is anything wrong?"

Paul leaned on the edge of his desk and pulled up his knee, hoping his relaxed approach would put the nervous woman at ease. "No. We just have a few questions. Have you ever noticed anything unusual in that office, anyone using it that you know doesn't belong there? Find anything out of order, like maybe the typewriter cover left off when it's usually on, or papers scattered about when it's neat?"

Bertha shook her head slowly. "I've never seen anyone suspicious roaming around. There's not much on the desk except the pad and phone. The typewriter sits on a stand in the corner, always covered." She looked up at him. "Wish I could be more helpful."

Paul did, too. "I appreciate your coming in."

The cleaning woman stepped toward the door, then stopped, her hand on the knob. "There is one thing that's kind of odd. Maybe it's nothing."

Chris smiled encouragingly. "What's that, Bertha?"

"The waste basket. Mostly, it's empty 'cause Mr. Leonard's out of town. Sometimes, it's full of papers so I know he's been in, like on Friday nights. But once in a while there's cigarettes in the basket, all neatly wrapped in a napkin or tissue. And the office smells real smoky."

"Maybe Mr. Leonard smokes only occasionally when he works late," Paul offered, looking at possibilities.

Bertha shook her head confidently. "That's the odd part. His wife died of emphysema some time ago. We talked about her one evening for quite a while. He's against smoking. That's why I air out the place real good when I find the basket full of butts. I've often wondered who puts their trash in his office."

"I wonder, too," Paul said. "I don't suppose you noticed the brand of cigarettes you've been finding?"

With a look of distaste, she shook her head. "Not the brand, but once when I pitched the smelly mess, the napkin opened. The butts were all different colors, like those fancy imported cigarettes."

"Interesting. The next time you find those cigarette butts, would you set aside the basket and call me?"

"Sure thing."

"Thanks, Bertha, for coming in." He watched the woman nod and leave before he walked back to his desk.

"Let's see, who among our suspects smokes? Come to think of it, I think they all do. Only you and I and Maggie don't. Do cigars come in colored wrappings? Jeremiah smokes them, and Steve those little cheroots," Chris said.

"It's possible. We may never know. The embezzler might have used that remote office to type the notes, maybe even alter the books. But, since he's obviously not playing with the ledgers anymore, he won't need it again." Paul exhaled dejectedly.

"Another dead end. Now what?"

"Now, I think we call it a day. We might see some fireworks tomorrow at Maggie's. I made sure Nancy's invited, and Steve will be there, too. I'm real anxious to observe those two together."

"Did you ever tell Nancy about the poison?"

"Not yet. I'm waiting for the right moment, to see her reaction. I did find something interesting in her desk last week."

In the process of locking her drawer, Chris looked up. "You searched her office?"

"I sure did. The evening our man from downtown was here getting typewriter samples. I found a receipt for a wedding dress that cost nearly two thousand dollars. And travel brochures advertising honeymoon cruises."

Chris picked up her briefcase. "Just like Dora Phillips mentioned."

"Right. I'd also like us to pay particular attention to Diane and Teddy tomorrow. He's rarely available when I want to talk with him, and Diane's too cautious to reveal much."

"What is it you're looking for?"

"Something, anything. They seem mismatched. He defers to her constantly, yet she acts indifferent to him. Everyone around here thinks she's one tough lady. Maybe she's masterminded this whole thing. The way two people behave with others around often reveals what kind of relationship they share."

Chris placed the strap of her bag on her shoulder. "Speaking of that, I'd rather we kept the change in our relationship between the two of us. I don't think it would serve any purpose to go public."

He raised a brow. "Leaving yourself an out?"

She should have known he'd see through her carefully worded request. "Maybe. I haven't lied to you, Paul. I've not made any promises."

No, she'd certainly been careful about that. He'd promised himself he wouldn't push, but it was damn difficult. He'd meant what he'd told her in Tucson. He had no intention of letting her go again. He'd have to find a way to make her see they belonged together. "I know. Let's take it one day at a time."

"That's fine with me." But she saw the determination in his eyes and remembered what Mike had said. Paul always got what he went after. Did she have the strength to fight that? she wondered as they left the office.

The late afternoon heat hit them as they stepped outside. Paul squinted up into the sun. "How do you feel about a cool drink at my place, followed by a charbroiled steak, then a dip in my pool when the sun goes down? Pete won't be there tonight." His brother had moved in with him recently, a temporary situation until he learned the results of the bar exam. After living alone for years, Paul found he enjoyed the company. But tonight, he had other things on his mind.

Chris stopped as they reached Paul's car. "Mmm, I don't know. I need to spend some time with Maggie."

"She probably wants some privacy in her own pool with Jeremiah."

Chris couldn't prevent a smile as she recalled his preference for nude swimming. "She might at that."

"Come on. Leave your car here, and I'll take you home later. Maybe."

Chris couldn't think of a reason to say no. So she let Paul help her into his car. One thing about skinny-dipping, she thought as he climbed in beside her. It usually made you forget all your problems, at least for a while.

"How do you manage to grow roses this beautiful in the desert, Maggie?" Steve asked as he stood at the edge of the garden.

"Why, Steve, I had no idea you were interested in roses." Maggie, wearing a vivid green jumpsuit with matching high heels, sounded pleased.

Paul watched Steve bend to inhale the delicate fragrance. He had to admit he was surprised to hear that a man like Steve would even comment on roses.

"Surely you know that many of the fragrances I work with come from flowers, Maggie," Steve said, falling just short of sounding condescending. "Are any of your roses used at the plant?"

"No, these are just for our enjoyment." She took Jeremiah's hand and pulled him closer. "Aren't they, dear?"

"Maggie has a way with all living things," Jeremiah answered. "Wouldn't you say so, Steve?"

"It would seem so." He glanced at the privet hedges that artistically divided the well-tended floral areas. "Do you mind if I wander around your garden? The sun's going down, and it's getting cooler finally."

"Not at all. Jeremiah and I will go with you."

Paul watched the three of them walk down the flagstone path and into the main garden. He turned to Chris, who was stretched out on a lounge chair on the patio bordering the garden. She wore terry cloth shorts and matching top and had her eyes closed to the waning sun. He saw faint smudges of fatigue where her lashes rested. She hadn't been getting enough rest, partly due to her concern over the embezzlement, partly because he'd kept her at his home till the wee small hours last night.

Even then, he hadn't wanted to let her go, wanting her to spend the night with him. But she wouldn't, worried about what Maggie would think. She was an intriguing mixture of passion and propriety. And he loved her. God, how he loved her. Sitting down on the corner of the chaise, he ran his hand along her slender calf. "Penny for your thoughts?"

She opened her eyes. "Mmm, I think you might get change. I was trying to let my mind go blank for a few minutes."

Another form of escape. She was good at that, always backing away from discussing their situation, from confronting their problems. ''Do you want to rest? It's a while before we have to get dressed for dinner.''

Today, Maggie had invited about half a dozen people from Lady Charm for a small celebration. She'd opened her home to them, asking them to come early and swim, if they wanted, or hike the scenic grounds or just relax in the sun until seven, when the dinner party would begin.

''No,'' Chris said, sitting up. ''I'm not sleepy. Where is everyone?''

''Here and there. Some are strolling around, a few are still in the pool around back. Maggie and Jeremiah just took Steve into the rose garden. Do you want to tag along, see what we can overhear?''

''I can't,'' she said, swinging her legs over the side. ''This time of year, the bees are everywhere in the flower garden. I'm allergic, so I stay away. You go ahead, if you like.''

''No, I'd rather be with you. I was inside a few minutes ago when Diane arrived. She told Maggie that Teddy hadn't returned from San Diego yet. She seemed pretty upset.''

Lazily, Chris got up. ''Mike had mentioned that Teddy sails his boat without Diane. I wonder who crews for him and whether it's a man or a woman.''

Frowning, Paul stood. ''I thought he was so nuts about her.''

''That's what everyone else thinks, too. I'm beginning to wonder. Or am I just suspicious of everyone?''

''Possibly. How about taking a walk with me along that path up the hill? I don't think there are any flowers up that way.''

Stifling a yawn, Chris nodded. ''Okay.''

Paul tucked her hand in the crook of his elbow. ''I didn't know you were allergic to bees. No wonder you were familiar with toxin poisonings.''

''It's not a problem most of the time. But when I lived here at Maggie's I got stung once, and I passed out in short order. That's when we discovered it. I almost went into a coma. After that, she kept serum for me here at the house. I don't know if she still does.''

They maneuvered around a rock, then met on the other side as Paul slid his arm about her. ''I guess there's still a few things I don't know about you.''

She looked up at him. ''Precious few.'' She warmed, remembering the hours they'd spent in each other's arms last night. He had a way of moving inside her skin, of looking inside her head, of touching her in places previously untouched. ''Yet you seem to want to know more. Always more. Maybe you want too much, Paul. Maybe I don't have that much to give.''

He pulled his gaze from her and drew her around the bend behind a huge red rock, out of sight of any passersby. Backing her against the stone wall, he cupped the base of her neck and began to knead the taut muscles as his eyes captured hers. ''Then again, maybe you have more to give than you suspected.'' Lowering his head, he nibbled along her jawline.

Already Chris could feel the weakness spreading to her knees, the pounding of her heart against her ribs. When they were locked like this in the gathering twilight, struggling with the mists of desire so easily aroused, she was sure they belonged together. It was when they walked out into the sunshine of reality that her doubts returned.

She turned her head and let his kiss fall at her temple. She wanted to keep her mind clear, to not fall prey to the heated male flavor of him on her tongue, the rich, musky scent of him surrounding her. If she gave in to another session of deep, mindless kisses, she'd not be able to think clearly.

Yet her body felt so welcome in his arms, her heart felt so at home. Could this feel so right if she didn't belong with him? Could her flesh fake the needs that clamored for his touch? Could her mouth want his kiss so desperately if it had not been fashioned to fit his? Unable to postpone the pleasure, she turned and brought his mouth down to hers.

It was always the same, yet always different, always unique. The thrill was somehow brand new, as if it were their first kiss. She felt the heat spread with exquisite slowness as she let her mind empty of all but him.

Paul had been aware of her solitary struggle, just as he was aware of the moment she surrendered to him. When he eased back and traced the shape of her mouth with his tongue, he saw her eyes open slightly, heard her soft sigh. He, too, knew surrender, the ultimate surrender of himself to the power she had over him. For a long moment, he let her see this new vulnerability. Then he pulled her into a kiss that was deep and slow and more moving than any they'd shared so far.

When he edged back to look at her, she again averted her eyes. She'd glimpsed the depth of his feelings that he himself had only just recognized and it had frightened her. Silently, he held her as she fought her demons, wondering if they could ever get past her fears.

Paul didn't know how long they'd been standing there when he became aware of the voices on the other side of the rock. When he was able to make out the identity of the speakers, he bent his head to listen closer as Chris did the same.

"Forget the dress, forget the trip, forget it all," Steve said, his voice hard and clipped. "I told you the wedding's off. Why can't you get that through your head?"

"But I don't understand why," Nancy wailed. "What have I done?"

"Nothing. We're just wrong for each other, that's all. I don't want to marry you or anyone. I've finally got my ticket out of here, and I'm moving on soon, leaving this provincial town and all the hicks in it."

There was a sound of a sob, then a hiccup. "I thought we'd planned to leave together. I did everything you wanted me to do, even though some of it was against my better judgment. Why are you walking out on me?"

"You're better off without me." Sounding like it was a gigantic effort, he tried for a reasonable tone. "We'd only hold each other back."

"I promise not to get in your way. Please, Steve. Let me go with you. I—I love you." Nancy had lost all sense of pride.

"No!" His voice lowered, became menacing. "And I'm warning you. Don't call me or try to see me alone again. Forget me. If you don't, you'll live to regret it."

The sound of stones crunching underfoot mingled with Nancy's muted sobs. Standing perfectly still, Chris raised her eyes to Paul's as the heated words hung between them.

Was Steve Thorn the embezzler?

Chapter Nine

Jeremiah leaned back in his dining room chair and caught Paul's eye. "Tell me, have you and Chris made any progress in apprehending the embezzler? Maggie and I leave on our honeymoon in another week, and we'd surely be pleased if this mess would be cleared up before our wedding."

Paul set down his coffee cup as he swung his gaze around the table. The usual group from Lady Charm. Teddy, who'd finally shown up unapologetic for holding up dinner, was seated at his mother's right hand, with a still simmering Diane on Maggie's other side. Next to Teddy was Angela, chugging down more than her share of wine, yet looking amazingly sober. Across from her sat Steve, his sharp eyes darting from one to the other throughout the meal. Except they never landed on Nancy, who sat on his left, looking sad and quiet. And on Jeremiah's other side was Chris, who was observing everyone as carefully as Paul. One of them, Paul was certain, was the embezzler. Though he had his suspicions, he still wasn't certain who that person was.

He turned his smile on Jeremiah. "I wish I could tell you that we'll have everything wrapped by the time you two leave," he said. He also wished he felt more convinced that

Jeremiah himself wasn't somehow involved and was now trying to see how much they knew.

The doctor who'd signed Jeremiah's wife's death certificate had finally returned his call, but had been rather abrupt with him, saying he wouldn't discuss his patient's death on the phone. Paul had pulled out the big guns at that point and told the doctor that he wanted a complete report, sent special delivery, or he'd be subpoenaing him and his records. Reluctantly, the man had agreed. He was now anxiously awaiting that report.

"Surely you must have made some progress," Jeremiah insisted. He sat twirling a new cigar between his thumb and forefinger, his eyes on Paul.

"Yes, we have. We've gone through every single personnel file at Lady Charm, and we've found some interesting leads that we're working on. I don't want to go into more on this until we have something concrete."

"But you are close?" Steve emphasized "close" as he leaned forward, his elbows on the table.

"Close is a relative term," Chris interjected, and saw the frown appear on Steve's forehead. "Let me put it this way. We still have things to sort out, but we're on the right track. We will apprehend the person responsible, and soon." She hoped she sounded more convincing than she felt.

"How soon?" Teddy asked.

"Why would the time factor bother you, darling?" Diane asked him through a cloud of smoke. "The money will probably never be recovered, isn't that right, Paul?"

Funny how she could make a term of endearment like "darling" sound insincere. "It usually isn't, in these cases. The funds have been filtered out of the company over a period of nearly two years. Chances are the embezzler hasn't squirreled it away, but has been spending it all along."

"It would seem to me, then, that a check into each suspect's finances and spending habits would reveal the guilty party," Diane went on. "An increase of four hundred thousand dollars spent within two years should be noticeable in someone's change of life-style."

"We've checked out each and every person's finances and have found no significant changes."

"Everyone? You've checked out all of us here as well?" Steve sounded offended.

"Yes, we have." Paul sent a quick glance around the table, but the only frown he saw was on Maggie's face.

"Oh, I hate this business." Chris's aunt sounded almost distraught.

"The only alternative is to let it go, dear," Jeremiah suggested calmly.

"You can't do that once the police are called in, can you?" Diane wanted to know.

"It's not a good idea," Chris said.

Maggie sighed heavily. "Michael would never let me drop the matter."

"Chances are, you're never going to find the guilty party, anyway," Angela added just before she drained her wineglass.

Chris turned to the model. "Why do you say that?"

Angela shrugged as she signaled for more wine. "I worked for a company once where funds were missing. Not on this grand scale, but nonetheless, missing. The police were called in, nosed around awhile, questioned us all endlessly. And to this day, they don't have a clue who cleaned out the till." She removed a cigarette from a gold case and leaned toward Teddy, who lit it for her. "White-collar criminals are pretty clever. Don't count on getting your money back, Maggie. Not beyond any insurance settlement you may get."

But Maggie didn't agree. "Christine goes after white-collar criminals often, and she's managed to expose quite a few or she wouldn't be Southwest Insurance Company's top investigator. I have faith in her and in Paul." She gave her guests a weak smile. "Now, shall we change to a more pleasant subject? Nancy, tell us about the centerpieces you've been making for the wedding. Did any of you know how talented she is with dried flowers?"

Reluctantly, Nancy raised her eyes from the spoon she'd been toying with and began a shy description of the floral arrangements Maggie had asked her to make.

Paul sipped more coffee as he sat back and watched the interplay between the people around the table. His gaze returned to Chris, and her eyes reflected his own troubling thoughts. It was disconcerting to realize that they'd just had dinner with at least one person who was not only a thief, but one who may not be above attempted murder.

When the party started to break up a few minutes later, Paul was relieved. As people straggled to their cars, Teddy took him aside.

"Have you thought of bringing in a handwriting expert to check those books?" he asked. "I understand there's a distinctive way people write numbers as well as the alphabet."

Paul's look was measuring. "No, I hadn't, but it's a thought."

Clapping him on the shoulder, Teddy smiled. "Hope it works."

Paul walked with him to the front doorway and outside where Diane waited, already seated in their car, her face a cold mask. He wondered if Teddy, who'd been almost chatty and friendly tonight, was going to hear a few well-chosen words from his wife on his tardy arrival.

Paul turned his head at the sound of Steve's wheels squealing as he aimed his little red sports car down the winding road. His was followed by Angela in a surprisingly beat-up older car, while Chris stood talking with Nancy at the door of her sedan. Quite an assortment of people, Paul thought. But which one was capable of theft and threats . . . and maybe more?

"Jeremiah and I are going for a little drive," Maggie told Paul as the Jaguar pulled up to the front door. "Why don't you stay awhile, and keep Chris company?"

"I just may do that," Paul said as Nancy drove off and Chris came strolling over.

Maggie gave her niece a quick hug before getting into the car with surprising agility. Arm in arm, Paul and Chris watched them pull away.

Paul glanced up at the stars already crowding the evening sky. "Beautiful night."

"Mmm, it is." Chris stifled a yawn. She walked with him to the stone ledge that bordered the yard. Before them was a magnificent view, the city of Phoenix winking and blinking in nighttime splendor. The sweet smell of oleander and honeysuckle hung in the soft summer air, and from a nearby tree, a night bird called to its mate. Standing close behind her, Paul's arms circled around and rested on her own as she stood hugging herself. Yes, a beautiful night. But her thoughts were churning with questions unanswered.

"Were you surprised when Angela spoke so freely about the money missing from the company she'd worked for previously?"

"No, not especially. I told you she wasn't a good suspect. I'm having that embezzlement at Four Seasons Modeling looked into again. Something's not right, but I don't think Angela's involved in that or in our problem."

"Then you think she's in the clear?"

"Yeah. I also think she's kind of pathetic, a woman who was once beautiful, who's getting older, drinking too much and desperately looking around for a last chance at fame. I doubt if New York will be her answer, either, but I don't fault her for trying.''

Chris leaned back against his firm chest and placed her hands on his, comfortable in his arms. "I wonder about Teddy's marriage. Diane hardly spoke to him all evening.''

"He did something that annoyed her, didn't arrive at the party as soon as she'd have liked. If Teddy likes to get away alone on his boat, that probably angers her. He looks like a solitary man.''

"Yes, he always has been. But then, she's not exactly overly friendly, either.''

"Teddy thinks we should bring in a handwriting expert to take a look at the ledgers.''

"What? Does he know how many bookkeepers have entered figures in those books?'' Dismissing that thought, she tilted her head back to look at Paul. "What do you make of the conversation we overheard between Steve and Nancy? That one remark of hers, about doing everything he'd ever wanted her to do even though some of it was against her better judgment. I'd sure like to know what she meant by that.''

"It could have a simple explanation, like he seduced her when she'd been holding out for marriage. Did she say anything revealing just now before she left?''

"We talked about her recent hospital stint. She's still in the dark about the poison. I think we should tell her, see what she says. As a chemist, Steve would know just what to put into the water to frighten, yet not kill.''

"For what purpose, unless he's the embezzler and wanted to scare us off?''

"Maybe he is. Did you check his bank holdings?''

"You bet. He's got under five thousand in assets. Not much for a man his age with a well-paying job. He rents a condo in Scottsdale, not bad but not luxury. That snazzy car he drives, which isn't paid for, is about all he owns. If he's the embezzler, he's got a secret Swiss bank account." Paul frowned as he remembered something. "I wonder what he meant when he said he finally has his ticket out of here. I spoke privately to both Maggie and Teddy and felt them out to see if Steve had mentioned leaving Lady Charm. They both said no."

"Maybe Steve and Diane are in this together and are running away soon."

He nuzzled her neck. "You have a romantic imagination."

Chris yawned again. "Think so?"

"I think you're tired. I should go."

"And whose fault is it if I'm exhausted? Who kept me up half of last night?" She turned in his arms, her look teasing.

Paul gave her a light kiss. "If you think I'm going to apologize, you're mistaken. If we both didn't have a lot to do tomorrow, I'd throw you over my shoulder and drag you off again."

She arched an eyebrow at him. "Caveman tactics?" Her face softened. "You don't need them with me. You never have."

He kissed her then, with an almost lazy thoroughness, before he moved his lips down her throat as he slipped his hands under her blouse. She squirmed a little, thrusting her breasts more firmly into his palms, sighing with pleasure. Then her fingers slid into his hair as she pulled his mouth back to hers.

They stood locked like that for long minutes, testing their endurance with deep kisses and longing touches until Paul drew back. He took in some air as he met her eyes. "We've either got to stop this now or go inside and finish it. Lady, I've never had such flimsy control with anyone but you."

Her smile was very female. She moved back reluctantly. "That's probably not a good idea since we don't know when Maggie will be back. I think we'd better say goodnight, for now."

Paul had to agree. He also had to get the hell out of there before he truly lost control. He gave her another quick kiss, then strolled to his Mustang and got in. She leaned on the door as he started the motor, her eyes suddenly serious.

"I wish I could be all that you need, all that you want," she said in a low voice. "I worry about that."

He touched his lips to hers briefly, then smiled. "Don't. You already are." With a wave, he headed down the mountain.

CHRIS HAD PLANNED to skip breakfast the following morning, but as she came down the stairway and saw Maggie alone on the terrace having coffee, she decided to join her.

"My, you're up bright and early," Chris said as she seated herself.

Maggie's eyes sparkled. "Yes. I was too excited to sleep. Jeremiah will be here soon. We're picking up the documents for our honeymoon trip this morning at the travel agency."

Chris poured her coffee. "You never did tell me where you're going since the Egyptian dig is postponed."

"Europe. A three-week tour. Everywhere from Rome to Scandinavia, including a segment on the Orient Express." Maggie chuckled in anticipation. "I can hardly wait. I've been there several times, as you know. But Jeremiah hasn't. It'll be such fun showing him my favorite spots."

Chris had trouble swallowing past the lump in her throat. Dare she give voice to her suspicions about Jeremiah? Maggie might not like to hear them, but if anything happened to her aunt because she'd kept quiet, she'd never forgive herself. Folding her arms, she looked at Maggie.

"Sounds like a wonderful trip, and I'm sure it's costing a lot. Are you paying for it?"

Maggie warmed her hands on her cup, her voice just a shade cooler than it had been. "What difference does it make who pays? The important thing is for us both to enjoy the trip."

Here goes, Chris thought. "Maggie, are you aware that Jeremiah filed for bankruptcy shortly before he left New England and came here?"

Slowly, Maggie set down her cup and raised her eyes to her niece's face. "Christine, have you and Paul been investigating Jeremiah also?"

"We had to. You know what Mike said. Everyone's background had to be looked into."

"My son as well?" Her voice was shaky now, and decidedly frosty.

Chris nodded, feeling miserable. She'd never wanted to bring that betrayed look to Maggie's face.

"I see. Yes, I did know about Jeremiah's bankruptcy. You may add that to your report."

Chris reached out a hand to touch her aunt's arm. "Please don't be angry. I'm only trying to look out for you."

But Maggie was staring off into the distance, her face unreadable. At last, she turned back. "Christine, Jeremiah would never do anything to hurt me. Never."

Chris let out a heartfelt sigh. "Are you so certain? He's been away from you for *forty years*. People change. Life sometimes changes them. Has he...has he ever told you how his first wife died?"

Maggie drew in a deep breath. "Go on."

She'd gone too far to back down now. She squeezed Maggie's arm, hoping she was doing the right thing. "It was very sudden. She died of anaphylactic shock. A fatal reaction to a drug.''

Maggie's face had gone white, but her eyes were fiery. ''I hope you're not suggesting that Jeremiah administered a fatal dose of drugs to his wife.''

''I'm not suggesting anything. I'm only relaying the facts so that . . . perhaps you might . . .''

''Postpone the wedding? I will not.''

From around front, the sound of the Jaguar's distinct horn drifted to them. Stiffly, Maggie got to her feet. ''There's Jeremiah. I must go.''

Chris stood. ''Maggie, I . . .''

''No, don't come with me. I'll talk with you later.'' A bit unsteadily, she walked through the archway, her heels clattering on the tile.

Chris sat down heavily. What had she done? Would Maggie confront Jeremiah? If he was guilty of something, anything, would he then grow angry and harm her? Or, if innocent, would he hate being suspected and perhaps leave again, which would forever remove the happiness from Maggie's face?

Rubbing her forehead, Chris stared off, focusing on the palm trees swaying in a soft morning breeze. In her anxiety to protect Maggie, had she tipped their hand, blown their case? Had she harmed her relationship with her aunt beyond repair?

She finished her coffee and rose. She had to see Paul, had to tell him what she'd done. Almost running, Chris went out the door to the car.

''POISON!'' NANCY EXCLAIMED. ''I don't believe it.''

Paul held out the police lab report. ''Read it for yourself.''

Nancy quickly skimmed the single sheet of paper. Her face went white, and she lowered herself to the chair alongside Paul's desk. "Oleander extract? That's one of the chemicals they use for... for some of our scents."

"Yes. Our guess is that you were probably just in the wrong place at the wrong time, that the poisoned water was intended as a warning to either Chris Donovan or me."

She raised bleak eyes to Paul. "The embezzler."

"Most likely. Do you know anyone well enough at Lady Charm who might need money badly or perhaps want a way out of an unhappy job situation enough to steal? Someone who'd have ready access to the chemical lab without suspicions being aroused?" He'd worded his question deliberately, giving her every reason to implicate Steve Thorn, if she suspected him. He waited while Nancy agonized. Finally, she shook her head.

"I don't know much about the lab. I stick pretty close to the accounting department."

Her loyalty to Steve, despite his rejection, wasn't going to let her say more. Paul thought he'd give it one more shot. "Would you want to hazard a guess, someone you feel is capable of serious theft or—"

"No." Nancy rose, shuffling a stack of papers nervously. "You'll have to excuse me. I have to have Teddy sign these." She started toward the door.

"I'll go with you. I'd like to get Teddy's opinion on this poisoning incident." He saw Nancy turn even paler, if that were possible, as they walked together. Paul gave one quick knock, then opened the door.

"... and your time is running out." Standing next to Teddy's desk, Steve Thorn abruptly turned around as the door swung open. "Don't you believe in knocking?" he asked, his lips a thin line as he snarled at Nancy.

"I did knock," Paul said as he followed the chief book-keeper inside. "Evidently, you didn't hear." He watched as Steve seemed to visibly collect himself. Teddy sat behind his large oak desk, looking as if he were glad they'd interrupted Steve's obvious tirade. Did the officious little chemist roar at everyone?

"I'll get back with you on this," Steve said to Teddy, then turned on his heel. As he marched past Nancy without so much as a glance, she seemed to flinch inwardly. No stranger to unrequited love, Paul felt sorry for her. They heard the door bang shut.

"What's got him so hot?" Paul asked as he urged Nancy closer to the desk.

Teddy's smile was patient. "He invented a new fragrance several months ago. We're test marketing it in several areas, but Steve's testy. He wants us to announce it with a big ad campaign, widely promote it—and him. He tells me our closest competitor has come up with something similar and that our time is running out if we want to get a jump on being the first. Steve doesn't seem to understand that that's not how we do things here at Lady Charm."

Paul was curious. "Is the base of this new fragrance oleander extract by any chance?"

"Matter of fact, it is. It was also used in Forbidden. How did you know?"

Nancy sank into a chair as Paul explained the poisoned water cooler situation. A small frown gradually appeared on Teddy's thin face, which Paul imagined was about as excited as Maggie's son ever got.

"You're certain? Is there a tie-in here with the embezzlement, do you think?"

"I think the embezzler got nervous and wanted to warn Chris and me that he meant business."

Teddy sighed as if the whole thought was too much for him. "This is getting messy. Have you told Maggie?"

"Not yet."

"Please don't, just yet. Let's let her enjoy her honeymoon, at least."

So there was a bit of compassion in him, along with some love for his mother. Paul nodded. "Unless she flat out asks, I won't bring it up until after her trip."

"Thanks." Teddy shuffled a paper aside. "Is there anything else I can do for you?"

"I need signatures on these," Nancy said, handing him the stack of papers.

Paul stood looking around as Teddy perused the sheets. Not as plush an office as Maggie's, but not bad. Rumor had it that Teddy would like to move into his mother's corner office, and he just might after her marriage. She already seemed disinterested in Lady Charm, though Paul wondered if that would hold true after the honeymoon glow wore off. Was Teddy capable of running such a big company, even one he'd worked for for years? A few people they'd interviewed had hinted that he was ineffectual, and one or two had come right out and said he didn't have what it took to keep profits increasing without his mother's guiding hand. What about Diane's influence? Hard to say.

"These look fine," Teddy said, taking a pen from his shirt pocket and scrawling his approval.

As Paul watched, something else on Teddy's desk caught his observant eye. A racing form, dated yesterday, with several horses circled. Had he been out of town yesterday or at the racetrack? And did he gamble a little or a lot? Another interesting avenue of thought. Paul stepped back as Teddy looked up and handed Nancy her papers.

"Thanks," she said, head down as usual. "I've got to get back to work." She shot them each a tiny smile as she left the room.

"You've got work to do," Paul told Teddy. "So I'll leave, too. Talk with you later." Frowning thoughtfully, he walked the several yards to the small office he and Christine shared down the hall. When he went inside, he found her pacing agitatedly.

"Oh, I'm so glad you're here," Chris said, coming toward him. "I need to talk with you. I may have messed things up royally."

Paul sat her down across from him and listened while she told him of her conversation with Maggie, her voice not quite steady as she finished with the fact that her aunt had walked away from her most unhappily. He leaned back and leveled his gaze on her damp eyes.

"In your situation, I'd have probably done the same thing. Maggie needs to know the facts. You once told me not to shield you from the truth, to be honest even if it hurt. Well, I think Maggie feels the same. She's just shaken. She doesn't want to suspect Jeremiah because she loves him. Give her a little time. You can't shoot the messenger just because you don't like the message."

But Chris wasn't convinced. "She'd been so happy when I first joined her on the patio. I sure took the smile off her face in a hurry."

"Better now than after they're married."

"She was emphatic. She's not postponing the wedding and doesn't believe Jeremiah would hurt her."

Paul sighed. "Let's hope she's right. To bring you up to date, I told Nancy about the poisoned water." And he told her all the rest, including Teddy's reaction and the racing form.

Chris looked pained. "If you think Maggie would be upset if she learns Jeremiah's guilty, that's nothing to how she'll feel if we discover Teddy's involved."

"I didn't say he's involved. So don't go jumping to conclusions."

"I don't blame him if he takes off alone to the race track now and then. That wife of his is something. Angela Knight was waiting to see me when I arrived. She had another quarrel with Diane, and she's turned in her resignation effective immediately. She wanted to tell us in person that she's leaving next week and will be staying with friends in New York for a while. She gave me their address in case we need her. I get the feeling she's telling us the truth."

"So do I, especially after what I learned this morning. I talked with Mike. It seems that the new investigation on the missing money at Four Seasons Modeling Agency has turned up something interesting. This is the second agency Alicia Morgan's had, *and* the second time a good deal of money's been reported missing. And she's had two insurance payoffs. Suddenly, our man can't find Alicia. She's moved and left no forwarding address. Packed up the same day you talked with her."

"I suppose that clears Angela's background and probably means she's not involved here. As to the others..."

They both turned as the door opened.

"They told me I'd find Sergeant Cameron here," the man in the postal uniform said. "Special delivery."

"That's what I've been waiting for," Paul said as he rose. "Do you need my signature?"

"Yes, sir, and some I.D., if you don't mind."

Paul showed him his identification, signed the form and ripped open the envelope as the man left.

Chris peered over his shoulder, then frowned as she read the form. "I'm not sure I understand. What is it?"

Paul drew her down beside him. With her deep love for her aunt, she wasn't going to take this well. He took her hand. "I acted on a hunch. I knew that Jeremiah had very little insurance, since he worked for a small university. After his wife died, he was almost thirty thousand in debt. I thought that was one reason he'd filed for bankruptcy."

"You mean Jeremiah still owes that money?"

"No. As the doctor states here in his letter, his bill and the one from the hospital were paid, and the date is about a month after Jeremiah arrived in Phoenix. Even though medical bills are low on the priority list for payment as unsecured debts, they were all paid in full after his bank-ruptcy debts were discharged.''

"How did Jeremiah get thirty thousand dollars in a month? He must have borrowed it from Maggie.''

"That's one possibility. Here's another. The first amount of money siphoned out of the accounts of Lady Charm, almost two years ago, was exactly thirty thousand.'' He ran his fingers along the tender skin of her wrist and felt her heart pounding.

Chris felt a quick rush of disappointment. "Maggie's heart will be broken.'' Then, she grew angry. "Damn him. How could he do this to a woman who's loved him for forty years?''

"We still don't have proof here, I want you to remember. We have bits and pieces of circumstantial evidence that—''

"That paint a pretty black picture of Mr. Jeremiah Green.''

Paul couldn't argue with that. He'd gotten to know Maggie better lately and knew her to be far more fragile when it came to her personal life than she let on. He, too, wanted to confront Jeremiah and demand some answers.

The phone rang, and Chris reached for it, answering almost absently.

"Christine?'' Maggie's voice was crisp.

Chris felt her heart lurch. "Yes, Maggie.'' Beside her, Paul squeezed her hand.

"Is Paul there with you?''

"Yes, he is. Did you want to speak with him?''

"I want to speak with both of you. Please come over to the house . . . right away.''

Chapter Ten

"How many others know about what you've discovered in your investigation of Jeremiah?" Maggie asked, a frown marring the smooth lines of her pale skin. There was a strained look about her as she leaned forward and took a sip of her Irish whiskey.

Paul shifted his weight and crossed his legs, a shade uncomfortable in the small Queen Anne chair. This parlor room was obviously Maggie's favorite, decorated in feminine pastels with sculptured roses on the carpet and a deep blue settee on the other side of the white marble fireplace opposite the antique chairs where he and Chris sat. Mendosa had slid shut the heavy mahogany doors, insuring privacy. By the look on Maggie's face, they would most likely need it.

"The doctor who signed the death certificate, of course," Paul began. "The clerk at the insurance company, the bank manager and the court—"

Maggie waved a manicured hand impatiently. "No, I mean who at Lady Charm have you mentioned this to?"

"No one. Just Chris and I have seen the papers."

She let out a shaky breath. "Thank goodness." Maggie tucked in a stray curl of hair, obviously gathering her thoughts. "This is my fault. It never occurred to me that you'd be checking on Jeremiah, so I didn't feel it neces-

sary to divulge certain...privileged information. I see now
that I must.''

"Maggie," Chris said, her voice sounding calmer than
she felt, "I want you to know we weren't just snooping into
his affairs—or anyone else's—for that matter. It was necessary to eliminate each and every person connected to the
company in order to—''

"I know, dear. I blame myself for not saying something
sooner. After our conversation this morning, I talked this
over with Jeremiah, and we both agreed we had to tell you
all of it." She took a deep, fortifying breath. "The truth is,
he and I have never really been out of touch over the years.
It wasn't something I wanted anyone to know, especially
my family. He was, after all, a married man. But it was as
good friends that we corresponded. We talked on the phone
occasionally, but he never visited—not once—until after
Annabelle died. I would never have interfered in his marriage.''

"Oh, Maggie, anyone who knows you would believe
that.''

"I certainly hope so. I want you to understand how it
was." She patted her brow with a white hanky before going
on. "Their marriage was not made in heaven. But then, so
few are. Yet Jeremiah respected his vows and tried to make
Annabelle happy. She was a spoiled young woman, vain
and given to temper tantrums when he married her, which
didn't improve much with age. He did the best he could
under the circumstances. In the end, her vanity killed her.''

"Her vanity?" Chris asked. She glanced at Paul and saw
he, too, was puzzled. "I don't see how a fatal reaction to a
drug could—''

"Let me explain. Annabelle had once been quite beautiful, but the years had altered her looks, as with all of us.
After all, she was sixty. She went to see a cosmetic surgeon
for a face lift, and she told no one. The problem was, she

wasn't aware she had a mild heart condition. When the surgeon administered a drug into her system during the operation, it triggered an allergic reaction that brought about a heart attack, and she died on the table.''

"Anaphylactic shock," Paul interjected.

"Yes. The doctor was as stunned as anyone."

"Do you mean Dr. John Whalen?" Paul asked.

"Yes."

"He's the one I spoke with on the phone. He never even hinted that her death had occurred on his operating table."

Maggie's lips thinned in disapproval. "I don't suppose he wants the information to be widespread. He should have probed more thoroughly into her medical history, but he didn't. In his defense, a patient dying from complications resulting from plastic surgery is highly unusual. He probably thought you'd drop the matter there. Does that clear things up?"

"It explains how Jeremiah's wife died," Paul agreed, "and obviously it was no one's fault."

"Unfortunately, her family and Jeremiah's don't agree with that. They feel *he* wanted her to have the surgery and therefore he's responsible for her death," Maggie went on.

"And that's why he didn't want us to invite any of them to the wedding," Chris surmised.

"Yes," she said. "He did everything they wanted him to do for years, and now they've turned their backs on him."

"Maggie," Paul said, wishing he didn't have to keep pushing, "Chris tells me that you knew that Jeremiah had filed for bankruptcy."

"Of course. He barely had enough money to bury Annabelle. I pleaded with him to come here, and he finally did. He arrived with only a pitiful collection of clothes, but I didn't care. He was with me again, and that was all that mattered."

Paul watched her face carefully. The next few questions were crucial. "Can you explain then how he was able to pay off both the doctor and the hospital to the tune of thirty thousand dollars one month after arriving in Phoenix? Or the fact that he has a great deal of money in the bank even now, plus expensive clothes, a new Jaguar, and yet still manages to show up almost daily with lavish gifts?"

"I believe I'd like to answer that," Jeremiah said as he entered and slid the doors shut behind him. He sat down alongside Maggie, took her hand and gave her a loving smile. No big juicy kiss this time, Paul noticed. He spoke but he never took his eyes off his fiancée.

"Maggie paid off all my debts. She didn't want the bankruptcy hanging over my head, so she paid everyone off, to the penny. She bought me a new wardrobe, the car—all of it. But all I ever wanted was to be with her. The only way I can begin to repay her for this new life we're to share is to spend the money she puts in my bank account on her."

His eyes shifted to Paul now, bright and intense. "I didn't want to move here at first. I didn't know how Maggie's family would accept me after I'd left her so long ago. And I was ashamed of the mess I'd made of my life. But she insisted. She saw to it I had everything, and she told no one, trying to preserve a bit of my shattered pride. But pride's not as important as love. I'm glad I came, even though all I had to give Maggie was me, in this somewhat shabby package. Me and this heart that's never stopped loving her."

"Dear man," Maggie said, drawing his attention back to her, "as if I ever wanted more than that." She kissed his cheek lightly before turning to Chris. "I tried to tell you when you first arrived. Money doesn't matter. Neither does pride. Love is all that counts. I'm sorry if I caused you unnecessary concern, but, as I told you, Jeremiah would never hurt me. Nor I him."

It was a quick couple of steps around the table and over to Maggie's side, and Chris covered the ground quickly. The last few minutes had lifted a heavy burden from her mind. She hugged her aunt fiercely as tears filled her eyes. "*I* should be apologizing to *you*. It's just that I was so worried and Jeremiah seemed so evasive." She drew back and looked at Jeremiah. "Please forgive me for doubting you. I should have realized anyone Maggie loved so much couldn't be guilty."

Jeremiah encircled her with his free arm. "Don't concern yourself, my dear. I understand. I'd have mentioned all this sooner, but you'll forgive an old man's battered self-esteem, I hope. Maggie's given even that back to me. Still, though it's her money to do with as she sees fit, there are people who might be critical of how she spends it. I hope, in time, everyone accepts me. It's true I don't have any money of my own. But I know I can make Maggie happy."

"I don't doubt that for a minute," Chris whispered. With a final squeeze of her aunt's hand, she got up and walked slowly back to her chair. She dabbed at her eyes with a tissue as she sat down, then saw that Maggie was doing the same. Simultaneously, they each laughed, breaking the tension. "We're a fine pair, mascara smudges and all."

"If you used Lady Charm mascara," Maggie said, her voice once again holding that hint of humor that had been missing earlier, "you'd find it doesn't run when you cry."

"I'll have to try some," Chris said. She leaned back in her chair, feeling enormously relieved.

"There is one more thing," Maggie said, "something no one knows, really. Years ago I was a little on the wild side, especially after Jeremiah married." She sent Chris a slightly embarrassed look. "I was probably headed for a less-than-wholesome life. At any rate, Jeremiah knew a man, Kent Brady, a brilliant chemist but someone whose arrogant ways had gotten him fired from several good firms. He thought perhaps Kent and I together could form a company." She looked into Jeremiah's face. "Actually, I think he was intent on saving me from myself."

"There's some truth to that," Jeremiah said.

"At any rate, I took what little money I had, hired Kent and established Lady Charm."

"I can see where you owe him for a fresh start," Paul commented. Maggie with her strong loyalty streak would feel that way.

"Oh, I owe him even more than that. The company did fairly well at first. But we'd expanded too rapidly. And then Kent was killed in an accident. I was devastated. Again, Jeremiah came to my rescue. He located another chemist and sent him to me. His name was Burk, and he came up with several new products. However, I was almost out of funds and couldn't produce the new goods." Maggie's eyes became misty. "Jeremiah cashed in his insurance policies, which were substantial, and sent me all of it. I didn't know where he'd gotten the money until much later. But it's because of *his* help and *his* funding that Lady Charm is what it is today. Now do you see why I don't feel, nor should he, that he's taking my money? He's only collecting on a long-overdue debt."

"Yes, I certainly do." At last, Chris felt she could relax. Maggie wasn't marrying a man who intended to live off her but one who'd had a hand in molding her life and her company from the sidelines. "Maybe it wouldn't be such a bad idea if everyone knew this story. It's nothing to be ashamed of." And perhaps Teddy would accept his stepfather more readily.

"No," Jeremiah said emphatically. "I think it's best to let sleeping dogs lie. It is, after all, no one's business. In time they'll accept me for who I am, or they won't."

"That's how Jeremiah wants it, so that's how *I* want it."

"Well, you needn't worry about us," Chris told them. "If you don't want people to know, we won't mention this conversation to anyone. Right, Paul?"

Paul nodded. Though Jeremiah had been a strong suspect, Paul was almost as happy as Chris to cross him off their list. "Absolutely. I'm glad it worked out this way. Both of us were hoping there was a reasonable explanation. You two deserve a world of happiness."

"I think so, too," Maggie said, her voice filled with emotion as Jeremiah put his arm about her and pulled her close.

Paul watched the two of them embrace. No one could mistake the depth of their feelings. Maggie was right, love *was* all that mattered. He turned to Chris and saw that her eyes were still shining. He couldn't help but hope that she too, had picked out the same message.

EVENING SHADOWS DANCED along his driveway as Paul pulled his Mustang close to his mountaintop house. It had been a long day, and he was grateful to be home. Lamplight arced from the family-room window, telling him that Pete was in. The nice thing about having his brother stay with him was that he was easy to get along with. If Paul wanted to be left alone, Pete made himself scarce. Yet if he wanted company, Pete always seemed willing to talk. They'd become better friends lately than they'd ever been, a fact that sat well with both of them. Paul unlocked the door and moved to the back of the house.

"Hey, Paul," Pete called as he jumped up from the couch where he'd been stretched out. "I was beginning to think you weren't coming home tonight." He hurried through the archway into the kitchen. "We're celebrating!"

"You passed!"

"Damn right I did." He grabbed a bottle of champagne from the refrigerator and held it up triumphantly. "Perry Mason, look out. Here comes Pete Cameron, attorney at law." Carefully, he unwrapped the cork and worked it out of the bottle. "And did you notice, I waited for you to start celebrating? Didn't want you to think your baby brother sat around drinking alone."

Paul took off his jacket and eased the gun case off his shoulder. Settling himself on the couch, he grinned up at Pete as he poured them each a glass of the bubbly. "Well, congratulations, on both counts. Does Dad know?"

"The question is, does Dad care?" Pete sat down. "We both know the answer to that, don't we?"

"Come on. Don't be so hard on the old man."

"I don't want to talk about him right now." He held his glass out. "Here's to the future, for both of us. May it shine."

Paul clinked his glass, then took a sip of the tart wine. "Not bad. So tell me, what are your plans?"

"Tonight, I may get drunk. Tomorrow, I go job hunting. I've got a line on this small law firm, midtown. They're looking for an associate.

"After the interview, I'll look for an apartment. After that, who knows? Maybe a steady girl. Speaking of girls, how's Chris?"

"Fine. Why do you ask?"

"Just curious." Pete scratched his day's growth of beard. "You two going to patch things up?"

Paul pushed off his shoes and stretched out his long legs. "I wish I knew."

"What are you doing about it?"

Frowning, Paul regarded his drink. "What do you want me to do, tie her to the bedpost until she agrees to marry me? Chris has a mind of her own, and it's dead set against my line of work."

"Do you love her?"

"Yeah, but that doesn't seem to be enough."

"Make her see that it is. Love, real love, is kind of rare, you know. If you're lucky enough to find it just once in your life, don't mess with it." Looking a little embarrassed at his own sentiment, Pete drained his glass.

Paul searched his brother's face. Usually lighthearted, tonight Pete was pensive as his gaze moved to the window and the darkening sky.

"I loved somebody like that once. That summer I spent in Italy. But her father didn't think I was good enough for her, and, frankly, neither did I. That was before I realized I could be. So I walked away. I still regret it."

"Stopping someone from walking away isn't always easy or possible." The conversation had somehow slipped away from him, Paul thought, making him feel oddly depressed.

Both men sat staring into space for long minutes before the sound of the doorbell ringing jarred them.

"I wonder who that is?" Paul muttered as he went to the front in his stockinged feet.

"Paul," John Cameron said in his usual exuberant manner, "I'm glad I caught you home. I've got some great news." The senator strode past his son.

"What's that?" Paul asked trailing after his father as he marched into the family room. "Pete's got some pretty impressive news, too."

"Hi, Dad," Pete said without rising.

"Hello." John was curt, obviously distracted.

"Pete's passed the bar," Paul told him, hoping he'd stir up some enthusiasm in the senator for his youngest son's accomplishment.

"That's great." He turned his gaze back to Paul, who stood with his hands on his hips. "I came to tell you some exciting news."

But Paul was looking at his brother, seeing the quick hurt flicker across his face before he averted his gaze. He turned angry eyes to his father. "Wait a minute. Is that all you have to say? I don't have to remind you how much work and studying goes into passing the bar, do I, Dad?"

John Cameron looked more annoyed than repentant. "No, of course not." He offered his hand to Pete. "Sorry. I had my mind elsewhere. Hearty congratulations."

Pete shook hands wordlessly and sat back down, his face expressionless.

"Now then, Paul," the senator went on, "as I was saying. Next Saturday's the night. I want you with me at the Biltmore, a dinner honoring a couple of the boys, plus fund-raising, of course. I've finally made all the arrangements. We'll make the announcement Saturday." He glanced at his other son. "You can come, too."

Pete rolled his eyes and poured himself more champagne and sat back.

"What's this all about?" Paul asked, wishing he could swallow his irritation with his father's behavior.

"Flanagan's resigning as D.A. I want you to throw your hat into the ring at the dinner. Four months to election, but it's in the bag. I've squared it with the boys. A lot of people owe me favors, you know, and it's time to collect my markers." He clapped Paul on the back. "My son, the district attorney. Then in two years, four tops, it'll be on to the Senate. From there, the sky's the limit."

Paul shot Pete a surprised look. He saw his brother raise his eyebrows and his glass in a toast. Slowly, he turned toward his father, who'd gone to the bar and was pouring himself a bourbon, neat. Paul had told Chris his father had only voiced his dreams to her. He'd had no idea that he was busily putting his plans into motion behind the scenes without even mentioning them to him. He waited until the senator tossed back his drink and turned around.

"Whatever gave you the idea I wanted to be D.A.?"

John coughed into his fist as he settled his lean frame into the easy chair. "Of course, you want to be D.A. It's not the best job in the world, but it's a stepping-stone, son. Then you can—"

"Dad, are you listening to me? I don't want that job or any other you've got in mind. I have the career I want. And I managed to get it on my own." Paul resumed his seat on the couch as his father glared at him. He should have recognized the signs. When he called him "son," it usually meant he wanted something.

"Are you crazy? Do you want to be a cop all your life, risking your neck, underpaid, overworked? You with a master's degree in law enforcement and a law degree. That's a criminal waste of talent. I won't stand for it."

Paul felt himself tighten. With effort, he kept his voice level. "*You* won't stand for it? Did you forget that this is *my* life we're talking about?"

The senator's long fingers worked the arm of the chair while his eyes narrowed. "It's all that woman's fault. She's filled your head with garbage. I warned her..."

"What?" Feeling his anger rise, Paul sat up straighter. So that's what he'd tried to do when he'd asked Chris to dance. "She has nothing to do with my decision. I'm not leaving the department—not for you, not for anyone." He took a cooling sip of champagne, trying to simmer down. He'd tried his best to please his father, tried not to disappoint him as so many others had, yet the man still wanted more. Always more.

John tried another tactic. "Son, if you'll just listen to reason," he began, his voice silky smooth now, the persuasive politician at work. "That woman has poisoned your mind."

Pete got up noisily. "Dad, you tried to get Chris out of Paul's life once before. It didn't work then, and it won't this time. Give it up."

Carefully, Paul set his glass down. "What did you mean by that?"

"You tell him, Dad." Pete strolled to the window and turned his back on them.

The senator's eyes became furious. "It's nothing, Paul. Just a small difference of opinion. She's not worth all this animosity she's causing between us."

Pete snorted as he swung around. "All right, I'll tell him. Two years ago Dad called Chris to his office, told her you were destined for great things and to get out of your life because she wouldn't exactly be an asset to a rising star."

Open-mouthed, Paul stared, first at his brother, then at his father. "Is that true?"

"No! She told me the other evening when we danced that she left because of your dangerous job, not because of what I said to her." The senator rose to get another drink, his hands not quite steady.

"But you did talk to her two years ago, told her to leave me alone?" As his father turned, Paul saw the truth on his face. "How could you interfere in my personal life like that?"

"It was for your own good. I didn't want you to marry some little policeman's daughter. She'd only hold you back." He carried his drink back to his chair. "I know lots of people in Washington. I can introduce you to all kinds of women who'll be an asset to you, to your career." John suddenly looked nostalgic. "I often wonder where I'd be today if I had married a woman who was well connected. I loved your mother, you both know that. But she was...small town."

"That did it!" Paul was on his feet, eyes blazing. "Don't you *ever* say one word against Mother. She was a better person than any of us. And she put up with a hell of a lot from you."

"Amen," Pete added.

Paul narrowed his eyes, fighting for control. "Has it occurred to you there are more important things in life than getting ahead?"

John Cameron looked up, genuinely surprised. "No, it hasn't. What else is there, for a man?"

A wave of pity cooled Paul down more thoroughly than if someone had thrown a bucket of water on him. His father really *didn't* understand—and probably never would. He sat down on the edge of the couch and leaned forward. "There's love, for one thing. There's sharing your life, *really* sharing. There's kids, doing things together as a family. We never did any of that because you were always too busy getting ahead."

John's shoulders slumped slightly. "I have regretted some of that." He studied the liquor in his glass. "I wasn't a good husband to your mother nor a good father when you two were young. We all make mistakes." He looked up, his eyes brightening. "Let me make it up to you now. Let me lead you to the Senate and then...well, who knows?"

Compassion softened Paul's voice, but the hard edge of anger was still there just under the surface. "There's something here you don't see. I appreciate what you're trying to do, but I don't want the Senate and whatever else you have in mind. You can't make your children's life decisions for them once they're adults. You have to stop trying to wheel and deal for them, trying to make them conform to your idea of the future. A father should—should care for his sons even if they choose paths he wouldn't follow." Paul fell back against the couch, feeling as if he were whistling into the wind. This old dog wasn't about to learn new tricks.

"I *do* care. That's why I want the best for you." He glanced toward Pete, who was watching him from the other end of the couch. "You, too. I'll make a couple of calls now that you've passed the bar. I've got friends in prestigious law firms. We'll get you in and..." He stopped as he noticed Pete slowly shaking his head. "You don't want a boost up the ladder, either? As I recall, you haven't done so hot on your own so far."

"Maybe not," Pete said. "But I did do what I wanted to do."

John drained his glass and sank deeper into the cushions of the chair, looking suddenly older. "All those years, do you know how many scrapes I got you out of? There was that incident in Quebec, and the weekend you and your drinking buddies wrecked that bar in Soho. Whose check do you think sailed over to clean up your mess?"

Pete leaned forward, his elbows on his knees. "Maybe you shouldn't have. Maybe you should have let me face my own mistakes, clean up my own messes. You can't grow up till you learn you're responsible for your own actions. It took me longer than some, I admit. I knew I couldn't satisfy you, so I stopped trying. Now I satisfy me. If that's not good enough for you, I'm sorry. I can't make up for the disappointments you've had in your life. You can decide to let us live our own lives our way, or you can let us turn into another disappointment. Your choice." Pete seemed tired after his speech. He poured some champagne and took a long swallow.

"I never said you were a disappointment to me—either of you. I just wanted to make life easier for you, better. I never had anyone fighting for me, someone with the ability to pave the way. But I guess you don't want my help. Fathers seem to become excess baggage as their sons get older." Slowly he pushed himself out of the chair.

Paul had never seen his father look quite so beaten or self-pitying enough to resort to melodrama. It wasn't a sight he relished. "Dad, we'll always need your help but in the form of encouragement in seeking our own way. I believe I speak for Pete, too. We want you in our lives. We just don't want you *running* our lives." He stood and held out his right hand. "Can we be friends?"

John Cameron smoothed back his perfect hair, then raised his eyes to his older son's face, studying him for a long moment. Finally, he grasped his hand and shook it. Pete stood, walked to his father and hesitated a long minute, then pulled him into a hug. Paul blinked back a rush of emotion as the two men held the pose for a moment, then stepped back, both looking a shade embarrassed.

John recovered first. Clearing his throat, he dug into his pocket for his keys. "I've got to run." He started toward the hall, his two sons following behind. At the door, he turned, his hand on the knob. "I always loved you both, you know. I tried to do the right thing. If I didn't, I'm sorry."

"It's all right, Dad," Paul said softly. Beside him, Pete stood with his hands in his pockets and nodded. The senator tried for a smile that didn't quite make it, then stepped outside and closed the door behind him.

Heaving a huge sigh, Paul followed his brother back into the family room.

Pete reached for the bottle. "Maybe I should have bought two of these," he commented as he poured the remaining champagne into their glasses. He threw himself onto the couch and looked at Paul, who was standing thoughtfully, fingering his mustache. "Well, what do you make of the whole scene?"

"You never told me he'd called Chris and told her to get out of my life two years ago. Why?"

Pete shrugged. "You probably wouldn't have believed me. You always thought Dad walked on water. Tonight you found out he's just a man, like the rest of us. He's made some mistakes, but hell, who hasn't? He doesn't belong on a pedestal, but he's not all bad, either. Sure he tried to interfere in your life and in mine. But in his mind, he meant well."

Paul took a soothing swallow, then sighed deeply. "You always understood him, didn't you? He was rough on you, yet underneath it all, you never stopped caring for him."

"He's my father. I can love him without agreeing with him. Maybe he'll learn to do the same with us. Tonight's a start. He left here looking like a man who had a lot to think about."

Pete ran a hand through his hair as if he were considering saying more, then plunged in. "You were programmed to believe you had to live your life in such a way as not to disappoint Dad, because he'd already had his fair share. I think you saw tonight that that's not your problem, it's his. As I see it, it's the same with Chris. She was programmed by her mother to believe that any woman who marries a cop can expect to live in fear and loneliness the rest of her days. She needs to learn that there are lots of ways you can lose someone you love. Think you can make her see that?"

Paul ran his thumb along his upper lip. "I don't know."

"You want to try? Or you want to give up?"

Paul's smile was slow in coming. "What makes you so smart, little brother?"

Pete let out a deep breath. "I may be a couple years younger, but I've been around. You get burned, you get smart."

"You may have a point there." Paul emptied his glass. "I think I'll turn in. All this heavy philosophizing has made me tired. Coming?"

"Nah. I think I'll throw together something to eat in a few minutes."

"Good night then." Paul strolled down the hallway and into his bathroom. Switching on the light, he stood staring for long moments at his mirror image. Gingerly he fingered his mustache.

He'd grown it as a kind of rebellion. To show Chris and his father that he was his own man. Tonight the need for defiance seemed to drain out of him. He'd learned there was a lot to admire about his brother, and he'd learned his father was human, too. He'd also learned a few things about himself. He no longer felt the pressing need to please others first. Maybe it was time he tried to please himself. Yes, high time.

Paul reached for his razor.

Chapter Eleven

The minister arrived wearing bright red pants and a golfing shirt for rehearsal. Chris had been expecting formal black and a turned around collar. She stood at the front window watching the reverend greet Maggie and Jeremiah.

She glanced up at the blue sky and hoped the next twenty-four hours would be free of clouds, in more ways than one. Maggie had invited selected members of her staff and a few old friends to stay the night, so Mendosa and her crew had been busily shining and polishing till the lovely old house gleamed. Three gardeners had been hired, and the grounds looked picture perfect. The wedding was to take place the next afternoon at one on the outdoor terrace, weather permitting. Chris stepped back from the window, realizing that while Maggie and Jeremiah had calmed considerably now that the big day was at hand, she had developed a case of the jitters.

"Chris?"

Hearing the unexpected voice behind her, she jumped, as if in proof of her last thought. She turned to see Teddy standing there, looking hesitant as usual. She gave him a relieved smile. "Yes?"

"I can't seem to get much out of Paul," he said, ambling closer in his somewhat stoop-shouldered shuffle. "I just wanted to know, is anything happening on the case?"

Paul had rehearsed her on what she was to say to anyone who asked about the case. She put on a confident look as she faced her cousin. "Yes, we're making progress, Teddy. We're very close and should have something to tell you soon." She said the words and hoped she sounded like she believed them.

"Is that a fact?" He moved closer to her, leaning one hand on the fireplace mantle. "So you pretty well know who embezzled the money, but you just can't prove it yet?"

Chris walked past him and sat down on the couch. "Something like that. I really can't discuss the details. I hope you understand."

For a moment he studied her eyes, then broke out into a shy smile. "Sure, sure. Has Maggie said what's to be done when this person is caught? I mean, is she prosecuting, or does she want restitution?"

"I would imagine, after two years, restitution would be unlikely. But yes, she has said she'll prosecute."

Abruptly Teddy sat down on the ottoman and leaned his elbows on his bony knees. "Even if the person turns out to be someone she knows quite well, someone who's worked for us a long time and been a good employee in every other way?"

What was he getting at? Chris wondered. "Teddy, do you know something you haven't told us?"

He jerked back, as if singed. "No, no. Maggie seems reluctant to discuss this with me. I was just curious."

She didn't know whether to believe him or not, so she decided to change the subject. "Where's Diane?"

"She couldn't get away. Maybe she'll pop in later or perhaps not till tomorrow at the wedding."

"You mean you're not spending the night?"

"*I* am."

So that's how it was. Poor Teddy. Or was it poor Diane? Hard to tell. At the sound of footsteps approaching behind her, Chris turned and saw Mendosa come into the room.

"A lady to see you, *nenita*. A Nancy Evans."

"Oh, yes. Show her in, will you please, Mendosa?"

Teddy hopped up and headed toward the door. "I'll see you later, Chris."

She was watching her cousin's purposeful strides carry him away when Nancy Evans came through the doorway, her face tense. She held a small package wrapped in silver paper.

"I saw Maggie out front, and she told me to bring this to you," Nancy said, holding out the gift.

Chris rose and took the package. "Yes, I've been put in charge of stashing the gifts until after the honeymoon. Thanks." She took in the woman's attire, even more dowdy than usual, and smiled encouragingly. "You are staying for the rehearsal and then overnight?"

"No, I can't." Suddenly, with a small sob, Nancy seemed to crumble, landing in the nearest chair. "I'm just not up to that much togetherness right now. I might embarrass myself."

Chris set down the present and pulled a chair closer to Nancy. Enough of the waiting game. She needed to zero in. "It's Steve, isn't it. You're in love with him."

The dam broke. Tears rolled down Nancy's pale cheeks, and her thin shoulders shook. Chris quickly closed the sliding doors and returned to Nancy's side. Squeezing the woman's hand, she waited for her to compose herself, remembering the conversation she and Paul had overheard on the mountain. She hadn't liked Steve Thorn from the first, but, more importantly, she had the insistent feeling that he'd used this poor woman. Maybe now she could find out how.

"Why don't you tell me about it? Sometimes it helps to talk."

From her pocket Nancy pulled out a tissue and dabbed at her eyes as her sobs diminished. "We were in love, or so I thought. At first I wondered why someone as important as Steve Thorn was interested in me. But he told me I made him happy." Her eyes darted to Chris's face, as if to check that she wasn't laughing at her. Reassured, she went on. "I live alone, you know, and Steve said he liked it best when we came to my house and we just sat and talked. He didn't want to go to crowded restaurants or parties. He wanted me all to himself."

It hadn't occurred to Nancy he didn't want to be seen in public with her, Chris realized as she listened. There was nothing quite so sad as a plain woman being romanced by a con man. "Go on."

"We talked mostly about starting our own company, him at the head, me taking care of the books. Steve said he needed to know every aspect of the business before we made the break. It made sense to me, so I brought some of the accounting books home and taught him how we did things at Lady Charm. He seemed fascinated." Nancy blew her nose, lost in her memories.

"Anyhow, one day he got real excited. He found something, some discrepancy or something out of order. But he wouldn't tell me what." She looked up at Chris. "You know, I'm pretty good with figures. I went over and over those books. I couldn't find anything. Then, next thing you know, there's an audit announced and we learn about the embezzlement. I was shocked. But not Steve. He just looked real smug and told me to forget we ever looked at the books. He told me to buy a wedding dress and start planning our honeymoon. So I did."

Chris watched her face cloud up again. "And then?"

"Then, a couple of weeks ago when you and Paul arrived, Steve changed. He became evasive, moody, and we argued all the time. Finally, he told me we were through, that he was coming into some money soon and he was getting out of this provincial town. Those were his exact words." She took a trembling breath.

"Nancy, do you think Steve is the one who embezzled the money?"

"No, I honestly don't. He's always broke. The first amount was taken nearly two years ago, you said. If he took it, he must have it stashed away somewhere safe."

"But he told you recently that he was coming into some money soon?"

"Yes, only last week. Maybe he's got a safety deposit box. Or maybe it's under his mattress. Did you search his condo?"

Another one who watches too much TV, Chris thought. "No. And it's doubtful that the money is hidden in his house." She looked at the distressed woman and felt a wave of compassion. "Nancy, I want to say two things. First, I know you're hurting now, but if Steve is as you described him, you're really better off without him."

"I tell myself that every day."

"And second, I must pass this information on to Paul. I hope you see that."

With a tiny sob, she nodded. "I know. I wasn't going to tell you, but somehow, I think Steve's involved in something bad. I don't want him to hurt another woman like he hurt me. And I want to help Maggie. She's always been so good to me."

Chris patted her hand. "You did the right thing. I promise to keep you out of it as much as possible."

Nancy stood. "Thanks, I'd appreciate that." She walked to the doors with Chris. "I don't know if I'll be here for the wedding tomorrow. It's really hard for me to be around Steve these days. He's so cold, like we're strangers. And weddings always make me cry."

Chris slid open the doors. "You come if you feel up to it." Sighing, she watched Nancy leave, wishing she could punch Steve a good one. Even if he hadn't embezzled the money, he had it coming for hurting such a nice woman.

Hurriedly, she checked the lower floor and wound up at the front door. Only an hour until rehearsal. Where was Paul?

CHRIS WAS STANDING in the archway leading to the patio, watching the Reverend Jamison walk all the principals through the wedding rehearsal the second time, when she heard a sound behind her. She turned to see Paul strolling in, wearing a lightweight tan jacket over a bright blue shirt and a new look. He'd shaven off his mustache.

She crossed her arms over her chest and smiled as she walked to meet him. "Well, well. Did it finally get to you, all that trimming?"

"Not really."

"Okay, let me guess. You did it for me?"

"Partly. I shaved it off because I no longer need it."

He stood there looking pleased with himself. There had to be more to it than that, but Chris decided to pursue it later. "I think it's quite an improvement. I also think I need to talk with you about a couple of things." She glanced over her shoulder and saw everyone still out on the patio. Taking his hand, she pulled him toward the library. "Come in here where we can be alone."

As soon as they stepped into the twilight-darkened room, its silent walls lined with bookcases, Chris turned to him. But Paul had other things on his mind.

With a swift movement, he curled his arm around her waist and brought her to him. "I like your thinking. I want to be alone with you, too."

She reached up and gave him a quick kiss, then moved out of his embrace and pulled him to the couch. "Mmm, hold that thought, and we'll come back to it. First, we need to talk. What took you so long getting here?"

Paul stretched his arm along the couch back and angled his body toward her. "I thought I'd linger around Lady Charm, since most of the big shots were over here, and see what I could learn." He grinned at her. "You tell me your news and I'll tell you mine." He kissed the end of her nose and rested his hand on her shoulder.

She never could resist Paul when he was in a light-hearted, teasing mood. She never could resist him, period. Chris leaned her head against his arm and told him about her conversation with the distraught Nancy Evans. "From listening to all that, I think our best suspect is Steve Thorn."

"Maybe. He's here, isn't he? Staying overnight?" He saw her nod. "Good. We can at least keep an eye on him. Coming into some money soon, he told Nancy? Was he trying to sidetrack her or telling the truth?"

"You've already checked out his finances, and Nancy verified that he's always broke."

Paul glanced at his watch. "It's too late tonight, but I'll make a call tomorrow and check something else out. Did you know that Lady Charm has a credit union it offers its employees? I found that out today. Maybe that's where Steve's stashed some cash."

"Wouldn't that be stupid, putting it through a company savings plan like that where it could easily be discovered?"

Paul shrugged. "Sometimes the most obvious place is the last place we look. At least that's what Diane must have thought. I found her account there today."

"Diane Muldoon? How much?"

"She opened the account, in her name only, right after she and Teddy were married, not quite two years ago. Started it with a deposit of thirty thousand dollars. And has been making regular deposits ever since. She's up to two hundred thousand."

Chris digested that piece of news. "I know she's well paid, but where would she be getting money like that?"

"That's a good question. Meantime, their joint savings account at the bank has been steadily depleted over the past year. At close of banking hours today, they had about seven thousand, period."

"But I know Teddy has stock through Maggie and probably a very nice investment portfolio. He was still in grade school when her company started making good money. I remember she started investing for him way back then."

"I can't find a record of Teddy's and Diane's investments, other than their Lady Charm stock and her credit-union account, which I wonder if he's even aware of."

Chris played with a lock of her hair. "I don't know what to think. We've eliminated Jeremiah and Angela. Certainly Nancy didn't do it. That leaves only Steve and Diane."

"And Teddy."

She shook her head. "Forgive me for saying so, but he doesn't have the brains or the guts. And I believe he really loves Maggie and wouldn't hurt her like that."

"But he's not crazy about Jeremiah. He may view his new stepfather as a threat. Frankly, I've never even seen the two of them having a pleasant conversation together."

"Nevertheless, all Teddy has to do is hang in there. His mother will transfer more and more to him, responsibility as well as stock. It's unlikely he'd risk all that. Diane strikes me as the impatient one. And quite volatile."

"That's true."

"Still, Steve gets my vote. He had the knowledge, the opportunity, the motive. I think we should keep an eye on him during this whole event, then question him extensively afterward. What do you think?"

"I agree we should question him again, but I'm holding off on guessing who the embezzler is just yet. All the facts aren't in."

"All right, you cautious cop. We investigators tend to go more on instinct."

Paul moved closer, nuzzling her neck. "And what is it your instincts are telling you to do right now?"

"Mmm, my baser instincts are telling me I wish we were alone, really alone."

He moved his lips along her jaw, then kissed the corner of her mouth. "We are alone."

The sound of voices and scattered laughter coming from the direction of the family room had Chris placing her hands on his broad chest, keeping him at bay. "Anyone could walk in. There are lots of people out there."

"To hell with those people."

And he took her mouth with the same fierce possession he'd taken her heart so many years ago, sending her senses whirling and her mind reeling. She'd thought she'd be accustomed to it by now. But she wasn't any better equipped to fight him now than she'd been at the beginning. Chris wondered idly if she ever would be. Giving in to the moment, she slid her arms up over his shoulders, around his neck and into the thickness of his hair and gave as good as she got.

Her long hair flowed down her back and laced through his fingers as Paul drove his tongue into her mouth, teasing her, tempting her. Her restless hands were kneading the tight muscles of his neck now, then gripping his shoulders with an intensity he could feel throughout his body. He wanted those same hands on his flesh, he wanted her beneath him on the oriental rug, he wanted her more than he'd ever wanted before. Deepening the kiss, he felt his tenuous grip on the civilized world rapidly slipping away as he shifted her in his arms.

With that small movement, Chris found herself pressed tightly to his chest and suddenly she was thrust back into harsh reality. The gun he always wore under the jacket he'd had tailored to conceal his weapon pressed against her breast and caused her eyes to fly open. The mood shattered for her. She pulled back. Feeling breathless and nearly limp, she waited for the mists to clear.

He'd felt the change in her and wondered at the cause. He raised her chin and made her look at him. Her eyes were huge and dark, filled with confusion. "What happened?"

Chris drew in a deep breath. "I don't like making love with a man when he's wearing a gun."

Paul sagged in disappointment. "Dammit, Chris!" The same old argument. He dropped his arms and angled away from her. Why couldn't they get past this? What could he say to make her see?

The door opened just then, effectively ending their confrontation, as Maggie bustled in.

"There you two are. I've been looking for you."

Chris tried to hide her dishevelment behind a shaky hand as she watched Paul rise and put on a smile for her aunt. Only the fists he shoved into his pockets revealed his agitated emotions. She shook back her hair and hoped Maggie was too caught up in her happiness to notice.

"How'd the rehearsal go?" Paul asked Maggie in a voice surprisingly level.

"Oh, just fine." She looked up at him, her shrewd eyes darting to Chris, then back to Paul. "Is everything all right?"

"Yes. I was just updating Chris on a couple of things about the case." He glanced through the open door. "I'll leave you two alone. I see someone I want to have a word with." Quickly he scooted past Maggie.

Slowly, Maggie strolled to the couch and sat alongside her niece. "We looked for you when it was your turn to walk down our make-believe aisle but no one knew where you'd gone."

"I'm sorry," Chris said as she watched her hand adjust and readjust the folds of her cotton skirt. "We had a lot to talk about."

"And it doesn't look as though your conversation has left either of you too happy." Maggie put her hand on Chris's, stopping the restless movements. "What is it, dear?"

Blinking back the sudden rush of tears, Chris shook her head. "It's nothing, it's everything."

"You love Paul."

She nodded. "Yes. That's the problem, not the solution."

"It so often is." Maggie sat back more comfortably, keeping Chris's hand in hers. "Christine, I'd hate to see you lose a good man because you're unwilling to compromise."

"Maybe in time I'll be able to accept his work. After this case ends, I'll go back to San Diego, do some thinking and..."

"You mean run away again?"

Chris raised her eyes. "That's not fair."

"Perhaps not, but it is the truth. Oh, Christine, I must tell you, I loved your mother dearly. She was my only sister. But she taught you by example so many things you'd have been a lot better off not learning." She held up her hand as Chris was about to protest. "Now, hear me out. Mary Muldoon loved Patrick Donovan fiercely, but she never learned to trust in him, to believe in him. Patrick was a very fine policeman. Yes, he died, but it wasn't through carelessness. He could as easily have died in an automobile accident on the way home from work. People die. It's a fact of life.''

Chris shook her head. "You weren't there, Maggie, at the hospital when they brought my father in. Four bullet holes. Or the night Paul got hit and I sat on the cement holding him, waiting for the ambulance while his blood flowed into my lap. You weren't there." She closed her eyes against the memory.

"No, I wasn't. But you're not listening. If your father had worked a nice, safe job and been in a head-on collision, hit by a drunk driver, would it have been any easier to go to the hospital and see him mangled from that accident?"

"Yes. I'd have known he didn't bring it on himself, didn't put his life on the line daily. He'd have just been a man in the wrong place at the wrong time."

"My point exactly. These policemen are trained and able to save themselves probably ninety-nine percent of the time. But that one percent of the time, they're in the wrong place and they die. Aren't those percentages better than that of a man up against a drunk driver? You must trust that Paul can do his job, believe that he doesn't want to die any more than you want him to. And you must confront your fears about this, Christine, not run away. Only then can you conquer them."

"I don't know. To live again with the constant threat of danger..."

Patiently, Maggie squeezed her hand. "Consider the alternative. You're young, bright and attractive. Sure, you can find another man. But will you love him the way you do Paul? Or are you like me, a woman whose heart made a choice the first time she saw that special man and who could not settle for second best, even if it meant living alone for years. Christine, I'm like some species of the animal kingdom I've read about. I mate for life, and I think you do, too. I'd rather spend one day with Jeremiah than a hundred years with a man I didn't love. How about you?''

The story of the humpback whales came to mind as Chris looked into Maggie's serious blue eyes. *You are my only choice,* Paul had said that night. *Don't let me swim alone for the rest of my days.*

Jeremiah chose that moment to give a quick knock on the open door as he stuck his head around. ''Maggie, Mendosa tells me dinner's about to be served.''

''Right away, dear,'' Maggie said. Leaning over, she hugged her niece and kissed her forehead. ''Stay here for a few moments, if you like, and collect yourself.'' She stood and gazed at Chris fondly. ''Please, think about what I said. I want nothing but your happiness.''

''I know.'' Chris heard the door close as she leaned back, closing her eyes. *I mate for life, and I think you do, too.* Could Maggie be right?

PAUL COULDN'T SLEEP. The restlessness was back, making his nerves jump at every sound that whispered through the walls as those who'd stayed the night at Maggie's settled into their rooms. He'd somehow made it through an interminable dinner and an exhausting several hours afterward, striking up conversations with this one and that, trying to pick up on something, anything that he could use to settle this case. Yet he hadn't heard anything, perhaps because he was concentrating so hard on avoiding Chris.

Shoving aside the sheet, he went to the connecting bath and stepped into the shower. Maybe a bracing dunking would relax him enough to turn off his mind. But she was there, behind his closed eyelids, in the layers of his memory. He remembered all too well the night in Tucson as she lay wrapped in his arms.

Grabbing a towel, he wondered what his next step should be. Tomorrow was the wedding, and though there were still some things to be checked out, their leads were slim, their suspects few, their chance of solving the case shortly not good. With Maggie and Jeremiah away on a long honeymoon, how long would Chris be staying if the leads dried up? Would good old Mark Emery call her home with some trumped-up emergency? And when they caught the embezzler, would Chris hop on the next plane, still unable to face her problems?

Almost savagely, Paul rubbed his hair dry, then hooked a clean towel around his waist. He'd promised himself he wouldn't let her leave again, yet could he really stop her? Did he want her if she wouldn't stay willingly, happily? He grabbed his comb and raked it through his damp hair. Why had he broken his promise to himself and fallen in love with her again? The man in the mirror stared back at him, in his dark eyes the answer. Because he'd never stopped loving her or wanting her. It was that simple—and that complicated.

He turned off the lights, stepped into the bedroom and saw his major complication seated in the chair under the window. Earlier he'd turned off the air conditioner and opened the window, inviting in the fresh mountain air. The soft breeze moved her hair lightly as she watched him in the dim light of the bedside lamp. Her robe was silk, pale peach, reaching to the floor and wrapping around her slim legs. This he hadn't expected. He stood still, waiting.

"I thought you might have trouble sleeping. I brought you some warm milk."

"I hate warm milk."

"I know."

"Did you think you needed an excuse to come to me?"

"I knew you wouldn't come to me."

"You're right about that." He hoped he sounded more certain than he felt. She uncrossed her legs, and the soft material fell away, revealing tan skin. Paul took a step and found his legs still worked. He went to stand beside the bed.

Chris rose, wondering if he could see the hammering of her heart. If he turned her down now, she didn't know what she'd do. "Actually, Mendosa brought me the milk, but I'm willing to share."

He raised a brow. "Mendosa knows you came here?"

"Yes." She took a step toward him, her confidence increasing as she saw him lose his.

"What did she say?"

"She told me to be careful with my heart." She was very close to him now, a breath away. She took his hand. "I told her I didn't own my heart anymore, that you had it." Slowly, she brought his hand to her mouth, bent her head and placed a soft kiss on his open palm.

The scent of her—something floral, something wild— drew him. He caressed the top of her dark head as she buried her lips in his hand and felt his pulse skitter out of control. She was doing it again, sending him mixed signals. Upset about his gun, indifferent to him all evening, then coming to his room and offering herself. It was what angered him about her and what fascinated him.

"Does your coming here mean you've changed your mind, that you accept me, badge and all?"

"My coming here means I want to make love with you, pure and simple. No more questions, no more deep discussions. Just for tonight." She put her hands on his shoulders, lightly touching. "Tell me you don't want me, and I'll go away."

He could have sooner scaled Mount Everest barefoot. "I can't, and you know it." His arms moved around her without his permission. "But this won't solve anything."

"Please, for tonight, I don't want to think. I just want to feel." She snaked her arms around his neck and found his mouth with hers. With a soft sound, she moved against him, letting him know how much she wanted him. Here was the only safe, only sane place to be in a world that so often seemed mad. Here was where her heart had led her.

She drew back from him and searched his face. "Can you handle loving me tonight without knowing where we're going from here?"

No, he couldn't. Yet he couldn't handle letting her go. Always choices. His had been made for him a long time ago. "Yes," he said softly, and saw her smile at last.

The sweet smell of gardenias drifted in from the garden below as he slipped the robe from her shoulders. His eyes darkened as he realized she wore nothing underneath. "You're more beautiful every time I see you. And tonight, more daring than I imagined."

"Let me show you just how daring." Her hand whipped the towel from him as her fingers closed over him.

Paul couldn't prevent the moan that escaped from him as he urged her onto the bed and lay down beside her. But he had to take control, so he brought her hand to his lips and slowly kissed each finger. On a soft sigh, she closed her eyes, and he stretched to kiss her lids, then the corners of her mouth. When at last he touched his lips to hers, it wasn't lightly.

She didn't want his gentleness tonight, Chris decided. Twin passions of anger and frustration had been building between them all evening, an intense foreplay. She was hungry for him, so hungry as she squirmed to touch him in every secret place while his mouth devoured hers. She hadn't planned this encounter, had come on an impulse, but, oh, how she'd longed for it.

Arms reached, legs tangled, mouths tasted while needs pulsed inside both of them. Paul had made love many times before, but had it ever been this savage, this untamed, this greedy? Her skin was tart on his tongue like the finest champagne, her scent intoxicating like the first rose of summer, her hair captivating his fingers like strands of silk. His eyes memorized her, his hands stroked and explored while his mouth tasted.

Chris no longer noticed the bedsheets she gripped nor did she hear the rustle of palm trees that brushed against the screen. She was only aware of pleasure, joy sweet and rare, as he catapulted her into a world of dark desire.

What little patience he'd had fled now as he drew himself up to her. Pounding within him was a need so primitive. He was overwhelmed by the magic of their lovemaking.

For a long while, they lay together, two hearts beating wildly, then gradually slowing. As soon as he was able, Paul rolled to his side and pulled her with him, cradling her head on his shoulder. When he opened his eyes, he saw her skin had the rosy glow of the aftermath of passion. Her hair lay in tangled disarray, and her hand curled in a small, loose fist on the hair of his chest. A wave of tenderness all but consumed him, and he tightened his arm about her.

"Stay with me tonight," he whispered.

Chris roused herself reluctantly. "I can't." She lifted her head and glanced at the bedside clock.

"What's the matter? Are you ashamed to have Maggie and the others know we're lovers?"

He was going to spoil it, damn him. She eased away and sat up. "Not ashamed, no. But I see no reason to flaunt it."

He took her hand, tugged at it until she looked at him. "You're right. I hate having you sneak down a dim hallway to come to me or have you crawl out of my bed to rush home before dawn. I hate having to hide behind rocks to kiss you when I want to stand with my arms around you in the sunshine. Marry me, Chris. Give us a chance."

"I don't know. I . . ."

"Look, this is a little humbling for me to admit, but I'm not as strong without you as with you. I've never loved any other woman but you. I've never asked one to marry me before, and if you don't think I'm as scared as you, you're wrong. But I'm willing to try."

Thoughtfully Chris moved her hand to the scar on his side, pale against his tan skin. She traced the ridge where the bullet had entered his body the night she'd witnessed the shooting. How many close calls had there been before and since that he'd kept from her? She hated herself for the doubts that wouldn't die, the fears that kept returning. And for what she was about to do. "It was a mistake to come here tonight."

Paul had felt her fingers on his scar, aware of the path her thoughts had taken. He sat up as his anger rose. "No. It was the first right thing you've done. You love me, you want me, you need me. What else is there?"

Quickly she leaned to pick up her robe and shrugged into it. "If I continue with you, marry you, the nightmare of your work will become *my* nightmare. I've had all the bad dreams I can handle in one lifetime, Paul. I can't go through that again, not even for you." With trembling fingers, she tied the sash of her robe.

Paul fell back, feeling defeated. Again. "Someone else asked me recently to stop being a cop. Now you're doing it."

"I'm not asking you any such thing. I know you love police work. You have the right to live your way, just as I have a right to protect myself from being hurt by your chosen life-style." She pushed back a heavy strand of hair from her face and stood looking at him. "I'm sorry, Paul. We should have stayed with lovemaking instead of conversation. We're great at the first, but lousy at the second."

"Do you know why I shaved off my mustache, the real reason?"

"No."

"It was a form of rebellion, a symbol. I grew it because I knew my father hated it and so did you. I wore it to show you both that I was independent, my own person. But I lied to myself. Well, I had a little skirmish with my dad the other evening, and I think I won. I shaved off the mustache because I realized I don't need a symbol. I am what I am, Chris, with no apologies and no guarantees. Take me this way or run back to San Diego. Your choice."

Chris let out a ragged breath. "I wish it were that simple for me. Maybe I should try to grow a mustache."

Silently she padded to the door and let herself out.

Paul placed his hands under his head and studied the ceiling. He'd done all he could, said all he had to say. The rest was up to her. Sighing, he wished he'd never heard of humpback whales.

Chapter Twelve

The bride was radiant. Chris felt a warm rush of happiness as she stood at the front and caught a glimpse of Maggie stepping onto the white cloth runner. As the maid of honor, Chris had preceded her aunt down the aisle, between the chairs set up on the sun-drenched terrace. She'd been escorted by Mike, who'd been pleased that Jeremiah had asked him to be best man. They both stood in front of the minister, waiting for the pianist to begin the wedding march.

Flowers in pots and hanging baskets were everywhere, and ivory satin ribbons hung from the aisle chairs. About fifty guests sat in chatty anticipation. Chris noticed Steve Thorn near the back wearing a red bow tie and a bored look. Across the aisle from him was Nancy Evans in a shapeless beige dress, already dabbing at her damp eyes. In the front row was Diane, beautiful in white silk, large sunglasses hiding her green eyes.

Next to her stood Paul, dressed conservatively for a change in navy blue, his blond hair moving in a light breeze. His gaze was fixed on her, his expression solemn and unreadable. She hadn't seen him since she'd left his room last night, and she wondered what he was thinking.

From the corner of her eye, she saw Jeremiah come out of the side door, and she turned to watch his approach. Tall and dignified in his gray cutaway, he stopped at the front of the aisle, shook Mike's hand, then stepped to Chris and kissed her cheek. Gently she touched his face, her own special welcome, and saw his eyes warm. He then nodded to the minister and aimed his smile toward the back of the terrace.

Chris shifted her gaze as well and saw Teddy fuss nervously with his tight collar as he moved beside his mother and offered her his arm. Looking more composed than anyone else, Maggie squeezed her son's arm as the pianist struck the first cord of the wedding march.

Maggie's eyes never left Jeremiah's as she slowly two-stepped her way down the short aisle. Her ivory antique satin wedding dress was simple yet elegant with a lace bodice resplendent with tiny seed pearls. She wore matching satin shoes with the highest heels she could find, as usual. Chris thought she'd never seen a more beautiful bride.

Reverend Jamison stepped forward as Teddy kissed his mother then handed her over to Jeremiah. Chris saw Teddy move to stand alongside Paul instead of his wife and wondered if he and Diane were fighting again. Maggie linked her arm through her groom's, and they turned to face the minister. The guests sat down as the music ended and the ceremony began. As her own eyes kept filling, Chris imagined that she wasn't the only one present who was fighting tears, each of them for reasons of their own.

Paul tried to pay attention, but his gaze kept returning to Chris. Flowers were twined in her hair as it hung down her back, the sun's rays highlighting the dark waves. The dress she wore was pale peach, contrasting beautifully with her tan skin. She looked lovely enough to be the bride, and he fervently wished she were and that he was standing alongside her, reciting vows. Reverend Jamison's voice was deep and rich as he addressed the groom.

"Jeremiah Green, do you take this woman to be your lawful wedded wife? Do you promise to love and to cherish her..."

Yes, Paul thought, I would love and cherish her. If only she would believe that I would do everything in my power to see to her happiness.

"...for better, for worse, for richer, for poorer..."

Chris felt her knees weaken as she stole a glance at Paul and found his dark gaze on her. She didn't care about richer or poorer. They could handle that. Would life with Paul be better? she wondered. How could it be worse than being without him?

"...in sickness and in health, from this day forward..."

Could she see? Paul wondered. See in his eyes the promise that he was silently making? From this day forward. If only she'd agree, he'd shout them out loud, for the whole world to hear.

"...till death do you part?"

As she heard Jeremiah swear that he would indeed promise all those things, Chris bowed her head. The last words rung in her ears, "till death you do part?" She could easily swear to love and cherish Paul, but how long would it be till death parted them? Was she a fool to even ask? Who knew how long anyone had left? Did she want impossible guarantees of a long and happy future together, as her mother had?

I'd rather spend one day with Jeremiah than a hundred years with a man I didn't love, Maggie had told her, and she'd proven the conviction of her beliefs. *Don't let me swim alone,* Paul had asked of her. Oh, God, she didn't want to swim alone, either, Chris thought as she blinked and raised her head.

Paul listened now to Maggie repeating the solemn promise, looking joyful and sure of herself. She'd waited a long time for this day, and he was certain that it had been worth the wait. For a moment there, he'd glimpsed something in Chris's eyes, a softening, an indication that the marriage vows had hit her as hard as they'd hit him. Dare he hope she'd reached the turning point?

The joyous chords of the piano filled the air along with the hearty applause of the guests as Jeremiah kissed his bride. Chris watched as they both broke into happy smiles, turned and walked down the aisle as Mr. and Mrs. Jeremiah Green. She smiled, too, as she reached to take Mike's arm and they followed them down the white runner.

"All the best to you both," Mike said, kissing his aunt and shaking Jeremiah's hand.

Chris followed suit, moved to do more than whisper her congratulations and hug them both. Hurriedly, she got out of the way of the other well-wishers and trailed after Mike into the family room. His big, comforting arm pulled her to him a moment before he angled his head to look into her face.

"Tears of joy, I hope?" he asked. "You okay?"

"Fine," Chris managed, brushing aside a few tears. "Pretty moving ceremony, didn't you think?"

"I always find weddings moving. As long as they're not mine."

Chris smiled up at him. "The confirmed bachelor. You wait, dear brother. Somebody will come along one day, and you'll fall hard. You big guys always do."

"Is that a fact? We'll see." Mike checked his watch, frowning. "I've got to get out of these formal clothes and run. I told Maggie I might get back before she leaves, but I can't promise.''

"A problem at the precinct?"

"There're always problems at the precinct. I hate to duck out on a good Irish party." He leaned to kiss her forehead. "I'll check with you later. I'm going to have a word with Paul and then I'm off."

"Bye." She watched him thread through the crowd and make his way to Paul, who was standing on the sidelines observing. At least if Paul was occupied with Mike for a few minutes, she could repair her makeup before he caught up with her. She saw Nancy heading for the front door and decided not to go after her. Undoubtedly she'd had enough, and Chris couldn't blame her.

Making her way toward the downstairs powder room, Chris remembered Paul's eyes on her through most of the ceremony. He'd seen how the words of the marriage vows had affected her and had probably guessed that her tears had been over their own situation. He'd bring it up as soon as possible, she was certain.

She opened the door and stepped in, then realized someone was seated on the love seat under the mirror. Sunglasses dangling in one hand, her head bent, the woman in white silk was softly crying.

"Diane?" Chris began, moving to her. "Is something the matter?" From the little she knew of Teddy's wife, she doubted if she was the type to get emotional at weddings.

Diane held a tissue to her nose as she brought her head up, but she didn't answer. She just sat while tears ran silently from behind her closed eyelids. Chris eased down beside her, uncertain what to say. Finally she seemed to get a hold of herself.

"I'm sorry," she said as she patted her cheeks dry.

"I'd like to help, if I can," Chris offered.

"I almost think it's too late."

Chris stretched her arm along the narrow couch and leaned toward Diane. "Maybe not. Tell me what's upset you."

"Marital difficulties, as usual. I'm not sure you'd understand."

Chris found it disconcerting to see Diane so upset. She'd always thought Teddy's wife had been the instigator in their arguments. "Try me. Did you quarrel?"

Diane gave a short, mirthless laugh. "We don't even quarrel anymore. He just walks away. Whenever I start talking about something he doesn't want to hear, he goes to San Diego, to his boat, where I've been forbidden to follow. Or he goes to the racetrack. Maybe he—he even goes to other women. I just don't know him anymore."

Stunned, Chris took a moment to think. "I didn't know he gambled."

"Oh, yes. On horses, dog races, anything. I've heard he has some pretty high-stake poker games on his sailboat."

Chris remembered how low Paul had found their bank balance to be. "Does he lose a lot?"

"Yes, a great deal. I've tried to get him to stop, and he won't. I've tried to get him to seek professional help, and he won't even consider it. I've threatened to tell his mother, and he—he struck me." She ended on a sob.

"No! Diane, how long has this been going on?"

"I didn't notice his addiction until we'd been married several months, but I believe he'd been gambling heavily long before that." She raised her eyes to Chris's, imploring her to believe her. "When I was sure this was a sickness in Teddy, I did something I'm not sure he'd forgive me for. I started taking money out of our joint savings account and placing it in a credit union account he doesn't know about. Just so he wouldn't gamble it away. Some of that money I earned. If Maggie knew..."

Chris touched her hand. "Let's not worry Maggie with this on her wedding day." She tried to think how to handle Teddy without her aunt catching wind of things.

"He's been worse since Jeremiah showed up. Teddy feels he should run Lady Charm, and he worries that Maggie's so crazy about her new husband that she's going to give him everything, that he'll be left out."

"Maggie would never do that."

"I know. But she really shouldn't give Teddy more money or more control. He'll only waste it. I don't know what he'll do next."

"When he hit you, was it bad?"

"Bad enough. A very hard slap. I had to stay home until the marks disappeared."

"I had no idea Teddy was violent."

"He can be. The thing is, no one suspects. He plays his role so well at the office, in public. Everyone thinks he's so mild-mannered and I'm the difficult one."

Chris just stared, wondering how much to believe.

"I know you hardly know me and that I've thrown this all at you suddenly. But I can prove it. I went to the doctor when he hit me. There's the bank withdrawals. I know he's sold most of our stock. The boat is mortgaged to the hilt and so is our house. All that money gambled away."

Chris rubbed a spot above her eye. "I just can't believe Teddy could be a split personality."

"I've had trouble believing it, too. And he's getting worse, always so nervous and fidgety. I'm really worried about him."

Chris felt her mouth go dry. A thought struck her that she wanted to push away. Gamblers were like alcoholics, she knew. They couldn't stop without help. Had Teddy gotten hooked, then moved to embezzling to feed his habit, having gone through most of the money he'd gotten from Maggie? And had he slipped poison into their water, left threatening notes, even taken a potshot at her on the mountain? Her cousin—quiet, gentle, introverted Teddy? Oh, God, if this was true, it would destroy Maggie.

Wearily Chris stood. "I have to go." She looked down at Diane and saw the pinched look around her mouth, the sadness in her eyes. She felt a pang of guilt, realizing she could have looked more closely at Diane, perhaps tried to be a friend to her. She touched her hand. "Will you be all right?"

"Yes." She smoothed her dress as she stood. "I've been coping alone with this a long while. Sitting through the wedding, everything just overwhelmed me. Thank you for listening. I won't say anything to Maggie. Not today."

"Perhaps we can come up with something." Chris went to the doorway, then glanced back at Diane. She hated to ask but knew she must. "What kind of cigarettes does Teddy smoke?"

"They're imported, very strong. I can't think of the brand, but they're rolled in thin colored paper."

Chris nodded, swallowing past a lump of fear. "I have to find Paul."

"How can he help? It really isn't a case for the police."

It was hard to believe that a woman as intelligent as Diane hadn't thought to suspect her husband of the embezzlement, given all she knew about him. Did she love blindly, this cool-looking woman Chris hadn't thought even cared for Teddy? Perhaps she'd been wrong—about a number of things. She'd make it up to Diane later. "I trust Paul. He has good instincts."

"And he loves you. You can see it in his eyes. I envy you."

Chris opened her mouth to comment, then changed her mind. "We'll talk more later."

As Chris entered the gaily decorated reception room, she took inventory. Guests were milling about, talking, sipping champagne, laughing. At the far end, Maggie and Jeremiah stood chatting with one of Maggie's old friends. Steve was talking with Mendosa at the hors d'oeuvre table. And Teddy was standing with some men from the office, a drink in his hand. But the man she was seeking was nowhere in sight.

She saw Mendosa leave the buffet table, heading for the kitchen with an empty tray, and intercepted her. "Have you seen Paul anywhere? I must talk with him."

"Sure. Few minutes ago, I see him go upstairs."

"Thanks." She dashed toward the stairs.

Please be here, Chris prayed as she gave a quick knock on his door. No sound from within. She had to see for herself. She turned the handle and walked inside. Bed neatly made, his suitcase spread open on it. Bathroom door ajar. No sign of Paul. With a muttered oath, she left the room.

She stood in the deserted hallway, wondering where to look next when it occurred to her that he might have gone to her room, looking for her. She hurried to her door and flung it open, then blinked in surprise. The room was in total darkness, the heavy drapes drawn on the window and across the patio doors. How very odd, she thought, remembering how she'd left it open to the sunshine. Perhaps the maid had thought dark rooms were cooler, but she hated the closed-in feeling. She reached for the light switch and was about to cross to the windows to draw the blinds when a faint buzzing sound stopped her in her tracks.

On the bedside table was a large vase of fresh flowers and swarming about them, as well as flying around the room, were what looked to be a hundred bees. All logic left her mind, all common sense fled as fear and memories mingled, making her heart thud and her lungs feel ready to burst. Chris's hand flew to her mouth as she let out a blood-curdling scream.

PAUL WAS HALFWAY UP THE STAIRS when he heard a scream coming from down the hallway. Taking the steps two at a time, he reached the landing and raced toward the sound. Chris's door was ajar. Bounding into the room, he saw her cowering against the wall, eyes wide with terror as she watched several circling bees.

"Here!" He grabbed her, sheltering her with his body as he hurried her into the hallway. Quickly he shut the door, locking the bees inside. He scanned the area to make sure no bees had flown out with them, then pulled her into his arms.

She was shaking, clutching the material of his jacket in tight fists as she fought the panic. Paul put his hand on her hair and murmured softly to her. "It's all right. You're okay now."

"I'm sorry. I just got so frightened I couldn't think." The words tumbled out as she sucked in gulps of air. "I was looking for you. My room was dark. I know I didn't leave it that way. I turned on the lights, and that's when I heard the buzzing. The bees weren't attacking, just sort of hovering around. But I remembered the last time..." A shudder raced through her.

"Let's go to my room." He steered her down the hall just as Mendosa stepped into view at the top of the stairs.

Frowning, she came to meet them. "It's very noisy downstairs, the music. But I thought I heard..." She took in Chris's white face. "You all right? What happened?"

"Just a little scare," Paul explained as he opened the door to his guest room. "She'll be fine. Mendosa, would you get someone to help you air out Chris's room? A cluster of bees got in, and they're all over the room."

"Bees? Christina's fearful of bees. How..."

"Just make sure they're all out, okay? And please be careful. There's quite a few."

"Sure. I will see to it."

Paul nodded and closed the door. She was sitting on the edge of his bed shivering, her arms hugging herself, her eyes closed. He took off his jacket and placed it over her, then sat down and pulled her close.

"I feel so foolish." Her voice was stronger now.

"Don't. It's a perfectly natural reaction." He angled his head to look into her face. Her color was improving. "You're sure you didn't leave the windows open?"

"Of course. Besides, there are screens. I left the drapes open. And the vase of flowers. It wasn't there when I left the room barely an hour ago."

Time for a few tough questions. Paul wished her eyes didn't look so vulnerable. "Chris, who knows about your bee allergy?"

"Just Maggie and Mendosa. That time I got bitten, I was in my teens. I was going into shock, and Mendosa held me in her arms in the car while Maggie drove to the hospital. Once they administered the adrenaline, I was all right in about half an hour. I remember the time because Maggie was worried that she hadn't left a note for Teddy and he was due home from some school event. Mendosa was the only one who worked at the house, and my cousin was always forgetting his key. When we drove up, he was sitting on the front porch."

"Did Maggie explain to Teddy what had happened?"

"Of course. She told him I could have died and..."

His arm tightened about her. The gut feeling had been there, but he'd pushed it away. He hadn't wanted to believe Maggie's son was guilty of anything. "So he knows that a bee sting could kill you if you didn't get the serum in time?"

Chris's hand went to her mouth. "Oh, God." She raised agonized eyes to his. "That's why I was looking for you. I just had the most frightening conversation with Diane."

"Tell me about it." As he listened and learned about Teddy's gambling, his resentment of Jeremiah, the picture became clearer. Paul felt the anger rise, but he had to stay calm for Chris. He tightened his hold on her, thinking they'd just had a very close call.

"Something else makes sense, now that we're discussing Teddy," Paul said. "Did you say he was educated in Europe?"

"Yes. Maggie was so pleased to be able to send him."

"Do you remember that I told you Teddy asked me if we'd gotten a handwriting expert to check the books?"

Chris nodded, looking at him with a puzzled frown.

"I studied those altered ledgers for hours. There were entries by several people in accounting, right?" Again, she nodded. "Are you aware that Europeans make their sevens differently than we Americans?"

"Yes, they put a short line through the stem." Chris eased back from him and sat up taller. "I remember now, there were some sevens like that. But wouldn't that be hard to prove, that Teddy made those sevens?"

"I don't think so. I think that was a test question when he asked me about the handwriting analyst. He wasn't smart enough to realize his sevens were a dead giveaway, but he still feared an expert could study all the entries and tell. When I brushed off his inquiry, he relaxed, believing we wouldn't bother."

The enormity of Teddy's plan was sinking in. "So what do we do now, spoil this lovely wedding day for two unsuspecting people?" Chris said.

Paul stood and straighted his vest, comforted by the familiar bulge of his gun tucked in the holster just under his shoulder. He hoped he wouldn't have to use it. "Let me handle things. I want you to stay here while I find Teddy. He has to realize you could stumble onto the bees at any moment. He has to be desperate to do this when there's a houseful of people."

"He's nearly out of money, his wife is hounding him, threatening to tell his mother—sure, he's desperate." The thought made her want to cry.

"I want you to stay right here until I come for you. Now, don't argue. He tried to kill you, Chris. He could try again. Didn't you just tell me that Diane said he's capable of violence?"

"I'm having a hard time taking this all in. It's so bizarre."

Paul placed a quick kiss on her forehead, then went to the door, his mind already leaping ahead to Teddy. "I'll be back as quickly as possible. Don't leave this room."

Lying back on the spread next to Paul's suitcase, Chris wrapped his jacket around her and inhaled his special scent as she closed her eyes. Poor Maggie, she thought.

PAUL WAS BEGINNING TO THINK he was too late, that Teddy had skipped out. For several minutes he'd wandered through the crowd, scanning each corner, pausing for a word here and there, trying to look like any other guest enjoying a wedding reception. Fortunately, the bride and groom were occupied chatting with well-wishers and hadn't noticed anything that had been going on. Muscles tense,

Paul moved to the other side of the house where none of the guests would likely have wandered.

As he came to each room, he paused to listen before carefully opening the door to look inside. No one was in Maggie's small parlor or in the den. As he put his ear to the door of the library, he heard the unmistakable sound of subdued voices, both male. Paul glanced around and saw that the corridor was empty. His heart pounding, he slowly turned the knob and eased the door open a crack as he leaned closer to listen.

"I don't give a damn about your financial problems," Steve Thorn said, his voice low and menacing. "I warned you the other day in your office. You're out of time, and I'm out of patience. I want the rest of my money today, in cash, like you promised. Then, I'm out of here, and no one's the wiser about your little scheme, pal. If I don't get it, I'm going straight to Maggie, wedding day or not."

"If you'll just wait until they leave on their honeymoon, I'll sell some more stock or get it out of the company somehow. You know I've got to be careful with that cop nosing around. Give me till Monday."

"No sale, pal. That's what you told me last week. I checked with Mendosa. Maggie and Jeremiah are leaving around five today. If I don't have my money by four, I talk." Steve let out a harsh laugh. "How do you think your mama's going to feel when she finds out her little boy's embezzled thousands from her, huh?"

Paul angled the door ajar a fraction more. He was every inch the professional now, nerves taut, his concentration absolute. But a knot of fear curled inside him nonetheless. Every cop knew that if a man attempted murder once, he would again. Teddy was not a soft-spoken, harmless introvert but a desperate and dangerous man. And, it would seem, so was Steve Thorn.

Peering through the slit, Paul could see the two of them now, standing by the fireplace, Teddy pale and fidgety, Steve's face a hard mask above his red bow tie. So the cocky little chemist had used Nancy to learn the books, then somehow had figured out that Teddy was the one siphoning the money. Perhaps he, too, had noticed the sevens and had guessed the rest. Blackmail. A neat little scheme. Teddy was sick, but greed alone motivated Steve. Setting aside his dislike for the arrogant man, Paul waited for the right moment to enter.

"I'll have your money for you. But please, don't tell Maggie. She . . . she . . ."

"You should have thought of her months ago when you started taking her money. I'm telling you, you've got till four."

Teddy ran a trembling hand over his sparse hair. "I can't have it until next week. I don't . . ."

Steve's hand whipped out of his pocket, a switchblade gleaming in the sunlight as he leaned closer to Teddy. "I mean business."

Teddy took a step back against the fireplace, his eyes huge, his hands clutching the rough stones. "Just a couple days."

The knife moved within a breath of his throat. "Too late."

Paul drew his gun and shoved open the door. As he moved in, he aimed it directly at Steve. "Drop it."

Steve swiveled around, startled as Teddy seemed to go limp.

"I said drop it," Paul told the man as he advanced into the room.

Breathing heavily, Steve took a step toward Paul, narrowing his eyes as if considering his options.

"Throw down the knife. Don't add murder to blackmail. There's no way out."

With lightning speed, Steve grabbed Teddy around the neck and held him in front of his body as a shield. "There's always a way. Put down your gun or I slit his throat. How do you think Maggie will feel when she learns you caused her little boy's death?"

Paul was close enough to smell the man's sweat and his own fear, but he held his gun steady and his eyes level. "You can't get away with this. Too many people are out there. Let him go."

Steve's watery blue eyes darted toward the door, then back to Paul. "Ease over to the window. I'm taking him with me. I won't hurt him if you give me ten minutes."

Paul raised his gun a fraction. He saw that Teddy's eyes were wide with fright as sweat dripped down his face. "No deals, Steve."

"You can't prove a thing."

"I think I can." He reached toward Teddy, got a grip on his forearm. "Let me have him!"

"Get back," Steve snarled. With a savage thrust, he slashed out, lunging at Paul, his one arm still around Teddy.

Paul felt the blade streak into his arm, followed by a fiery pain. His mouth a thin line, he concentrated on ignoring the wound as he brought his gun back up into firing position, but he couldn't shoot without hitting Teddy.

Teddy's hands clawed at Steve's arm, which was cutting off his air supply. As he struggled, Steve lost his hold, and Teddy stumbled forward onto the floor.

In that instant, Paul squeezed off one quick shot that caught Steve in his left shoulder. He landed on one knee, the knife still clutched in his right hand. He tried to grab Teddy again, aiming the blade at the center of his back.

"Oh, my God," Maggie shrieked from the doorway.

"Paul!" Chris cried from beside her.

Paul's second shot went through Steve's hand. He screamed and fell atop Teddy, his knife clattering onto the hearth. Teddy groaned as Paul moved to free him. Unsteadily he sat up as Paul checked Steve. The man had passed out, but his pulse was strong, Paul ascertained before stepping back.

Maggie rushed to her son's side, followed by a startled Jeremiah, who'd just come in the door.

"What's going on in here?" Jeremiah asked Paul.

"It's a long story," Paul said as he put his gun away and held up his arm to stem the flow of blood as Chris rushed to his side.

Her heart still pounding, Chris recalled how it had missed several beats when Mendosa had come to her and told her she'd better hurry to the library. She'd imagined a hundred terrifying scenes in her mind's eye in the few minutes it had taken her to reach the room. She took a deep breath as she realized Teddy wasn't hurt and Paul was all right. Going to his side, she put her arm around Paul and held on, her head falling to his shoulder. He rested his cheek on her hair for a moment.

When Teddy moaned, she looked over at him. Maggie huddled beside him as he ran shaky fingers over his hair.

"Teddy, what's happening here?" Maggie asked. "Why was Steve holding a knife on you?"

Teddy's eyes were drained of life as he looked at his mother. "I'm so sorry." He bent his head and covered his face with his hands. Maggie looked up at Paul.

Paul helped her to the couch. There was no way to soften the blow. "Steve was blackmailing Teddy about the embezzlement." He saw what little color there was left drain from her face as she gasped. "You sit here a minute, and

I'll fill you in on the rest shortly.'' He motioned to Jeremiah to sit with her. As the news sank in, Maggie let her husband comfort her.

Steve groaned as Paul picked up the phone. "I'm going to call this in and request an ambulance." Glancing up, he saw Mendosa at the door, her dark eyes wide and frightened, as several guests who'd undoubtedly heard the shots hovered in the hallway behind her. "Could you find Diane, Mendosa, and tell her to come here, please? And don't let anyone else in for now."

She nodded wordlessly and closed the door.

While Paul cradled the phone under his chin and talked to headquarters, Chris went to the corner bar and pulled out a small towel. She returned to his side and gently wiped the blood from the cut on his arm. When he finished and hung up, he looked at his wound.

"Not too deep," she told him, "but it'll require stitches." How many times had he been stitched up already, and how many more sutures would he face in his lifetime? she wondered as she raised her eyes to his. Yet she'd stood in the doorway and watched him save Teddy's life. Despite all her cousin had done, she was sure Paul thought a few stitches a small price to pay for a man's life. She swallowed hard as she realized she thought so, too.

She'd lain upstairs on the bed that held his scent, wrestling with her thoughts. She'd run from Paul before so she wouldn't be hurt. But what day had gone by, what hour, that she hadn't thought of him and all she'd left behind? What did she have to show for those two long years? She'd thought her arguments for leaving had been rock solid, but they'd been flawed. She hadn't taken into consideration how very much she loved him.

Chris slid her hand up his chest and rested it over his heart. It was still beating rapidly. "Were you frightened?"

"I'm always frightened in a situation like this. Hopefully that fear keeps me on my toes." Paul watched her silently for a moment longer. "You're handling this pretty well."

"Not well perhaps, but I am handling it."

He smiled at her. "A tough lady, are you?"

"No, not yet. But tougher than I was yesterday." She reached up and gave him a soft, gentle kiss. "I love you."

He slipped his good arm around her waist. "The feeling's mutual."

They looked up at a sound from the doorway. Diane came in, her face as pale as her dress. Slowly she walked to her husband and knelt beside him. Chris felt her eyes fill as she watched Teddy, wearing the face of a broken man, reach out his arms to her and pull her tightly to him as he gave in to his tears.

"It's all over, finally," Chris whispered.

Paul's gaze went from Teddy and Diane to where Maggie and Jeremiah sat. "Yes, for us. For them, it's just beginning."

"I'M SORRY THAT MAGGIE and Jeremiah had to cancel their honeymoon," Paul said, his head turned toward Chris as he lay on the table at the emergency room of the hospital.

"Postpone not cancel. They wanted it that way. I don't blame Maggie. She can't enjoy being away until she knows Teddy's in good hands."

Chris saw him wince and heard a muffled oath.

"Just a few more stitches, Sergeant," the doctor assured him. "You just keep talking to the lady, and we'll be done before you know it."

"Comforting," Paul grumbled.

"You're a bit of a baby, you know that?" Chris teased. "There's a six-year-old in the next cubicle getting twenty stitches, and we haven't heard a peep out of her."

"Females are stronger."

"Mmm-hmm." She held his hand nonetheless, and had a feeling this might become a familiar scene to her, sitting in hospital rooms watching Paul get stitches. Hopefully, that would be the worst of it.

Chris didn't know when exactly she'd decided to risk everything and give herself completely to Paul. She only knew this felt right.

She tugged her mind back to the embezzlement. "What will happen to Teddy? I've never really run across someone with a gambling addiction. Can he be helped?"

Paul grimaced as another pain shot through his arm. "He can, if he wants to be. Maggie's assured him she'll see to his treatment. She's not prosecuting, of course, and she's forgiven him the money he's lost. She's convinced that he was only trying to frighten us off the case and meant no serious harm. How do you feel about that?"

She and Teddy had shared a tearful few minutes before she'd driven Paul to the hospital. Her concern had mingled with pity as he'd begged her forgiveness. "I tend to agree with her. Did you talk to Maggie about Steve?"

"She's furious with him and will prosecute. The blackmail was one thing, but when she saw him intending to knife Teddy, that did it."

"That did it for me, too. How did Steve discover that Teddy was the one embezzling?" If she kept him busy talking, he wouldn't feel the discomfort.

"Well, Maggie didn't bring Mike and the police in on things for some time, thinking the outside accounting firm she'd hired would discover a discrepancy instead of a crime. But crafty old Steve got wind of it and smelled a blackmail victim. He romanced poor Nancy into explaining the books, then threw her aside when he no longer needed her. Steve reports only to Teddy, so he'd had ample opportunity to see his handwriting, including the numbers. The sevens must have rung a bell with him, and he probably gambled and confronted Teddy.''

''I suppose my cousin was so fearful of exposure that he started paying him.''

''Right. And the notes, the trace of poison, even the shotgun blast were meant to frighten us off the case.'' Paul's mouth became grim. ''But Teddy saw himself losing ground and thought the bees would send you packing.''

''Didn't he realize you'd never just drop the case?''

''We weren't dealing with a rational mind at that point, but a desperate one. I hope they're able to help him. And Steve will recover and be able to stand trial.''

Chris squeezed his hand. ''Did I tell you that you're a damn good shot, Sergeant?''

Her eyes told him even more. Paul smiled, then winced as the doctor pulled and cut the suture.

''There you go. We'll give you something for pain, if you like. Don't get that arm wet for a few days. Come back in a week, and we'll take the stitches out. The nurse will finish bandaging you.''

''Thanks, doctor.'' Paul sat up and let the nurse take over. When she left, he reached for his shirt, frowning at the stained and ripped sleeve.

''I should have thought to grab you a clean one as we left the house.'' Chris watched as he slid off the table and stood up, a bit wobbly. ''Here, lean on me.''

Paul drew her close with his good arm, touched his forehead to hers and took a deep breath. He was glad the case was settled. Now he desperately wanted to settle things between Chris and him. He searched his mind how to begin, afraid to trust the signals he'd been receiving from her.

"Did I tell you how proud I am of you?" she asked, her voice soft, her mouth a breath away from his.

"I was pretty proud of you, too. I understand how much you hate guns and shootings and—"

She placed a finger on his lips. "Shh. I understand a little more now. Without you there today I don't know what would have happened. Maybe Steve would have gotten away. Maybe he and Teddy would have fought until they both got hurt worse, or killed. I see how very necessary your work is, how important. I've not allowed myself to see the good you do because I've been so busy focusing on all the negatives. In that regard, I've been wrong.

"Paul, I'll never be ecstatic that you have to occasionally face maniacs like Steve. But I'll always be proud that you're able to save disturbed men like Teddy. To give him and his wife and mother another chance."

"I only hope he makes the most of it. Maggie's love and support could make the difference. She's very strong in the things she stands for," Paul said.

"Yes, she is. She told me something yesterday. That she'd rather spend one day with Jeremiah than live a hundred years with a man she didn't love." Chris smiled into his eyes as she saw them warming. "I'm like my aunt. I mate for life. I took one look at you and that was it, even though I fought my feelings."

"Tell me something. Why didn't you ever mention that my father called you in two years ago and told you to leave town?"

She raised an eyebrow as she looked at him. "Would you have believed me? I didn't think so. You admired your father so much. I saw no point in toppling him from the pedestal you'd put him on. I figured he'd do it himself in time.''

Paul sighed. "He did. I suppose, as Pete maintains, Dad means well. I just don't like his methods.''

"I want you to know I didn't leave because of what he said. He could never push me away from you, nor could anyone else. I left because of my own fears. I think I've conquered those, at least somewhat. Please don't let me swim alone, Paul. Marry me.''

He shifted his gaze to the ceiling. "Let me think about it awhile...''

Chris jabbed an elbow into his ribs.

"Ouch! I've thought it over. I'll marry you—on one condition.''

"And that is?''

"That we honeymoon on the East Coast. I want to show you that humpback whales really do swim in tandem.''

Chris slid her arms around his neck as she gave him a lazy smile. "I don't care if we honeymoon in your backyard and prop a picture of a whale alongside the pool. Let's just do it *soon*.''

"You got a deal, lady.'' And he lowered his head for her kiss.

Epilogue

"Well, big brother," Pete began as he fussed with his tie, "how do you feel about walking down that long, white aisle in front of all these guests and swearing to love, honor and obey?"

"Uncomfortable," Paul admitted as he stood in the open doorway of the great room alongside his brother. "Chris and I wanted to have a quiet family wedding, but Maggie wouldn't hear of it."

"Looks like she invited most everyone she knows, to say nothing of all those cops out there. Who's in charge of law and order in the big city today?"

"Guess it'd be a good day to rob a bank," Paul said with a grin.

He'd been smiling a lot lately. People had even commented on it. Well, hell, why not? he thought. He had a lot to be happy about. In a few minutes, Christine Donovan would stroll down that aisle and become his wife.

She had been worth the two-year wait, though he hadn't waited with patience. Two months had passed since Maggie and Jeremiah had gotten married in this very house. Since then, Steve Thorn had recovered from his wounds and was in jail, awaiting trial. Teddy was on an extended leave of absence and undergoing treatment for his addiction with private counseling. To everyone's surprise, Diane had remained steadfastly loyal and lovingly supportive of her husband while continuing to work long hours at Lady Charm.

Paul saw Teddy and Diane enter from the double doors at the back and sit unobtrusively off to the side. She looked beautiful, as usual, and he a bit pale and somewhat strained. But they held hands and sat close together. It was a start, Paul thought, and perhaps a new beginning for them.

"Maybe they'll make it," Pete commented following Paul's gaze. "Think so?"

"Time will tell. They've got a good shot at it."

"Look at that rain come down," Pete said as the wind whipped a wet swirl against the glass patio doors and the early morning sky darkened.

"Let it pour," Paul said. "I like it." It had been raining the night he'd met Chris, and raining again the night he'd lost her. It was only fitting that it showered the day she became his forever.

None of the guests seemed to mind, either, as they sat and admired the peach-and-ivory flowers and satin ribboning that decorated the large room. Paul saw many of the people he'd gotten to know from Lady Charm, including Nancy Evans, who'd waved to him shyly a moment ago. She looked prettier today, her hair shiny and her complexion pink and healthy. She sat next to one of the men in accounting, and they leaned toward each other with occasional whispered comments. Maybe he was the reason why Nancy was suddenly glowing. Love. It made the world go round.

"Well, I'll be damned," Pete said as he looked toward the back where a slight commotion had heads turning. "He showed up after all."

Paul watched his father shake a few hands on his way to his designated seat at the front, looking hale and hardy as befitting a U.S. senator, his politician's smile in place. "Did you think he'd miss a chance to win a few more voters?"

"Who knows? Maybe he's really changed."

"I'd like to think so." After that night of confrontation, John Cameron had eased up in his campaign to push and nudge his sons where he wanted them to go. He still offered strong opinions on everything in their lives, but then Paul hadn't really expected a total about-face. Though he knew his father wasn't crazy about Chris, he seemed to accept her. It was compromise behavior Paul could live with.

"And here come the newlyweds," Pete commented as one of the ushers escorted Maggie to the front row, followed by a dapper Jeremiah.

Paul watched Maggie smile greetings to several guests as she settled the folds of her pale pink dress. Very few redheads could get away with wearing that color, but leave it to Maggie to carry it off with style, he thought. Only those close to her could tell by the addition of tiny stress lines around her mouth and an occasional nervous blinking of her eyes what toll the last two months had taken on her. As the pianist began the strains of "Here Comes the Bride," Paul smiled at Chris's aunt with genuine fondness.

"Okay, old buddy," Pete said. "It's time. You ready?"

"I've been ready for months. Let's go."

As he and his best man took their places in front of the minister, the guests all rose to watch the bride walk down the aisle on the arm of her handsome brother. But Paul neither saw them nor heard the music. He saw only Chris, a vision in her antique wedding gown, the one her mother had worn. She moved toward him with sure steps, her eyes shining with love.

When Mike handed her over, Paul clutched her hand in his and never let it go until after they'd spoken their vows. Then he lifted the delicate lace veil and arranged it back over her dark hair. Huge blue eyes brimming with happiness watched him as he dipped his head to hers.

"Forever yours, Mrs. Cameron," he whispered for her ears only.

"Forever," she promised, then reached for the kiss that would seal their pledge.

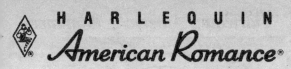

HARLEQUIN
American Romance®

COMING NEXT MONTH

#305 MOTHER KNOWS BEST by Barbara Bretton

Author of the "Mother Knows Best" helpful-hints column, Diana had a master plan: finish her book, lose ten pounds and on Labor Day, begin the Great Husband Hunt. But then a month at seaside Gull Cottage fell in her lap, and two months early, at exactly the wrong time, Diana met Mr. Right. Don't miss the second book in the GULL COTTAGE series.

#306 FRIENDS by Stella Cameron

As children, Tom, Shelly and Ben had been inseparable. Then they became adults and their friendship faced a challenge. Ben was destined for fame, while Tom and Shelly were destined for love. But would their love break the bonds of an unbreakable friendship?

#307 ONE MAN'S FOLLY by Cathy Gillen Thacker

Diana Tomlinson was justice of the peace in Libertyville, Texas, but her life was far from peaceful. Newcomer Mike Harrigan was insistent about his foster ranch—even though the town was up in arms, all hell had broken loose and there had been a rash of burglaries. Diana knew that where there was a will there was a way—but as she got to know Mike and his trio of boys she found her will rapidly fading....

#308 WHITE MOON by Vella Munn

Lynn Walker was a championship barrel rider without a horse—her dream was just out of reach. Then Bryan Stone found her a mare to match her spirit and her strength: proof that he believed in her and her dream. There are many ways to say "I love you," and White Moon was Bryan's.

Harlequin American Romance®

Gull Cottage

SUMMER.

The sun, the surf, the sand...

One relaxing month by the sea was all Zoe, Diana and Gracie ever expected from their four-week stays at Gull Cottage, the luxurious East Hampton mansion. They never thought they'd soon be sharing those long summer days—or hot summer nights—with a special man. They never thought that what they found at the beach would change their lives forever. But as Boris, Gull Cottage's resident mynah bird said: "Beware of summer romances...."

Join Zoe, Diana and Gracie for the summer of their lives. Don't miss the GULL COTTAGE trilogy in American Romance: #301 *Charmed Circle* by Robin Francis (July 1989), #305 *Mother Knows Best* by Barbara Bretton (August 1989) and #309 *Saving Grace* by Anne McAllister (September 1989).

GULL COTTAGE—because a month can be the start of forever...

Have You Ever Wondered If You Could Write A Harlequin Novel?

Here's great news—Harlequin is offering a series of cassette tapes to help you do just that. Written by Harlequin editors, these tapes give practical advice on how to make your characters—and your story—come alive. There's a tape for each contemporary romance series Harlequin publishes.

Mail order only

All sales final